Who was this woman

Drawing back, he stared down at her, dazzled by the fierce urgency that had consumed them, locking them in a moment rife with power and need.

A witchy little smile tinged those bee-stung lips. "You look surprised, Lancelot."

"Lancelot?"

That smile broadened as she cocked her head. "You were the one with the white-knight complex this morning."

"I'm not feeling very pure and honorable at the moment."

"That makes two of us." Her temptress's smile shifted, gentled, as she released her hold on his waist. "But it doesn't change the fact we don't know each other very well."

He knew he stared, unable to look away from the vivid, bright woman standing before him. But he also knew she had secrets.

***

Be sure to check out the rest of the books in the Dangerous in Dallas miniseries—
Dangerous in Dallas:
Danger and desire fill the hot Texas nights...

***

If you're on Twitter, tell us what you think of Harlequin Romantic Suspense!
#harlequinromsuspense

Dear Reader,

Have you ever heard the history of a place and it got you thinking? After working in Dallas's Design District I knew I needed to set a book there.

For the longest time the area was home to many warehouses, then a few decades ago the design community overtook the space, resulting in a series of interesting galleries and wholesale shops.

About five years ago, the area went through another renaissance and in that short time has become one of the city's crown jewels. Trendy and full of residential and business development, the area has remained bohemian enough to be interesting yet trendy enough to attract young entrepreneurs.

And that's where we find my heroine, Cassidy Tate, wedding dress designer and part-owner of Elegance and Lace with her two best friends. Unbeknownst to them, there is a secret hidden in the floor of their shop. Fortunately, they've got some rather attractive neighbors—ex-military men who have an architectural firm in the same neighborhood—who are more than willing to help them figure out what it is.

I love the adventures my imagination takes me on when I'm writing a book, and it took me on a whopper with this one. I hope you'll join me on the adventure *and* forgive my flight of fancy—and creative license—when I happened upon an idea about the British crown jewels. I'd like to think the Queen Mum would approve.

Best,

Addison Fox

SILKEN THREATS

Addison Fox

HARLEQUIN® ROMANTIC SUSPENSE

Recycling programs
for this product may
not exist in your area.

ISBN-13: 978-0-373-27907-4

Silken Threats

Printed in U.S.A.

Addison Fox is a Philadelphia girl transplanted to Dallas, Texas. Although her similarities to Grace Kelly stop at sharing the same place of birth, she's often dreamed of marrying a prince and living along the Mediterranean.

In the meantime, she's more than happy penning romance novels about two strong-willed and exciting people who deserve their happy-ever-after—after she makes them work so hard for it, of course. When she's not writing, she can be found spending time with family and friends, reading or enjoying a glass of wine.

Find out more about Addison or contact her at her website—addisonfox.com—or catch up with her on Facebook (addisonfoxauthor) and Twitter (@addisonfox).

Books by Addison Fox

HARLEQUIN ROMANTIC SUSPENSE

Dangerous in Dallas Series
Silken Threats

House of Steele Series
The Paris Assignment
The London Deception
The Rome Affair
The Manhattan Encounter

Visit the Author Profile page at Harlequin.com for more titles

For Girlfriends.

One of life's truest joys.

Chapter 1

Tucker Buchanan heard the scream as he moved into the last quarter mile of his run, his boxer, Bailey, beside him. He'd always shunned earphones, favoring the subtle din of early-morning ambient noise and abstractly solving quadratic equations in his head. The run both soothed and invigorated him and he was rigid in keeping this time to himself each day, even if the incessant solving of formulas only proved his geeky beginnings.

While his business partner would suggest he was still a geek, he knew damn well an early-morning scream of terror definitely did not solve for x, y or z.

Years of training kicked in and with a glance, in unison with Bailey's, they both ran harder in the direction of the noise. As a second scream echoed through the warm, hazy Dallas dawn his gaze narrowed in on the only shop lights visible in a nearby row of storefronts.

Slim shoulders that still balanced a large tote bag and an oversize purse stood quaking as he closed the last few feet down Dragon Street. "Miss!"

Another scream died on her lips as she turned toward him, her vivid blue eyes wide. He lifted his hands as he called Bailey to a halt, and they both came to a stop a few feet away. "Are you okay?"

She took a few steps back, the fear still visible in her gaze, and he and the mutt remained in place, waiting for her to calm. Bailey dropped to a seated position, his tongue lolling, and that final action seemed to do the trick.

The woman blinked, the fear receding slightly from her eyes. "They… It…" She pointed toward the store. "Someone was in there. I can see the destruction from here."

Tucker wished he had his gun but figured an eighty-pound dog would provide some measure of menace. "Stay here and I'll go check it out. Do you want Bailey with you or would you rather I took him?"

"I'm going in there with you." Her voice had calmed another notch and now that fear faded fully, replaced with sheer, stubborn grit.

"You seem pretty shaken up."

"I only screamed the second time because I saw movement from the corner of my eye." Her voice grew stronger, more aware. "Something skittering down the street from the garbage."

"You're still shaken. Why don't you wait here?"

"My store. My rules."

He shrugged. The likelihood anyone was still in the store was slim—especially with the clear signs of destruction evident in the window—but he pointed toward the phone in her hand to buy a few additional minutes. "Why don't you call the police first and then we'll check it out."

He gave her space to make the call, moving up toward the windows with Bailey by his side. The storefront was still dark but the early-morning light brightened it enough for him to see the destruction that littered the floor in a morass of white material and what looked to be dress-makers' forms.

Storefront, Tucker knew, wasn't the most apt description. Dallas's design district had evolved out of a series of old warehouses along the banks of the Trinity River. Or what had become the Trinity River after the Corps of Engineers had outfitted it with a series of levees in the 1930s.

From the detritus on the floor, he quickly processed that the woman owned what looked to be a wedding store. As his gaze took in a lavish wall of gilt-edged mirrors and lush couches, he figured he'd hit it spot-on. Any number of designers and decorators had chosen to make this corner of Dallas their own, and with the district's renaissance in the past five years several businesses were thriving.

Hell, it was the reason he and his partner had opened their firm here. Max's grandfather had given him an old warehouse on the south end of Dragon Street and it had seemed as good a place as any to set up shop. The past eighteen months had proven the decision was a good one and they'd worked themselves to the bone.

If those same eighteen months had been rather light on female companionship, well, starting a business was tough work. He'd heard about the neighboring wedding business—and had seen the pink truck delivering cakes all over Dallas—but hadn't yet met the women who owned the place.

"They're on their way. The police and my partners." Her husky voice broke into his musings and Tucker turned, registering the tightening in his stomach at the sultry tones.

"Do you want to go in?"

"Might as well." A small smile quirked her lips and he was pleased to see her fear had fully faded, replaced by what looked like grim determination. "So you've introduced Bailey but not yourself. I'm Cassidy Tate."

"Tucker Buchanan." He held the slim fingers, firm under his palm, and wondered how he'd missed seeing her around the neighborhood. Those blue eyes were set off by pale, creamy skin and long, curling red hair. The shade was so vivid—so full of life—there was no way he'd have passed by the delectable Cassidy Tate and not noticed.

"You and your partner own the architectural firm at the end of Dragon."

Her quick confirmation surprised him. "We do."

Her smile broadened, a slight hint of mischief evident. "I have two female partners in my business. It hasn't escaped our landlady's notice that some single male and female shop owners are only separated by a few blocks."

"So that's why my partner, Max, came back complaining after the last community leaders meeting."

"*My* partner Violet came back hot to trot about the same thing."

Tucker glanced up at the wide windows. "Let's hope this wasn't quite what your landlady had in mind to get us introduced to each other."

Cassidy gestured toward the door, her smile fading as she neared the destruction once more. "I suspect it wasn't."

"Come on, then. Where's your alarm keypad? Or will you need to get across that mess to disarm it?"

"Oh, no."

If possible, her pale, ethereal features turned whiter as her eyes widened until they threatened to fill up most of her face. "We never got a call. Whoever did this disarmed the system."

Cassidy swallowed past the renewed lump of panic that tightened her throat. The initial shock of seeing the showroom floor had faded and all that remained was a sick ball of lead that seemed to grow by the second in the pit of her stomach. She raced toward the small keypad inside the door and saw the bright green lights indicating it was disarmed.

"How?"

Had she forgotten to turn on the alarm last night before leaving? She'd been the last to head home; Violet had been out on a date and Lilah on a delivery in a northern suburb. A tight weight settled on her chest and she struggled to calm and regulate her breathing.

The destruction was even worse than she'd originally thought, yet another swift reminder that whoever had been here had meant business. Several delicate chairs, designed for those waiting to fuss over a bride-to-be, were scattered on their sides, and a wall rack of gowns lay on the floor. Since she'd done a few chin-ups on that bar to confirm it was solidly attached to the wall, it must have been pulled down with considerable force.

Her gaze caught on a large pool of shattered glass—the remains of a small crystal bowl she used to keep pins in for alterations—and that small act of destruction penetrated her panic. With one hand on Tucker's arm, she reached past him to grab Bailey's collar. "He's going to get something in his paws. Stay here and I'll get something to gate him up."

Tucker's easygoing, friendly manner from the street had vanished the moment they walked through the door. "You stay here and tell me what to look for."

Her hand tingled where she touched his arm, and she snatched it away as if singed, using the momentum to point toward the far end of the showroom. "I've got a baby gate in the back storeroom, just inside the door. We use it every so often for guests."

"Be right back."

She watched him move, the tight outline of his butt evident just beneath the hem of his gray T-shirt. A large outline of a dragon filled the material over his back, and she watched, fascinated, as it rippled with his movement. The words *Dragon Designs* spanned the width of his shoulders.

This was the last moment she should be noticing her rangy neighbor with the broad shoulders, but that subtle spark of interest went a long way toward making her feel a bit more settled.

More normal.

It was normal to feel a subtle flutter of attraction for an attractive man. It was *not* normal to walk into one's store and find it burgled and destroyed.

Bailey—momentarily forgotten next to her—nudged her knee as he sat down.

Dropping to a crouch, she pulled him close, her hand still wrapped in his collar while she stroked his short, brindled fur with her free hand. "You're a sweet boy."

His tongue lolled once more as his solemn brown eyes roamed over her face.

A protector.

The word flitted through her mind, swift and immediate, and she somehow knew Bailey had a lot in common with his owner.

"He likes you."

"The feeling's mutual." She glanced up to see Tucker heading her way with the baby gate. "I've got a small dressing area over here, and we can put him in one of the rooms."

"First time you've had a dog in your dressing room, I'd wager."

"Only if you don't count the handbag dogs several society matrons have carried in here. Oh, or the cheating fiancé I caught in there with a bridesmaid a few months back."

Tucker's eyes widened as he leaned over and took Bailey's collar in hand. "Seriously?"

"There's something amorous about the smell of tulle, I'm told."

Confusion stamped itself in the depths of his brown eyes, and she put him out of his misery. "Sorry. Bad wedding joke. But you would be surprised what I've caught people doing in here."

"In a dress shop?"

"Yep. Something about the thought of happy ever after seems to bring out the strangest reactions in people. Sex. Fights. Makeup sex. My partner Lilah has had it worse, I think. She caught a couple in her kitchen having sex with a vat of icing."

Tucker fastened the baby gate to the fitting-room door and patted a whining Bailey on the head. "Sounds like a break-in is the least of your problems."

The reminder of what had happened hit her with swift fists, and Cassidy let her gaze roam around the room. "I'm not so sure about that."

"I'm sorry. Really sorry. That was insensitive. Come on, let's take a look. The damage in the back doesn't look nearly so bad and I did a quick look around when I got the gate. No one's here."

She let out her first easy breath and followed him toward the back of the store.

"You mentioned your partners but I don't see their stuff."

Cassidy kicked a seed pearl with the toe of her shoe, the small bead tinkling as it lightly skimmed the floor. "Violet uses an office in the back next to my studio, and Lilah's store is technically next door, even though it's the same building. We keep her kitchen officially separate."

"Health codes?"

"Yep."

"Or should I say, health codes so long as no one's having sex in there."

"Pretty much."

He halted in front of a large rack of wedding dresses. "Any idea why someone would target you? Do you keep a lot of cash on hand?"

"No, hardly any."

"How much are these gowns worth on the black market?"

Cassidy turned his words over in her mind. She carried merchandised stock from several major designers, as well as her own creations. Although she'd been written up in several bridal magazines and had been steadily building her reputation since getting out of college, she hardly considered her store a mecca of high-value goods.

"A fair amount, I suppose, if you added up all my current stock. But it doesn't make sense. If someone wanted the dresses, then why didn't they take them? I'll have to do inventory, but I don't immediately see any that are obviously missing. And that one over there—" she pointed out one of the well-known designers "—is worth quite a bit and is untouched. Other than a heck of a lot of destruction I don't see what they were after."

Another round of anxiety coated her stomach in acid. She had several fittings this week and three bridesmaids were scheduled to pick up their gowns later that day. She raced toward the small area where she kept completed alterations, pleased to see the dresses were all there.

One or two might need pressing, but she didn't have to brace herself for upset phone calls with stressed-out brides.

"A competitor, then? Someone who would want to see your business suffer."

Cassidy pulled her attention from the rack of gowns, mentally cataloging the ones she'd press first. She knew his was a valid question—had already run through any number of similar thoughts—but it just didn't play. Her showroom felt as if it had been searched, even if she couldn't quite put her finger on why she felt that way. "I can't explain the instinct, but it seems like a long shot that someone would do this out of competitive spite. I haven't even spoken to anyone in the business since a local bridal show in June. Two months is a long time to hold a grudge without any escalating behavior."

"Anyone who would have the code to your alarm?" His voice was quiet—steady—and she appreciated he didn't shy away from the difficult.

"No one beyond my partners and myself."

He rubbed a hand over her shoulder, the small gesture as soothing as it was intoxicating. "I'll call my buddy down. We'll help you get everything cleaned up after the police go through here."

"You don't need to do that. Lilah and Violet can—"

His gaze narrowed, drinking her in, and she swallowed the last of her words.

"We'll help." A small smile crinkled the corners of his eyes. "If you won't allow me to get my white knight on, then consider it a matter of giving your landlady a thrill."

A loud bark pulled her attention from the warmth of his touch, and she saw the flashing lights of the Dallas PD outside her front windows. "I'd better go get that."

"I can't believe the hottie down the lane is the one who came to your rescue," Lilah Castle, baker extraordinaire and one of Cassidy's two partners in Elegance and Lace, uttered for the third time from around her large latte.

"It must have been the tall one." Violet Richardson, partner number two, had her own coffee and a specula-

tive gaze as she stood with a notepad near a rack of ruined gowns.

"Define tall." Lilah pushed a strand of cotton-candy
pink behind her ear—her current color streak of choice
amid a sea of blond—before letting out a rather lusty sigh.
"Both owners I've seen are deliciously taller than average."

Violet turned from her inspection, her eyes lighting up
like a kid's on Christmas morning. "Let me amend my
comment, then. Were you rescued by the long, rangy man
with the sigh-worthy derriere and ugly dog?"

"Hey. Bailey was cute." Although his mushed-in face
with a steady line of drool earned the term "only a mother
could love," Cassidy had a soft spot for the boxer. "And I
will be forever grateful for the sense of protection ema-
nating from that large body."

"The dog's or the man's?" Lilah's smile was even faster
than her retort.

Cassidy reluctantly grabbed a small broom to start picking up scattered seed pearls. "You're as bad as Mrs. Beauregard. She's been going on and on about the men who
moved in down the street and how we need to meet them."

"I can only hope to be as spry as Mrs. B. when I'm
eighty. She's got a good eye and she can spot a douchebag
loser at twenty paces."

"Lilah has a point," Violet pointed out. "Mrs. B. has
impeccable taste *and* knows her hotties. And I've met the
other owner, Max Baldwin."

"Oh. Oh!" Lilah broke in. "Is he the one with the tool
belt?"

"I believe he's a structural engineer." Violet's voice had
gone prim, a distinct sign, Cassidy knew, that she'd noticed the tool belt.

"I bet Mrs. B. already has visions of matchmaking

floating through her sweet little head." Lilah downed another slug from her ever-present coffee cup.

"I suspect it's more than matchmaking." Violet brightened. "Rumor has it she had a wild affair with Max's grandfather years ago. Maybe she sees it as renewing the sexy for another generation."

"Where do you get this stuff?" Cassidy knew she should be surprised, but her friend had more information in her head—and significantly better connections—than half the data streams on Facebook.

Violet's cat-'n'-cream smile matched her equally catlike green eyes. "I'm a pillar of the community and our business representative to the neighborhood. I hear things."

"If 'pillar of the community' is code for 'wicked gossip' then I concur." Lilah righted a fallen mannequin before dropping cross-legged to the floor next to it.

"None of it changes the fact that I've not yet met Cassidy's rescuer, which, if his promise to return is kept, will be remedied soon."

"I'm not a damn damsel in distress." Cassidy reached for a small band in her pocket and dragged her hair into a thick ponytail.

"No, but you did have a scare." Lilah's normally quick grin had faded. "I'm really glad he was here when you needed him. And I'm baking an entire tray of cupcakes for you to take there as a thank-you gift."

Cassidy couldn't hold back the smile. Or the blessed feeling of normalcy that her friends could impart with a few teasing words.

Where would she be without the two of them?

She'd met Lilah Castle and Violet Richardson on their first day of their freshman year of college and they'd been a trio ever since. These women *knew* her. Got her.

And they always had her back.

"I bet it's Anastasia Monroe. She's been jealous of your latest line for the past three months."

Cassidy couldn't quite hold back the shocked look at Lilah's words as she rekeyed in to the conversation. "One, it's not nice to go around accusing people. And two, I hardly have a line."

"Lilah sort of has a point. You did have three designs featured in the *Brides of Dallas* magazine." Violet held the dressmakers' dummy in place while Lilah made quick work repairing the base with a small handheld screwdriver.

"Let go, Vi, and let's see if it's sturdy." Lilah sat back on her heels and pressed a hand to the base. With a satisfied nod, she stood after it held firm. "Better than before. Which is more than I can say for this place."

Cassidy glanced around at Lilah's words, their truth more than evident. The police had come and gone, leaving behind a couple of business cards and paperwork for her to fill out if there was anything missing. They had perked up when she'd mentioned the alarm and promised to look into the situation with the shop's security provider, confirming if she'd forgotten to set it or if it had been turned off at some point. Beyond adding it to their investigation and promising a report she could turn into her insurance agent, there was little else the police could do.

All in all, relatively small comfort or help now that she was staring at two thousand square feet of destruction.

Tucker had left after the police departed and Lilah had arrived, but he'd promised to return with coffee and his partner, Max. Her friends' continuous glances toward the front door weren't lost on her.

Violet held up a delicate veil, a large rip evident in the center of the lace. The simple veil was one of Cassidy's favorites and—unbidden—a well of tears filled her eyes before cascading over her cheeks.

"Why would someone do this?" Cassidy knew full well the tears were useless, but suddenly, the knowledge her sanctuary had been violated crashed over her in a wave. On a hard sob, she dropped the contents of her dustpan into a garbage can Violet had dragged to the middle of the room, then sat on one of several couches strategically positioned through the shop.

"Oh, Cass!" Lilah moved first, her thick Crocs thwapping on the floor as she crossed the room. "It's all right."

"No…no—" Another hard sob gripped her throat at the comforting arms that wrapped around her. "What if they come back? They know the alarm codes."

The thought had slithered through her mind, taking root as she'd begun the slow slog of cleaning up the mess left by their intruder.

Or intruders.

The thought of more than one criminal traipsing through the store only brought another hard knot in her throat and another hot wave of tears.

"What if we'd been here? What were they after? And the destruction—" She broke off, struggled to catch her breath. "It's mean. Vindictive. Evil."

Lilah and Violet stayed by her side, flanking her both physically and emotionally, as the tears fell. And as the moments ticked past, the adrenaline fading along with her sobs, Cassidy knew another emotion.

Anger.

Raw and white-hot, its steady drumbeat filled her as she slowly dried her tears.

Someone had done this to her work. To the business she shared with her friends. To the neighborhood that had scratched and clawed its way from obscurity into a glittering jewel of commerce within the city she loved and called her home.

The light tinkle of shop bells rang out, dragging their collective attention toward the door. Tucker stepped through first, followed by another man Cassidy assumed was his partner, Max.

She took in their intimidating size, both large and impressively built, and could only feel their arrival somehow punctuated the moment.

"Looks like the cavalry just arrived."

Violet's voice was low, but Lilah managed to keep hers even lower, tinged with a breathless edge. "You know that saying. About cowboys. I think I finally understand it."

"What saying?" Cassidy turned toward Lilah and brushed at her cheeks, dashing off the last few lingering tears.

"I could definitely save a few horses and be more than happy to ride those cowboys."

Chapter 2

Tucker took note of Cassidy's red-rimmed eyes and the supportive stance of her friends and knew her adrenaline rush had faded in full. Something primitive tugged at him, tightening his hands around the toolbox and drill he carried.

She could have been hurt. Worse, had she walked into her shop at the wrong moment, while someone was bent on destruction, she could have been killed.

Collateral damage to whatever else had taken place.

The Design District was an up-and-coming neighborhood but it still had some dodgy edges. Although any number of apartments and restaurants had sprung up around those edges in the past few years, slowly reclaiming the area as a trendy spot for work and play, the warehouses themselves could be prime picking for thieves. On their walk from their own offices, he and Max had thrown out various ideas as to who might benefit from robbing a store focused on weddings.

And when they came to the humbling realization that they knew next to nothing about weddings, Tucker knew they'd be a far better resource as a repair crew than as detectives.

That still hadn't stopped him from placing a gun in the bottom of his toolbox for extra protection.

Tucker gestured his buddy through the door for introductions, and Max settled the large ladder they'd carried between them before turning to the women. He'd met Lilah earlier and had pinned her as the lighthearted one of the group, with her pink streak of hair, baker's uniform and ready smile. She didn't disappoint in that respect, that quick smile reappearing immediately along with a promise to provide goodies before she disappeared through the door that led to her half of the shop.

The other woman—Violet, with her long sweep of black hair and serious eyes—finished off the triumvirate, as he was quickly coming to think of them. She already knew Max from the neighborhood business meetings and Tucker finished off the introductions before setting his tools on the floor. "We came to help, so put us to work."

"As far as we can tell, the main damage seems confined to up front in the showroom area." Cassidy's voice still held a slight quaver but he heard a note of steel clearly underneath. With each step and gesture toward destroyed merchandise or littered debris, the warrior goddess who had marched into her store this morning more fully reappeared.

Max followed Violet toward a heavy rack of dresses that needed righting, leaving Tucker a few moments with Cassidy. Her smile was warm and genuine and faded the last vestiges of her crying jag. "I can't imagine Bailey was too happy to be left behind."

"Since I left him with a rather large bone I suspect all's right with his world."

"Let him know a second one's headed his way. A small token of my gratitude for the reassurance this morning."

His gaze drifted toward a small corkscrew curl that had fallen out of her ponytail. The urge to reach out and tug that curl—as much to watch it spring back into place as to assuage his curiosity that her hair was as soft as he suspected—gripped him. With a step back, he let his gaze drift deliberately around the shop. "How long have you been in this space?"

"Almost three years now."

"And you and your partners go to all those weddings?"

"Violet more than either Lilah or I. She's a wedding planner so she's much more involved in the actual event, as well as all the activity that leads up to it. Lilah mostly handles wedding cakes and I've got the bride's dress and trousseau."

Their business was pretty much what he expected, but it still didn't explain why they'd been targeted for a robbery. Especially when it appeared as if the would-be thief was more hell-bent on destruction than any actual burglary. "I can't imagine you make a lot of enemies in the wedding business."

"You'd be surprised. It's a competitive market."

He heard the pride—and the unspoken words underneath the comment. "A lucrative one, as well?"

"It's not nice to brag."

"Facts are facts." He shrugged it off but was curious about her response. With an attentive eye, he pushed past her beauty to focus on her more wholly.

There was an elegance to Cassidy Tate. A subtle grace that suggested good breeding and a veneer of class. Yet here she was, in one of Dallas's up-and-coming neighborhoods, building a business with her friends.

He'd met more than his fair share of Dallas socialites, and while it wasn't fair to paint them all with the same brush, his overall impression had been of money, polished beauty and the raw ambition to marry well. Beyond the polished beauty, he saw very little resemblance between that venomous set and the woman standing before him.

"Lilah thinks a competitor did this." Cassidy fingered a length of lace in her hand. "I just don't know if I agree."

"The destruction suggests something personal."

She shrugged. "Like the bragging, it's not nice to go around accusing people of bad behavior."

"And like I said, facts are facts."

A loud shout from the back of the store had both of them rushing in the direction of Violet and Max. Tucker took off first, Cassidy in his wake, as they threaded their way through the destruction.

"What is it?"

"Look at this." Max was on his knees in front of a small, squared-out area in the floor.

"A trapdoor?" Cassidy moved from her position behind him, and Tucker didn't miss the way the casual brush of her arm lasered through him in a hot, heated rush.

"Have you ever seen this, Cass?" Violet stood on the other side of Max, pointing toward what appeared to be a filled-in hole.

Cassidy shook her head, confusion blooming in her eyes like a ripe flower. "No. Besides, I assumed this entire place sat on a slab of cement like all the other warehouses down here."

Tucker had grown up in New York, so it had come as a surprise to him on one of his earliest architectural jobs that no one in Texas had basements. The region's soil composition simply wasn't conducive to a below-ground layer of structural support.

"It is strange." Violet shifted around the perimeter of the small square of concrete, her heels clicking on the exposed slab of floor where they had pulled away the rug.

Tucker held back a smile at the way Max's gaze tracked over the woman's long legs before Cassidy's voice pulled him back to the situation at hand. "Mrs. B. already had the rug in here when we moved in. Remember?"

Violet tapped a lone high heel. "That's right. One of her selling points for the lease. Fresh carpeting throughout the office areas."

Tucker glanced at Max, well aware the man's thoughts matched his own. "Why'd you think to pull it up?"

"The rug had a tear in it when I came back here to inspect the office," Max said. "If I hadn't been looking for anything out of place I'd likely have missed it."

"We didn't even see it until I noticed that my desk was out of place." Violet pointed toward the floor, and Tucker could see the indentation of where the leg of the desk had left an outline in the carpet.

Cassidy dropped to her knees and ran her fingers over the handle built into the concrete. "You think this is what the burglar was really after?"

At her light frown, Tucker dropped to his haunches beside her. "It appears so. Do you have any idea what your landlady might be hiding?"

"No." Cassidy's gaze never left the handle, but he saw the moment her puzzlement shifted to something more. "But if this was what the burglar was looking for, that means his first trip was unsuccessful."

"Mrs. Beauregard can't be responsible." Lilah stood over the sealed entrance, her hands on her hips and a stain of chocolate smeared across her white chef's coat.

"And she's certainly not the type to hide things," Violet added.

"How do you know?" Max piped up from behind her. "She's your landlady, not your grandmother."

Lilah and Violet turned at the same time, their eyes flashing. Where Lilah's gaze was purely defensive, Violet's held something more. Challenge?

Anxious to diffuse the situation, Cassidy stepped in. "Because she wouldn't do that to us."

"And, well—" Lilah broke off. "She's *old*."

Cassidy wasn't sure age had anything to do with it but had to agree with Lilah that their sweet, twinkle-of-mischief-in-her-eye landlady seemed unlikely to be hiding secrets.

Especially secrets that would lead to danger.

Unwilling to let the jarring impact of the break-in further color her judgment of others—the accusations against Anastasia Monroe already sitting uncomfortably on her conscience—Cassidy held up a hand. "I was already planning on running this month's rent check over to her during lunch. I'll ask her about the hole when I go."

"You can't go alone." Violet's normally calm features were lined with concern. "Especially not about this."

"Look. I'd already promised her I'd repair that tear in her grandmother's wedding veil, which I was also planning to bring with me. I'll use that as my way into the conversation. Besides, someone needs to stay here and wait for the alarm people to come check the system and reprogram a new code."

"I'll go with you."

A small shot of pleasure wove through her at Tucker's offer before she brushed it off. "I'll be fine. I don't want to make too big a deal out of it."

"You already said earlier the woman has matchmaking on her mind. We'll drop a few hints and make eyes at each other to keep her distracted."

The image he painted was far more tempting than she wanted to admit, but Cassidy opted for casual nonchalance.

"She didn't get to eighty and remain wily as a coyote because she was dumb and easily played. We're making too big a deal out of this."

A slight grunt from the floor pulled their attention to Max, who tossed a wrench into the box by his side. "Damn thing's shut tight, cemented into place."

The challenge spurred Tucker into action and he joined Max on the floor, both of them searching the small area for a way to get underneath it. Cassidy didn't miss Violet's speculative gaze or Lilah's breathless expectation as the men went to work attempting to get to whatever lay beneath the concrete flooring.

When they'd made no headway after ten minutes of prodding, tugging and putting their backs into it, the talk drifting to blowtorches and drills, Cassidy finally stepped in. "I'm not comfortable continuing to do this. It's obvious whatever this space was created for has been sealed over for a reason. We shouldn't keep prying. I'll ask Mrs. B. about it."

"And I'll go with you." Tucker gathered up the various tools he'd pulled out for their attempt at the sealed floor and dropped them into his toolbox, then stood.

"I really can go alone."

"Humor me. You had a big scare this morning and while I believe you when you say your landlady is a sweet woman who is incapable of doing harm, I'd like to see for myself."

"Tucker's got a point," Lilah piped up. A wicked light filled her dark chocolate gaze, and Cassidy fought the blush that crept up her neck, her cheeks going warm. "Distract Mrs. B. with visions of matchmaking and she'll answer whatever you want."

When Tucker only shoved his hands in his pockets, a small, impish smile on his face, Cassidy gave in. She'd learned long ago how to put a smile on her face and go with the flow.

She might as well put the skill to good use.

Tucker followed Cassidy's directions as he threaded through downtown traffic toward one of East Dallas's oldest and most well-heeled neighborhoods. The trapdoor Max and Violet had discovered in the floor continued to fill his thoughts. "Have you had any other problems since you moved into the shop?"

"Nothing. We get the same alerts as the rest of the neighborhood when a crime has happened, but for the most part we've been left alone."

"And no one's happened by or stopped in to casually ask questions? Maybe ask for directions, then start asking about the building?"

Tucker stopped at a light and glanced over toward her. The vivid blue of her eyes turned thoughtful before she shook her head. "No, nothing, but I will ask Vi and Lilah if someone's come in."

He didn't want to scare her but after spending time inside the shop and seeing the destruction with his own eyes, he couldn't quite chalk it up to a run-of-the-mill burglary attempt.

"I keep playing it over and over in my mind. I make wedding gowns. Why would someone want to destroy that?"

"Which takes us back to a competitor."

Cassidy let out a hard sigh. "Which doesn't play for me. I don't have enemies."

Tucker knew it wasn't that simple, but he opted to hold his tongue as she tried to work through the angles.

"And then I come back to the alarm. No one has the code except Lilah, Violet and me."

"Could either of them have given it out?"

"Nope. Lilah doesn't even give it to her delivery teams. If she's sending a cake out with someone else, she meets them at the store."

"You've been in business awhile. There's no chance she gave it to someone she trusts? Someone who's been dependable trip after trip."

"I just don't see it. In fact, Lilah's been the one of us who has been the most insistent about not sharing our alarm codes."

He filed that one away, as well. The bright, happy baker seemed as if she didn't have a care in the world, but someone that maniacal about giving an alarm code to what he'd expect were trusted employees seemed a bit off. "Yet someone got the code."

"Yes."

Cassidy tapped her fingers on her thigh, the nervous motion spearing through his chest. Tamping down on the surprising—and altogether uncomfortable—sensation, he pointed toward an upcoming light. "This is the turn, right?"

"Yes. Left at the light and then a right at the next one."

Tucker moved through the light and drove toward one of the most elite neighborhoods in East Dallas. The homes were old—some of the oldest in the city—and the structures had great bones. Even more apparent was the fact that the owners in Mrs. Beauregard's neighborhood took care of what was theirs.

Although he knew he and Cassidy could keep going round and round like this, there didn't seem to be any answers to their questions. Recognizing this downward spiral, Tucker latched on to the opportunity to shift their focus. "I haven't been over here before. These homes are spectacular."

"Swiss Avenue was one of the city's first Historic Districts, if not the first." Her gaze drifted from the passenger window toward a home about half a block away. "Each one's more beautiful than the next, but that one there on the corner is my favorite."

He took in the neoclassic architectural style on the pristine white home that rose three stories and had to give her points for style. "It's gorgeous."

"A glittering diamond among diamonds, but extraspecial somehow."

Her murmured words only added to his curiosity, especially combined with his observations of her earlier. Although she gave off the impression of wealth and that subtle society-girl vibe, maybe he was mistaken. "Are you from Dallas?"

"Born and raised."

"What part of the city?"

"Not too far from here, actually. My mother grew up knowing Mrs. B., and I've known her my whole life. She knew about the business we wanted to start and offered us a great deal on the space we lease from her."

Bingo.

Tucker prided himself on his ability to read a situation, and his impression of elegance and money was spot-on, especially if she had grown up nearby.

"What about you?" Her question pulled him from his musings, and he thought about how to answer what was—at its core—a simple question.

Even if his ability to give a casual answer would be a hard-won victory.

"A bit of a mutt. I moved around as a kid, then settled in upstate New York for high school before going to West Point. And then it was into the military."

"You and Max were in the armed forces, right?"

He couldn't hold back the cheeky grin at her clear knowledge of his background. "More details from Mrs. B.?"

"And Violet. That woman's a walking social network. Not much escapes Vi's purview."

"Yes, we were. Part of the Army Corps of Engineers."

As the words came out, Tucker waited for the inevitable drop in her smile—that subtle gesture that indicated she was disappointed he didn't say they were with the Navy SEALs or Special Ops. His father still wore that look of disappointment every time his career came up.

"That's so cool. So you went around blowing up bridges and building dams and stuff."

He fought off the surprise at the interest sparking in her words. "A few times. Although I suspect the protectors of said bridges weren't quite so happy with our efforts."

She laughed at that—a deep, throaty chuckle that speared him down deep—before gesturing to the next driveway. "You've got a point there. The next one's Mrs. B.'s."

The house was a vision, and his innate appreciation of architectural lines and good old-fashioned home design approved of what he saw. They parked and he came around to help Cassidy out of his SUV.

The light scent of her—something along the lines of sweet lemons—greeted him, and his gaze caught once more on the vivid color of her hair. Shaking off the flight of fancy, he turned to stare up at the three-story home. "Does Mrs. Beauregard live here alone?"

"She does now. The girls and I have tried to convince her to get a live-in companion or consider moving but she claims she's fine."

"Max fights the same battle with his grandfather."

"He used to date Mrs. B., you know."

"How would I know that?"

A spark of mischief lit her eyes before she concealed them with a pair of sunglasses. "Consider yourself further informed on the Design District gossip chain."

"So noted."

Cassidy carried the fragile lace veil she'd mentioned earlier in both hands so he moved on ahead to knock on the door. The wide, thick entrance was offset by a large porch. He took in its simple comforts—an oversize porch swing, several plants and a pair of mud-caked garden shoes neatly lined up near the door.

When no sound echoed from inside, he knocked once more. "She knew you were coming, right?"

"Yes. I talked to her about it yesterday. She was so excited about getting the veil back." Her voice remained level, and all hints of mischief in her gaze were gone, replaced by a thin sheen of concern.

"Is there a back entrance?"

"Knock once more."

He did as she asked, then moved to look in the windows. "I don't see anyone."

"Would you hold this for me?"

He took the veil, the thin material weightless in his hands as she dug out a cell phone. She tapped the face and in moments he heard the ringing echo through the house. After four rings the phone went to voice mail, and Cassidy redialed once more.

When the ringing stopped a second time, Cassidy shoved the phone back in her purse and reached for the door. "This isn't like her."

She knocked before trying the handle, a small moue of surprise springing to her lips when the door slid open.

"Wait." Tucker handed back the fragile lace before moving through the door. Concern had filled him on his walk through Cassidy's shop this morning, but a decided sense of menace crept down his spine as he moved through Mrs. B.'s neat home. Foyer. Living room. Kitchen.

Cassidy saw the woman a split second before he did. She cried out before racing for the prone figure lying in front of the oven.

Chapter 3

Cassidy fought back the wave of terror creeping up her throat as she raced toward Mrs. Beauregard. *Please let her be okay. Please. Please.* The words pounded through her mind with the heavy tread of Thoroughbreds as memories of another day rose up and threatened to swamp her with grief.

"Mrs. B.!" The older woman had a sturdy frame, and Cassidy knelt beside her, running her hands over her shoulders, arms, then face. "Mrs. B.!"

Cassidy probed still-warm flesh, her limbs shaking as she sought evidence of life. Abstractly, she heard Tucker on the phone calling for emergency assistance.

Nothing…nothing…and *there.*

Thin and faint, she paused until she could calm herself enough to finally recognize a pulse.

"She's alive."

Tucker knelt on the other side of Mrs. B. and leaned his head toward her face. "I can feel her breath. It's faint and slow, but I can hear it, too."

Her touch was gentle, but Cassidy kept pressing Mrs. B.'s arm and squeezing her hand, all the while murmuring the woman's name to get her to wake up. Tucker vanished, but returned a few moments later with a thick throw that had lain over the sofa in the living room. "Let's get her wrapped up."

She sat back on her heels as he wrapped the blanket around Mrs. Beauregard, then settled a small couch pillow under the woman's head. The soft sound of sirens echoed in the distance, growing louder by the second.

"Stay here with her, I'll go meet them."

She watched him leave the kitchen, her gaze trailing after his large, capable form. They'd met under the strangest circumstances—shocking ones, even—yet she was more than grateful for his presence.

For how *right* it felt to have him there.

A light moan pulled her from her thoughts, and she squeezed Mrs. B.'s hand as another moan—louder this time—fell from the woman's lips. "Shh. Shh now."

Thin, blue-veined lids fluttered open, Mrs. B.'s normally vibrant green eyes filled with pain and confusion. "What happened?" She blinked once. Twice. "Cassidy?"

"It's me, Mrs. B. Shh, now. You're all right."

Mrs. B.'s eyes darted left and right and her breathing hitched as she grew more agitated. "But what happened?"

"It's okay now. We don't know what happened, but the ambulance is almost here. We're going to get you checked out and you'll be fine."

She crooned a few nonsense words, pleased when she heard Tucker's directions echoing from the front of the house.

The paramedics moved in, and she stood up to give them access. A large man, his dark blue T-shirt stretched tight against his chest, took charge immediately as he knelt next to Mrs. Beauregard. Cassidy gave the team room to work and took a spot beside Tucker.

It was several long minutes later that she looked down to realize her hand was firmly clenched in his.

Tucker and Cassidy followed the paramedics from the house. The ambulance had just pulled away, the team having confirmed the emergency room where they were taking Mrs. Beauregard, when Max pulled up in his sports car. The two-seater was anything but practical, but Lilah and Violet didn't seem to notice as they tumbled out of the passenger seat.

Questions carried across the yard as the women raced toward Cassidy before they surrounded her in a tight embrace.

"What the hell's going on?" Max's gaze stayed steady on the trio of women before giving Tucker his full attention.

"I'll be damned if I know."

"Did you get anything from their landlady?"

"She was pretty out of it." Those first few moments in Mrs. B.'s kitchen rolled through his thoughts, the shock and horror of finding the woman. "I'm just glad she's alive."

Max's face set in stoic lines, concern etching his tanned skin. "Don't tell me you're thinking this was a coincidence."

"I've never put much stock in coincidence."

"I fiddled a bit more with that panel in the floor."

"And?"

"Nothing. It's cemented tight and won't budge." Max paused a moment before pressing on. "I stopped short of jackhammering it but it smacks of something curious."

"So why now? Unless they're damn good actresses, Cassidy and her partners obviously weren't aware of the hole. Besides, they've been there for a few years already. If they were responsible, they could have dug it up at any point and without destroying things. So who suddenly decided to go digging for whatever's been hidden?"

Snippets of the conversation between the women floated toward them on the rising heat of the day. Their concern for Mrs. Beauregard had faded to speculation on what might have happened. Tucker missed the specifics of their discussion, but he didn't miss Cassidy's hard head shake or the shrug of her shoulders in response to her friend's questions.

He suspected she didn't believe in coincidences, either.

"They make quite a sight." Max's voice was low, hovering in the register he'd perfected when they were on active duty. Only this time there was a layer of intrigue that spoke of anything but the enemy.

"A beautiful trio."

Tucker wasn't sure if he realized it, but Max mentioned Violet every time he came back from one of the Design District's business meetings. He'd never mentioned the other women, but now that he'd met them all, Tucker saw what a team they made.

A competent and beautiful one.

Their conversation faded as the women moved toward them as a unit.

"We're going to head to the hospital. Would one of you mind taking us?" Cassidy's brow furrowed. "Mrs. B. doesn't have any children and we don't know who else to call. We don't want her to be alone."

"I'll do it." Tucker ignored the subtle lift of his friend's eyebrows, satisfying himself that his quick reaction was tied to the knowledge his SUV offered better transportation than Max's two-seater. "Max can follow us with the keys after the locksmith gets here."

In minutes they were loaded back in his car, Max's lone figure left standing on the porch. As he took in his friend's speculative gaze, Tucker instinctively knew Max's thoughts matched his own.

Someone thought Mrs. Beauregard was sitting on a secret. What bothered him was what that nameless, faceless threat would do to possess it.

Charlie McCallum slammed the door to his apartment and stalked toward the bottle of bourbon that sat on the bar divider between his kitchen and living room. Heat radiated off him, the thick, long-sleeved sweatshirt he'd donned for the job a bitch in the Dallas heat.

Debating between pouring his drink and stripping, the heat won out as he dragged the sweatshirt over his head. The thick ski mask bulged from his back pocket and he threw that across the living room after the rest of his clothes.

Damn old woman. That crotchety old biddy was a useless dead end. He hadn't gotten a single thing out of her and had shaved about ten years off his life in the process.

The moment when he'd let himself in her door and had come face-to-face with her, shock and horror lining her features…

It'd nearly had him running in the other direction.

He grabbed a glass from next to the sink and poured a generous portion of the bourbon with shaking hands. Damn it, he had the stones to do this.

He *did*.

He slugged back the drink and let the heat of the liquor wash through his system as the list of his sins piled up. When had it gotten so bad?

And why weren't the pieces where he'd been promised?

His late wife had been vague, the rumor of a cache of jewels something she'd heard as a child. But he'd done his homework. Had hunted up that old appraiser and knew what he was looking for. Jo Beauregard was sitting on a boatload of jewels, and they were all hidden in the floor-boards of his former sister-in-law's shop.

And what were the freaking odds of that?

Charlie poured a second glass, calmer now as he worked through the problem.

Cassidy didn't know he'd been in her shop. She had no reason to suspect him, and after the number he'd done on her dresses there was no way she'd think it was anything but a standard break-in.

Mrs. B. didn't know it was him today, either. He'd seen the fear in her eyes and not a single moment of recognition it was him under the wool. He knew he could have gotten the location out of her if she hadn't panicked and slipped in her kitchen.

Calming, he nodded as the liquor went to work on his system. He was okay. Fine. Better than fine.

He was clean with Cass and he was clean with the old bat. There was absolutely nothing to tie him to either place. Add on the fact that no one in the Tate family had seen him in three years and he was golden.

Of course, since the damn hole he'd finally found was shut solid and he hadn't gotten a whiff out of Mrs. B., he was going to have to find a way to play buddy-buddy with freaking Saint Cassidy or lure her away from the shop somehow.

On a sigh, he figured he'd better start thinking up a good way to get her and her friends out of the shop. Attempting to contact her needed to be a last resort.

She'd never liked him and was certain not to have lost any sleep over him these past several years.

Especially since he was a living reminder of what she'd lost.

Cassidy noted the detective's sharp gaze as the man scribbled another note into a small black folio. Detective

Reed Graystone had arrived about an hour after the doctors had wheeled Mrs. B. back for tests and had quickly commandeered a private room from the information station.

Where Cassidy had initially appreciated the privacy and the detective's ready attention to details, they were going on hour two and the repetitive questions had grown tedious.

"Please take me through this morning's events, Miss Tate."

"Detective Graystone. I appreciate the time and your need for answers, but as I told you, the police who arrived at my business this morning showed very little interest in the break-in. They were kind, did their job and left, assuring me there'd be a report as a follow-up."

"And then you happen upon the owner of your establishment after she was assaulted in her own home. Please don't tell me you think it's a coincidence."

"Hardly." Cassidy bristled at the implication she was slow on the uptake but kept her smile firmly in place. "What I'm questioning is why we keep going over the same events."

"Witnesses often remember things they forgot."

Or detectives can ask different questions to trip those witnesses up, Cassidy thought ruefully.

"That's fair, Detective. But I've spent all day racking my brain to understand why someone would target a bridal boutique and my landlord. Other than Mrs. Beauregard's ownership of the location, she has nothing to do with my business."

"So why did you go to Mrs. Beauregard's?"

"As we discussed, I owed her our rent check as well as a bridal veil I was repairing for her. My partners and I also felt it was proper to tell her about the break-in this morning."

"And Mr. Buchanan? What's his relationship with the victim?"

The detective's gaze grew sharper as he turned his attention toward Tucker. Speculation ran rampant in the man's enigmatic gray gaze and Cassidy called on every shred of Southern charm and decorum she possessed not to call him out and request the name of a supervisor. "Tucker is one of the owners of another firm in our neighborhood. He found me this morning outside my shop."

"Found you?"

"I was shaken up. He was out running with his dog and happened upon me."

Detective Graystone didn't smile as his gaze landed fully on Tucker. "So the two of you never met before today?"

Before she could reply, Tucker cut in, smooth as spun cotton candy at the state fair. "Our partners have met at neighborhood events but Cassidy and I had never met before today."

"Yet you were more than willing to take her to her landlady's?"

"My mama would expect no less. Cassidy had a scare this morning and I offered moral support."

Cassidy held back the snort—she suspected that was the first time a New Yorker had ever called his mother his "mama"—but she had to give him points for style. The aw-shucks routine had the detective standing down a notch or two, even if he appeared no closer to believing the coincidence.

"What were you doing outside her store at—" Graystone consulted his notepad "—a little after 6:00 a.m.?"

"I was on my morning run. My dog and I stumbled across Cassidy as she stood outside the store."

"And you accompanied her inside?"

"After Cassidy called the police, yes, we did."

The detective's gaze skipped between Tucker and Cassidy before coming to rest on Tucker. "And you weren't scared?"

"I served in the army. I assessed the situation and felt it was okay to go in." His smile brightened and edged toward celebrity wattage before he added a cocky grin. "And I have a big dog."

Detective Graystone bared his teeth in a gesture that bordered on a snarl—as if he were irritated at being thwarted—but his words were deceptive as he spoke. "I think that's all my questions for now. I plan on following up in the morning. I'd like to talk to your partners, too. Will you be at your shop?"

"Yes." Cassidy nodded. "We won't be open for business in order to finish dealing with the damages, but come by anytime. I'll be there."

"I'll see you in the morning then."

Tucker waited until the door had closed behind the detective before he spoke. "He believes you."

"Why do you think that?"

"He didn't want to, but every question he asked, you had an answer for."

"He sure didn't act like he believed me. In fact, he sort of resembled the big bad wolf, just before he ate Grandma."

"Don't mistake standard interrogation tactics for lack of belief. Every volley the good detective tossed your way you sent right back. Nice job."

"Thanks. But I think you get the award for bringing Bailey into it. I still owe him that bone."

Tucker's easy smile—the one that kept snagging her pulse—fell away so suddenly she blinked at the rapid change. "You didn't tell him about the alarm."

The words weren't quite an accusation, but she heard the note of disapproval all the same. "He didn't ask."

"You didn't mention the hole in the floor, either."

"It's Mrs. B.'s building. As far as we know, it's empty."

"They were both omissions."

"It wasn't relevant to the questions."

Panic bloomed, chasing away the light, airy butterflies he'd created with his smile.

She'd been questioned before. Remembered how it felt to have someone stare at you as if you were nothing. Or worse.

As if you'd done something to be ashamed of.

She'd lived through that once and she'd be damned if she was going to go under the microscope again.

Tucker leaned forward, his dark eyes urgent. "Can you honestly sit there and tell me you think a hidden, sealed hole in the concrete floor of your office is empty? That you're not in danger and that whoever was in there once won't try again?"

With swift efficiency, she bricked up her emotions. This wasn't the same as before. No matter what they ended up discovering about the break-in and the concrete floor and even Mrs. B.'s attack, this would *never* be the same.

"It's not my building. It's not my business to say anything until we've spoken to Mrs. B. Besides, we've been there for nearly three years and nothing's happened."

"Yet someone came and ruined your things—*your* business—to make a point."

"We'll get to the bottom of it."

"By keeping the cops in the dark?" His big shoulders hunched, and he stood to pace. She watched the long, trim lines of his body and couldn't help wondering what had suddenly spooked him.

"You've been my partner all day and suddenly you're playing judge and jury. What gives?"

"This isn't a joke. Someone with access to your building wants something inside of it. I'd think you'd take it a bit more seriously."

"I am taking it seriously." The shift from easygoing flirt to fierce protector caught her more off guard than she wanted to admit, and Cassidy heard the quaver in her voice. Swallowing hard, she firmed up her tone. "I just spent two hours with a cop taking it seriously."

"Then prove it."

"I don't need to prove anything and I don't appreciate round two of an afternoon interrogation. While I appreciate the partnership, this isn't your problem. Violet, Lilah and I are more than capable of handling it."

"Handling it?"

She knew sparks arced between them—could practically see them float in the air—but Cassidy held her ground. It was embarrassing enough to be treated like a criminal by the detective. She'd be damned if she was going to take it from the one person who'd been with her all day.

Before she could say another word, those same sparks thickened, then exploded in a rush.

Tucker had his hands on her shoulders and hauled her to her feet. Somewhere inside she knew she should protest that she'd be fine. That she could take care of herself. That she could deal with whatever the hell was going on.

But as those large, capable hands pulled her close, she had to admit that Tucker Buchanan might be a bit more than she could handle.

Chapter 4

Tucker had no idea why her omission to the detective had him so riled, but now that it had, he couldn't quite stop the raging need to touch her and assure himself she was whole.

Unspoiled.

He'd seen the destruction this morning in her shop. And he'd seen her corresponding fear, sharp and pointed in that bright blue gaze. Someone had violated her space and ruined her work. And then they'd found Mrs. Beauregard.

What had seemed like a run-of-the-mill break-in at her shop had morphed into something far more serious. A threat hovered around Cassidy and, by extension, her partners. For reasons he couldn't name or begin to understand, that nameless, faceless danger had every instinct he possessed on high alert.

His gaze roamed over her face once more. Although that wild-eyed fear from earlier was nowhere in evidence, she had gone still, her gaze too bright as she anticipated his reaction.

Tucker gave himself that moment to simply look his fill. Her skin was so pale, a soft cream that spoke of elegance and refinement. His fingers gentle, he ran the pad of his thumb over the fine bones of her cheek. "You need to take this more seriously."

"I am taking it seriously, but I want to give Mrs. B. a chance to explain what we found." It was as though wisps of smoke curled around the edges of her voice, the register low and husky. "I owe her that much."

Fascinated by the softness of her cheek, he skimmed his thumb toward her jawline, tracing the firm length. "Don't you think she owes you the truth of why it's there in the first place?"

The moment hovered between them, their bodies close even as their battle of wills kept them at an emotional distance.

"She's an old woman. I hardly think she's hiding secrets."

"Everyone has secrets, Cassidy." He shifted closer before bending his head to press his lips along the same path his thumb had traveled. The light sigh that floated between them encouraged him, and he ran his lips over her slightly open ones, capturing the end of that small exhalation with his mouth.

Her hesitance vanished, and suddenly she was as in the moment as he was as they explored each other. Her hands settled on his hips before tangling in the material of his shirt where it bunched at his waist, and she moved closer in his arms.

Their bodies flush, Tucker felt that age-old rush of satisfaction as she came to him.

And in mere moments, he had to admit to himself that he was lost. His role as frustrated he-man—not his usual style *at all*—faded as he went from actively aggressive to humbly enthralled. The slim woman in his arms had turned his attraction on its ear and now stood toe-to-toe with him, giving as good as she got.

Their mouths met and clashed with a fierce urgency that gripped them both, drove them both.

Destroyed them both.

Her soft lips were lush under his, begging him to drink his fill. But when she turned on him, taking his bottom lip between hers, Tucker knew a moment of such deep-seated weakness his knees nearly buckled.

Who was this woman?

Drawing back, he stared at her, dazzled by the fierce urgency that had consumed them, locking them in a moment rife with power and need.

A witchy little smile tinged those bee-stung lips. "You look surprised, Lancelot."

"Lancelot?"

That smile broadened as she cocked her head. "You were the one with the white-knight complex this morning."

"I'm not feeling very pure and honorable at the moment."

"That makes two of us." Her temptress's smile shifted, gentled, as she released her hold on his waist. "But it doesn't change the fact we don't know each other very well."

He knew he was staring, unable to look away from the vivid, bright woman standing before him. But he also knew she had secrets.

And some level of fear that ran deeper than even she likely understood.

Willing his raging blood to cool, Tucker took a step back of his own, seeking some sort of equilibrium in that extra degree of space.

"I can at least buy you dinner. You up for burgers?"

"A man after my own heart."

A funny little tingle settled low in his gut at the mention of her heart, but he ignored it. Instead, he grabbed her

hand—unable to *not* touch her after what they'd shared—
and pulled her toward the door. "Let's go."

Cassidy snagged a crisp French fry, loaded with cheese,
bacon and ranch dressing, and avoided a low moan as the
combination passed her lips.

"These are good." Tucker shoved about three fries to
her one in his mouth, his head nodding as he chewed.
"Really good."

"Angry Dog makes one of the best burgers in town.
And their cheese fries are to die for. I have to promise
cleansings and salads for a week to even get Vi to consider this place."

A lone eyebrow raised across the scarred wooden table.
"Do I dare ask what's involved in a cleansing?"

"Not if you want to enjoy that burger that's about to be
set in front of you." Cassidy glanced at their waitress, who
hovered over them with two plates loaded with juicy burgers and even more of those delicious golden French fries.
Their waitress settled the plates, and Cassidy didn't miss
the appreciative glance the young woman gave Tucker.

Nor did she miss Tucker's abstract smile when he nodded for another iced tea.

Cassidy waited a beat until the woman was out of ear-
shot before she spoke. "I think you wounded her."

"I'm sorry?" He glanced up from the ketchup bottle,
confusion stamped clearly in his dark eyes.

"Our waitress. She was getting her flirt on and you
seemed oblivious."

"She wasn't flirting. She asked me if I wanted a refill
on my drink."

"Could have fooled me."

"She wasn't flirting, and even if she was, I'm here with
you. Why would I make eyes at her?"

Cassidy nearly fumbled her bun as she layered on her own spread of ketchup. Who was this man?

She'd been single longer than she wanted to admit, but even in her periods of active dating she'd struggled with men who seemed to have a wandering eye, always looking for something better to come along. Hell, even Robert had always acted like there was something better waiting around the corner.

And then he'd gone and proven it.

When she said nothing, Tucker pressed his point. "You look confused at my statement."

"I'm not confused. Surprised, maybe, is a better word."

"I'm full of them." A cocky grin quirked his lips along with something else she couldn't quite name.

Courtesy?

Humor?

Or maybe it was just another facet of that air of chivalry that seemed to hover around him like a cloak.

Either way, she couldn't hide the fact that she found it appealing. Found *him* appealing.

"So tell me about your business." Tucker split his attention between his juicy burger and her, and again Cassidy couldn't quite fight the sense that he was unique. "Violet made a few comments about the business while we were cleaning up this morning but I didn't get a full sense of your place."

"We started Elegance and Lace several years ago, snagging jobs where we could. Violet's always been an event planner and was working for a woman who can only be kindly referred to as a bitch."

"Ow."

"Exactly." Cassidy nodded, remembering more than one round of after-work martinis that involved as many tears as anger-fueled words. "And Lilah did some time in a restaurant before going to work for a bakery and then doing her own stuff on the side where she could."

"And you?"

"I've always designed but never thought I could make a career of it."

"Why not?" Half his burger had vanished and she hadn't even started on her own. Her uneaten dinner gave her a chance to hesitate for a moment as she figured out how best to answer his probing question.

Even as she worked through what she wanted to say, long-ago fights sprang up as fresh memories.

You're meant to wear a wedding dress, not design them for spoiled socialites.

If you want a career so damn bad, the least you could do is invest in something worth your time. Law or banking instead of fripperies and lace.

My sister, down on her knees before Dallas's brides, hemming their skirts.

"Cassidy?" The dim lighting inside the pub had turned Tucker's eyes such a dark brown they were almost black. The color was rich and inviting, as were the small crinkles that bracketed his mouth in a smile. "You in there?"

"Yes. Sorry." She fiddled with a fry before taking a deep breath. "Designing dresses was seen as a frivolous thing to do. In my family's estimation."

"Frivolous?"

"In the extreme. While waiting to marry well a woman should make herself useful by doing some staid, corporate thing like working at a bank. Then you'll be sure to make enough money to squander it properly on a variety of items no one really needs."

The words were out before she could pull them back. And where the *hell* had they come from?

She did okay for herself and had the benefit of pursuing

something she loved at the same time. And she'd stopped worrying long ago about other people's choices, even if they were her family.

So she had no small measure of surprise when Tucker bypassed the money comment completely.

"You would look cute in a button-down blouse and pencil skirt." His gaze roamed over her face, and she felt the heat rising at the careful perusal. "But it doesn't suit you."

Surprise at his quick assessment banished the storm clouds that thoughts of her family always brought. "Most don't agree."

"Then they don't see what I do."

The urge to ask him what he meant rose up on the swiftest of feet, but before she could ask what he saw, he pressed on.

"So how'd you break free?"

"I designed on the side and got lucky."

"Nothing wrong with a little luck. Especially when you've done all the prep work in advance."

Flashes of silk and seed pearls drifted through her thoughts as she popped another fry in her mouth. Cassidy still wasn't sure Violet hadn't had a hand in things, despite her friend's denials to this day, but Tucker was right about one thing.

She *had* been prepared.

"A girl I went to school with had to stop by my apartment to pick something up. My father had made a donation to a Junior League function and I had an envelope for her."

"What exactly is Junior League? And do you graduate to senior varsity or something?"

"I keep forgetting you're not from the South."

"No, ma'am." His grin was broad and she saw the mischief that had replaced concern in his gaze. "Which is why

I walk around in a perpetual state of confusion every time I attempt polite conversation with a client."

"Junior League is a charity organization, not a sporting event."

"And here I pictured sweet, refined young women mud wrestling."

She laughed at that, images of the women she'd grown up with rolling around in mud and ruining their perfectly manicured hair and nails.

"We only sling mud of the verbal kind, and even then, it's rare. Most of the women I know are dedicated to the cause."

"Be that as it may, I still don't understand how that ties to a wedding dress."

"It was a silly coincidence, nothing more. But Suzy had come for a check my father had made out for a table at an upcoming function and I said I'd get it to her. I had a dress I was making laid out on the dining-room table. I hadn't even expected her to come in, but we'd started talking and she was excited about having gotten engaged the weekend before."

"Decibel levels too high to keep the conversation in the hallway?"

His smile was broad, and she couldn't quite fault him for the tease. In fact, she realized, back to her earlier thought, most men wouldn't have even given the story another moment of their time, yet he seemed genuinely interested.

"Pretty much. So she comes in and sees the dress I was making and that was it. She demanded I design her wedding dress for her on the spot."

"Off to the races, then."

"Off to the races. It didn't hurt that her spring wedding was one of the most covered in Dallas. Nor did it hurt that Violet was her wedding planner. It gave me a bit of street cred to get some interest in dresses from other brides, and gave us the experience to pitch for a small-business loan."

"Funny that your father making a donation took you on a path away from a 'proper' life, especially if he didn't support what you were doing."

Tucker's words were casual, his gaze focused on his last few fries, before he glanced back up at her. But way down deep in those dark depths, she saw just how serious he was.

They'd spent all day in each other's company—a day full of any number of intense experiences, from danger to attraction—yet this moment seemed the most significant somehow. Because in that moment she *knew*, without a doubt, that Tucker Buchanan wasn't casual. Or simple. Nor did he miss much.

And he fully understood the irony of seeing her success come out of the simple action of an unsupportive parent.

"He's gotten over it."

"Parents usually do. The bigger question is, have you?"

Josephine Beauregard came awake to dim lighting and the dull scent of antiseptic. She became aware of a steady beeping somewhere behind her head and tried to figure out where she was. Recognition hovered just out of her reach—like she should know where she was but was too happy floating in a sea of blissful ignorance.

Should she open her eyes? Wait…they were already open.

With a series of rapid blinks she tried to pull the room into focus but her pupils hadn't adjusted fully to the darkened room.

She wanted to panic. Should she panic? But the blanket around her was warm and she felt an odd sense of safety surrounding her.

Blanket?

The question hit her, tunneling through her disorientation and the fierce edges of a headache she was slowly coming to realize she had.

Why did she have a blanket? It was Dallas in summertime and she hadn't had a blanket wrapped around her since the freak ice storm they'd battled the previous March.

So why was she wrapped up?

Underneath the antiseptic she became aware of something else. A scent she remembered from so long ago. Strong. Masculine. And mind-numbingly alluring.

Turning her head, she took in a dim shape in the corner of her room. "Max?"

Now that she was aware of it, pain throbbed in her skull with all the finesse of a jackhammer. Despite the searing pain, she couldn't hide the rush of awareness and excitement at the figure she sensed in the dark. "Is that you?"

"Been wondering when you'd wake up."

"Why are you here?" Why *was* he here? He never came, and she'd stopped expecting him to long ago.

"That's the question I've been waiting to ask you." He moved slowly—wasn't that the way of it now?—before coming to stand beside her.

Despite the age that tinged his features, she saw the young man she'd loved so well underneath. The firm jaw that had added folds of age still begged for her touch and those bright blue eyes saw as much now as they had fifty years ago.

"What happened to you, Jo?"

"I don't know." Confusion warred with the sweet memories of Max and again, the pain rose up in her head with sharp claws. Through the haze of hurt, a dim memory registered. "My house… Someone broke into my house."

She pulled at the blanket, the warm cocoon turning suffocating. "In my house. There was someone in my house. Someone hurt me."

He moved closer, his large hand on her shoulder to steady her. "Shh. Don't move like that. Take it easy."

A wave of panic stuck in her throat, choking her, as hot tears pricked the backs of her eyes.

Were they tears for the sudden realization she'd survived an attack, or were they for the fact that he was finally touching her? On a hard exhale, she admitted to herself she had no idea.

But it was probably both.

"Who would do that?"

"We don't know who."

"We?" The word struck her as strange since she'd been the one hurt.

"My grandson and his friend are helping out your girls. Seems like trouble's found its way to their door."

Max leaned closer, his gaze firm as those blue eyes lit with understanding. She'd seen those same eyes on his grandson—his namesake—and it never failed to choke her up.

Never failed to remind her of things best left buried.

"What aren't you saying, Max?"

"We don't know who attacked you, Jo. But I think you and I both know why."

Cassidy closed her front door behind Tucker, touched he'd walked her to her door. She'd purchased her small bungalow in East Dallas two years before, her home quickly becoming her haven, and it was odd to see his large frame in her doorway.

Odd, yet lovely, she thought now as she watched his long-limbed strides through the glass pane that edged her front door frame.

Maintaining his streak, he'd been the chivalrous gentleman, escorting her home and doing a quick check of her house to ensure the problems they'd battled all day hadn't found their way to her door.

She'd known the moment they walked in no one had been inside the house, but that knowledge hadn't negated how nice it felt to be looked after. Nor had it kept her from allowing him to roam through her kitchen and living room, bedroom and studio, confirming all was well.

If he'd noticed the thick duvet and red silk accent pillows that covered her bed she didn't know. But a girl could hope the sight had been what put the slight hitch in his stride as he walked from her home.

Yep. Tucker Buchanan had *gentleman* written all over him.

And why was that so damn appealing?

He pulled away from the curb, and she turned to focus on her home. The warm, almond-colored walls set off by bright, vivid prints of various sketches filled her with pride. This was her home. She'd earned it through hard work and the determination to make something of herself.

To make something of her life.

And with a soft sigh, she acknowledged she'd better get her mind off her attractive escort and back to work. She might have started the day early, but the unexpected twists ensured she still had a fair amount to get done.

With a cup of hot tea in hand ten minutes later, she made her way into her studio and assessed the dressmaker's dummy that stood half-clothed with her latest design.

Although the bride wasn't getting married for a year, the young woman was in the mood to experiment, and Cassidy had promised a preview of some mocked-up designs by the end of the following week.

The opportunity was a new one and she enjoyed the

challenge of designing something with the wearer in mind. Even so, she was still struggling with the sweep of silk she'd planned at the waist.

Gaze speculative, Cassidy kept her distance from the dummy, considering the angles as she stood across the room. The cut of the neckline negated an empire waist-line but the gathers she'd planned didn't quite fit, either.

The dress looked like every other dress and the carefree artist she was designing it for was anything but traditional.

Unlike Tucker Buchanan.

She settled her now-empty mug on the edge of her desk and considered her neighbor. The man had *traditional* and *old-fashioned* stamped across every inch of him. He was smart, strong and capable, with that damnable streak of chivalry she'd have never known she even liked until he found her standing in the middle of Dragon Street.

"He even has a dog," she muttered to herself as she padded back to the kitchen to make a second mug of tea. "A freaking dog. With a smooshed-in face and a big loyal gaze."

Other than Vi and Lilah, commitment and lasting bonds were not her strong suit. And a man with a dog had *commitment* painted across every inch of him.

There was no way she was getting herself mixed up with a modern-day version of the Lancelot she'd teased him about. Nor was she a tease, so their hot kiss would have to be the end of things.

When she saw him next—and based on what they'd discovered she knew more time with each other was in-evitable—she'd keep her distance.

She'd be polite.

Friendly.

Warm, without being a tease.

It was only right. They were neighbors, after all, running up-and-coming businesses.

The whistling teakettle added a smooth punctuation to her thoughts, confirming the finality of her decision. She had no real interest in Tucker Buchanan. They'd shared nothing more than a luscious lip lock between two healthy adults, capping off a tense and action-filled day.

It was understandable. And really, it could happen to anyone.

She'd nearly convinced herself as she carried her steaming mug back toward her office, once again determined to figure out the lines of the gown.

But when images of Bailey—curled at her feet while she sat with a sketch pad working on dress designs—floated through her mind, Cassidy had to admit the truth.

Who, exactly, was she trying to convince?

Chapter 5

Tucker dropped Bailey's leash on top of his drier as the mutt beelined for his water bowl. Loud slurping sounds echoed behind him as he headed for a bottle of water in the fridge.

Damn, but it was hot. Sweat covered him and he could have sworn he was giving off steam.

And it was only six freaking o'clock in the morning.

Just when he thought he was getting used to Texas, more heat leaped up to slap him in the face. It was a stark reminder of why Max had enticed him to take the job in the cool, arid month of January.

"Calculating bastard."

Even as the epithet left his lips, Tucker knew full well Max wasn't to blame for this morning. He'd earned his own personal heat wave all by himself, pushing the two of them through their paces. Bailey had delighted in the jog, his year-old boundless energy undeterred by the increasing heat. Although Tucker enjoyed his morning runs, he'd adjusted his schedule since getting the dog, ensuring they left early enough to miss the heat of the day.

Clearly he underestimated the power of August in Texas.

The lolling tongue and thick pants from where the dog now flopped on his belly against the cool kitchen tiles only reinforced the thought.

"Good run, boyo. Even if I am still thinking about the woman and all that gorgeous red hair."

That tongue continued to loll but Tucker could have sworn he saw a subtle head nod as well as clear understanding in that solemn brown gaze.

"And now you're convinced the dog understands you," he muttered to himself before gulping down a glass of orange juice, willing the natural sweetness to bring some equilibrium back to his thoughts.

He obviously had none if he was talking to himself all while assuming his dog understood his words. With brisk motions he snagged another glass of OJ from the fridge, along with the milk and a large box of cornflakes from the counter.

Sustenance and a shower would set him to rights. Then it was back to his drafting board to get a bit more done before heading into the office. Although Cassidy had filled more of his thoughts than anything else, the depths of his subconscious did manage to work through a bearing-wall problem he hadn't quite figured out on his latest project. He'd focus on the designs and get the luscious redhead out of his mind.

It was a good plan, and Tucker was convinced he'd have managed it until he caught sight of Bailey once more as he headed off for his shower.

He'd be damned, but if he wasn't mistaken those large brown eyes had a twinkle of a smile that dared him to keep Cassidy Tate out of his thoughts.

With images of his mocking housemate dogging his steps, Tucker pulled into the street parking in front of

Dragon Designs. Heat filled his lungs the moment he stepped from his vehicle's air-conditioning, and he glanced over to see Max's silhouette in the doorway, a mug in hand. "You're late."

Tucker shrugged and slammed their office door closed, amused despite himself at his friend's perpetual scowl. "Thanks, Mom."

"You're never late."

"So I was today. Got caught up in a design problem and did some drafting at home. I live three blocks away. If it was that important you could have called me."

"I'm just curious is all. You're never late."

"I was today."

Tucker brushed past Max and headed straight for the coffee. Heat be damned, there was no way he was skipping caffeine. After selecting his usual, he hit the button on the Keurig machine and settled in for whatever had Max extra surly this morning.

He didn't have to wait long.

"How the hell did we manage to get involved in what is happening down the street?"

"Define *involved*."

"Come on, Buck. You know as well as I do those girls are in a ton of trouble."

His nickname always reminded him of his time in the service—*Buck* an amalgamation of *Tucker* and *Buchanan*—and Tucker tamped down on the corresponding memories. He and Max had known each other for a long time, and there were few people—hell, there wasn't anyone—he trusted more.

But he didn't like the frustration roiling in his friend's tone.

"For the record, I think there's something going on, too. And I also think they need our help."

"This wouldn't have anything to do with your attraction to Red."

Tucker watched Max over the rim of his mug, curious at the very real frustration he saw lining his friend's jaw. "If we're going to start giving them nicknames, I didn't miss you eyeing Killer Heels every chance you got."

Max backed off at the pointed reference to Violet, his tone ratcheting down a few notches. "We don't need this. It's a distraction and a hassle. We're trying to get a business off the ground, not play protector-slash-detective for our neighbors."

"I'd say it's more than off the ground. We put in three new bids last week and won two others. The hard work's starting to pay off."

"So we can't put it at risk."

"I'm not putting anything at risk. And I'm not interested in playing detective."

"Could have fooled me."

Tucker fought the slight itch that settled in the dead center of his back. Max Baldwin was a straight arrow. He liked things his own way in his own time and the man had the role of curmudgeon down to a T.

But he was also as honest as Abe Lincoln, so whatever had his eyes darting away had Tucker's senses on high alert.

"What the hell's really going on here, Max?"

"Nothing."

"You started it, man."

"I just think you need to watch your step. We both do."

"What aren't you saying?"

Max settled his cup on his drafting station, his attention drawn to the messy surface before taking a deep breath. "This whole area—the Design District. It's got ghosts."

"Oh, come the hell on." Tucker fought back a laugh by

sheer force of will, the misery stamped on his friend's face the only reason he didn't let go with a series of mocking insults. "Don't tell me you believe in that."

"Hell, no. I'm not talking literal ghosts. I mean remnants of bad things. My grandfather's had property down here for more than half a century and some bad stuff's run through here. These warehouses have hid a lot of things in their time."

"So you're talking ghosts. Worse, you believe them. Yet you chose to set up shop here. Build a business. Become a freaking pillar of the community."

"Pop's been cagey about it all, but when he gave us the space for the business I figured it was a sign he finally believed the neighborhood was turning a corner."

"And now?"

Max ran a hand through his hair, tugging on the still-military-short ends. "Now I'm starting to wonder if he put us here to keep watch."

By midmorning Cassidy had made a significant dent in the cleanup. Although by no means done, she could now see an end in sight, with the majority of her studio set to rights. She'd intended to make a quick visit to Mrs. B. but Violet called a team meeting to discuss the upcoming Baker-Sullivan nuptials.

"What happened here?" Gabriella Sanchez stepped through the front door, her gaze sweeping over the space. Although Gabby owned her own business, Elegance and Lace had formed a loose partnership with her catering firm and they had three weddings they were working on together.

Cassidy caught her up on the events of the past day and in moments found herself pulled into a tight hug. "You could have been hurt."

"I keep going over it in my head, doing my best to ignore that part."

Gabby gave her another tight squeeze before standing back. "Then we won't talk about that part. But we will talk about why."

"That's just it, Gab. What would anyone want with us? We create weddings. We don't even sell bridal jewelry except for some nicer rhinestones and crystals. We're hardly a high-dollar smash-and-grab."

Gabby shrugged, her long, dark hair curling around her shoulders in an oversize, gorgeous mass that Cassidy had admittedly envied from the first day they'd met. "Because weddings are expensive, others often think we're flush with cash. I fought off a cousin about that very fact two weeks ago."

Despite the hair envy—which Cassidy was still working on getting over—she knew her friend had borne her fair share of struggle as she worked to build her business. Family criticism from one corner and unrealistic demands when she'd begun to see some success from another.

"This is why we drink wine."

Gabby patted her arm. "You're not kidding. And I have a new vineyard I've been sampling from up in the Panhandle. Wait until you taste this guy's Malbec. He's really got something."

"Let's get through this wedding and then we'll dive into a case."

The click of Violet's heels interrupted the mostly casual conversation and in minutes, they'd moved into a business meeting, each of them itemizing the status of their responsibilities for the upcoming event. They moved through the details quickly, each of them well versed in their roles.

Gabby finally had an approved menu and had confirmed her staff for prep and on-site. She and Lilah would work to bring in the cake and the same team Gabby had hired would assist in plating and distributing the cake to guests. Cassidy was on the final stages of the dress and would shift to run point on coordination with Violet since the wedding attendance numbered over three hundred.

Violet closed her laptop, a subtle satisfaction humming around her in the air. "Last bit of business. Rumor has it Sullivan's got cold feet."

"He's a dog." Gabby frowned, her gaze knowing. "We went to school together."

"And?"

"And he's had a roving eye since puberty."

"Lovely." Cassidy fought the groan. "Guess I know how I'll be assisting Violet. Checks of the bride's and groom's suites every fifteen minutes for a rogue groom."

"That's what backup to Vi usually entails anyway." Lilah patted Cassidy's hand, her grin broad. "What is it about a wedding?"

"I told Tucker it was the scent of tulle. He—" Cassidy broke off as Gabby leaned over the table.

"Tucker who?"

"The guy down the street who found me yesterday outside the shop."

"Wait. Wait." Gabby waved a hand. "Is this the other half of the duo Violet complains about every time she comes back from a District business-owners' meeting?"

"I don't complain." Violet took a sip of her tea, her gaze focused on the small cup. "Although Tucker's considerably nicer than Max."

"You do complain," Gabby pressed her, "but that's beside the point. Is he hot?"

"You've seen Max at the same meetings I have."

Gabby rolled her eyes but no one missed her sly grin at Violet's protests. "I meant Tucker, the neighborhood hero."

"Hot. Definitely." Lilah added a sigh. "And he's got a dog."

Cassidy felt three pairs of eyes settle on her, the weight of those expectant gazes suddenly oppressive in the airy space. "He's a nice guy. And he helped when I needed it."

"And?" Lilah pressed.

"And what?"

Cassidy knew she was being stubborn—and in her obstinacy she was making this more than it needed to be—but what did they want her to say? Tucker Buchanan was a nice guy. And he'd definitely shown up at the right time.

But—

But what?

Had she stopped believing she didn't deserve a nice guy? Or worse, had she stopped believing they existed altogether?

"He drove you home last night," Violet pointed out. "Made sure you were safe."

Gabby sighed. "Who does that?"

"No one I've been able to find." Lilah stood, the memories that normally stayed buried hovering like specters around her. "And on that note, I've got a cake to finish up. Gabs, I'll see you at the blessed event."

"You got it, *chica*."

The three of them watched Lilah go, and it was Violet who finally spoke. "When did the concept of finding a nice guy become a fairy tale?"

"I have no idea." Cassidy shook her head.

"Me, either," Gabby added.

Violet's gaze drifted to the doorway to Lilah's kitchen before she spoke. "Does it make me nuts for still believing in them anyway?"

Gabby laid her hand on the center of the table, palm up. "I'm right there with you."

Cassidy laid her hand in hers and Violet followed. "Look at us. Sappy wedding planners."

Cassidy couldn't hold back the smile—the first real one she'd had since the morning before. "I wouldn't have it any other way."

Since Lilah was neck-deep in a cake and Violet was out on appointments, Cassidy opted to move up her visit to see Mrs. B. from after work to lunch. Their morning business meeting had been productive and she'd made a good dent in a new design she had in development.

All in all, a break was in order.

With a bright bouquet of Stargazer lilies in hand, Cassidy navigated her way along the sterile hospital corridor, ignoring the paintings of pastel-hued abstract art that were somehow meant to soothe and calm hospital visitors and patients alike.

And walked straight into a wall of testosterone when she turned into Room 482.

Any sense of calm the paintings may have imparted vanished as she caught sight of Tucker, seated at the head of Mrs. Beauregard's bed like a sentinel. Max flanked the door, further adding to the image of the two of them as guards, and Cassidy suddenly wished there had been far more to clean up at the office.

"Cassidy, dear. Come in." The deep lines of Mrs. B.'s face creased in welcome as she waved her in, and Cassidy knew there was no easy escape. And when she realized how delighted Mrs. B. seemed by all the attention, she didn't have the heart to go.

"How are you feeling today?" She kissed the older woman's cheek, concerned when she saw the dark circles marking the tissue-thin skin.

"Right as rain, my dear. I should be out of here in no time."

Cassidy didn't miss Tucker's sharp gaze or the subtle shake of his head so she allowed Mrs. B. her illusions. "Can't keep a good woman down, you know."

"Of course not."

They made small talk over the flowers, and Cassidy couldn't quite hide her smile as Max and Tucker fought to stay interested. She did see a small yawn from Max as he shifted from foot to foot at his post.

Although her initial observation had been somewhat in jest, it did dawn on Cassidy there was a protective nature to how Tucker and Max manned the room, one at the bed and one at the door. Taking pity on them, she gave a small wave. "You guys look starved. Why don't you run and grab something to eat? I'm taking an extralong lunch hour today and would love to play hooky catching up with Mrs. B."

"The benefits of being the boss." Her landlady patted her hand.

"Exactly."

"If you're sure." Max's relief was palpable. "Can I bring you anything?"

"Nope. Go on." Cassidy waved them away before shooting a pointed glance at Tucker. "Go ahead, Aramis. Join your fellow Musketeer."

A small spark lit the depths of his eyes, nearly imperceptible in the dark brown.

Nearly.

"First it's Lancelot, now Aramis. Who's next?"

"Since you look ravenous, I'd say Cookie Monster."

"Porthos will do just fine on his own. I'll stay here, if you don't mind."

Reluctantly impressed he could conjure up the name of another Musketeer so quickly—especially since she only knew Aramis because of the men's cologne—Cassidy also didn't miss the look of clear interest stamped across Mrs. B.'s face.

Unwilling to let that scrutiny stay too long on her and Tucker, Cassidy focused the conversation on the older woman. "What did the doctor say?"

"You know doctors. They say I have a concussion." Mrs. B. snorted. "Like that kept Troy Aikman down."

Their former Dallas Cowboys quarterback might have had his share of concussions, but he'd also been about sixty years younger when he'd sustained them. Ignoring that simple biological fact, Cassidy used the man's near-legendary status in Dallas to her advantage. "Well, Troy also took care of himself and followed doctor's orders."

Mrs. B. snorted again, but this time the sound was a bit more delicate and far less emphatic. "I suppose."

"You're in good hands here and I didn't miss snagging another glance at your doctor when I spoke to him in the hallway. I'd stay firmly put, if I were you, and enjoy his attentions."

Cassidy smiled to herself as she caught sight of Tucker's grimace from the corner of her eye and laid it on a bit thicker. "He certainly enjoyed being the center of our attentions yesterday."

The discussion of an attractive young man of marriageable age did the trick and Cassidy was able to entice Mrs. Beauregard into a conversation that lasted until the woman's eyelids fluttered in exhaustion about twenty minutes later.

"You should get your rest, Mrs. B. I'll come back tomorrow for lunch."

When her departure was met with a small smile and nod of acknowledgment, Cassidy pressed soft kisses to the woman's cheeks and backed out of the room, Tucker at her side.

"How'd you manage that? No matter how we shifted the conversation we couldn't get her to take a nap."

Cassidy took in the solid form beside her and marveled yet again that she'd only met him the morning before. It seemed as if she'd known him far longer.

She supposed it was the fact that the neighborhood grapevine had abounded with chatter about the eligible bachelors—ex-military—who had taken up residence in the Design District.

But if she were honest with herself, she knew it was something more.

Knew that *he* was something more.

Despite her repeated self-assurances the night before that she did not need to get involved with her very attractive neighbor, the bright light of morning had shifted her wayward thoughts. Yes sirree, she'd left the Land of Determination and Self-Reliance and headed straight back to the true north that was Tucker Buchanan.

He fascinated her, with his chivalrous streak and his adorable dog and his willingness to step in and help.

They stepped into the elevators, and Cassidy fought the little voice in her head that noticed he hadn't shaved this morning and how that added a decided sense of danger to his smile. "You missed your chance to escape with Max."

That smile widened before growing the tiniest bit wicked. "He's an amateur."

"Amateurs. Didn't he get out of listening to girl talk while the getting was good?"

"He'll be back. He's got a few questions for his grandfather and he hasn't been able to get him alone." He settled a hand at her back and guided her into the waiting elevator. "I say he's a moron for walking away from two beautiful women."

In spite of herself, her heart softened another notch at the fact he'd added a woman old enough to be his grandmother into his assessment.

But it melted at the obvious sincerity in his voice.

"Be that as it may, you all didn't need to give up so much time. Between yesterday and now today I can't imagine you've gotten much done."

"We do okay."

"But I've been an awful imposition. We all have."

His gaze roamed over her face. "You giving me the bum's rush?"

"No. But—" The door slid open and Cassidy realized her purse was still in Mrs. B.'s room. "I need to go back up. I left my purse."

Tucker stabbed at the button for Jo's floor, and Cassidy couldn't help but think she'd overstepped in some way. "Problem?"

"We may be men, but we're certainly capable of helping out a neighbor. That's not solely up to you and your friends."

"That's not what I meant." When he said nothing, his penetrating, deep brown gaze the only indication he was listening, she pressed on. "You've been so helpful and we don't know each other and I've taken up so much of your time. You even came to check on Mrs. B. and she's got a great team of doctors watching her. I just spoke with her doctor before I came in, and he said she's going to be fine. A bit rumpled, but a full recovery."

Whatever fumbling had gotten her to this point morphed into something else entirely as she alluded to the doctor.

"Yes, I believe you mentioned the doctor already."

Violet had suggested for years Cassidy was unable to see the forest for the trees.

She'd also suggested—on numerous occasions—that Cassidy wouldn't know a man who was interested in her if he walked up and gave her a love bite.

If only she'd spent more time listening to Vi and less living inside her own head. "Of…of course."

"And maybe if he focused on caring for his patients instead of giving you puppy-dog eyes, your landlady might be getting out of here right now."

"She's getting excellent care!"

The elevator pinged as the car came to a stop, and she snapped her jaw shut. Whatever idiotic direction their conversation had taken, it wasn't anyone else's business.

The elevators slid open and two men stood across the hall, both dressed in dark suits, their gazes sharp as they stared into the elevator.

A subtle shiver at odds with the comfortable temperature in the hospital gripped her, and Cassidy had the strangest urge to shrink into her skin. Before she could say another word or make room for the new additions, Tucker had his hand on the door, pointing toward them. "You want in?"

One of the guys shook his head and uttered a hard "no" before he and his friend hotfooted it down the hall. They moved out of view, and Cassidy was surprised to see Tucker surge forward.

"What is it?"

"Something I don't like. Stay in there."

"What?" He was already into the hall when she pressed on the sliding doors and squeezed through into the hall. "What's going on?"

"Damn it, Cassidy."

Before he could say anything further the men took off

at a heavy clip, running along the long corridor. Tucker's shouted request for them to stop had no effect, and he took off after them, his long runner's strides eating up ground as he moved.

Without thinking twice, Cassidy took off behind him.

Tucker heard the staccato clip of her heels as she ran behind him but he ignored it. A nurse shouted, and as Cassidy's footfalls faded he figured she'd been slowed by the staff.

Good.

He'd rather she stayed in their grasp and far away from whatever problem was currently running in the opposite direction. Hell, let her go cozy up to that damned doctor with the perfect teeth if it kept her out of trouble.

Ignoring another round of shouts from the hospital staff, he hit the stairwell door before it fully closed, following his quarry.

The tops of their heads faded from view as they rounded the squared-off stairwell, and Tucker heard the heavy thrum of feet as they booked it toward the ground-floor door.

He shouted again for them to stop but they never even slowed. The first guy blew through the ground-floor door, followed by his partner. Bright light lit up the space before going dark once more, and Tucker knew the second guy had slammed hard on the door when it stuck tightly closed, the doorjamb clicking into place as his hands hit the thick metal.

Pressing on the release bar, he barreled through the heavy metal. The two men moved on swift feet through the lobby, picking up speed as they caught sight of him once more. Tucker ducked around a slow-moving patient with a walker, frustrated as he pivoted around the older woman, who skewered him with her gaze.

An order to stop lit up the serenity of the lobby and Tucker felt a hard fist wrap around his wrist before turning to face a security guard with considerable girth to match his meaty hands.

"Where's the fire, son?"

"I need—"

The man cut him off, before exerting subtle pressure to pull them both away from watchful eyes. "You need to slow down."

Although he'd never got off on intimidating others, Tucker moved up in the man's grill, his own height adding a measure to his message, even though his opponent outweighed him by a good hundred pounds. "I suggest you let me go."

The man dropped his arm and took several deliberate steps back. Whether the good ole boy was surprised by the fight or saw the obvious seriousness in his eyes Tucker didn't know, and he didn't care. What he did know was that two men who took off like that in the middle of a hospital were there to cause trouble.

He took off the moment that ham-fisted grip slackened and sprinted toward the hospital entryway.

And saw a nondescript black sedan lead-footing it out of the parking lot, the smell of hot asphalt and burning rubber hovering in their wake.

"What was that about?" Max's voice hit his ear, breaking up the lingering shriek of tires.

"I have no idea." He turned toward his friend, Max's face set in grim lines.

"What the hell are you doing running through the hospital?"

"Those two guys were on Mrs. B.'s floor. They just seemed shady and when I spoke to them, they got shadier."

He ran through the quick interaction from the elevator, his instincts humming with the knowledge something was off.

Without warning, a memory of the missions they used to run in the Corps filled his mind's eye. Recon, advance planning and any number of operations designed to weaken the defenses of known enemies.

As Tucker and Max well knew, the ability to understand a structure's weak points made it exceedingly easy to blow up.

Sort of like the current situation they found themselves in.

Blown to bits and looking a hell of a lot more dangerous than they could have ever imagined.

Chapter 6

Cassidy stood at the door to Mrs. Beauregard's room, pleased to see her still sleeping peacefully. The excitement from the elevator had faded over the past hour, but she knew Tucker's chase through the hospital had frayed what was left of all their nerves. Although Tucker had promised repeatedly that the police were keeping a watchful eye on her landlady, Cassidy couldn't shake the lingering sense of unease.

Nor could she shake the litany of questions whose answers remained elusive no matter how many times she turned them over in her mind.

What was their landlady hiding? Who could possibly have a vendetta against the woman, especially now, as she approached eighty? And what were they after?

Violet stepped off the elevator, several cups of coffee in her hands, and gestured toward the visitor lounge with her head. With one last glance at Mrs. B., Cassidy moved down the hall toward her friend.

"Lilah's not coming?" Cassidy took one of the coffee cups from the holder, the heat seeping through the thin paper warming her ice-cold hands.

Violet passed over several packets of sugar, that sweet reminder of how well her friend knew her going a long way toward calming Cassidy's nerves. "She's finishing up the delivery on that eightieth birthday cake she was working on earlier. I told her to text when she left the restaurant where she's dropping it off and we could either have her swing by here or come back and meet us at the office."

Cassidy nodded as she doctored her coffee, the mundane action doing little to calm her nerves as she watched the large men pacing a rut in the floor, before each stopped in turn to pick up their cups. It didn't escape her notice that Max repositioned himself at the glass doorway to the lounge, his line of sight clear to Mrs. B.'s room, as he sipped his coffee.

The move struck her for what it was—protection detail—and the streak of fear she'd tried to fight skittered up her spine.

What had they suddenly fallen into? And what had Mrs. Beauregard gotten herself mixed up with?

Again, more questions, round and round like an out-of-control roller coaster. Because whatever the problem was, her sweet, doddering landlady was smack in the middle of it.

The room was empty except for the four of them and with one last glance at the closed doors, Violet launched in, her tone all business. "So what are we dealing with here?"

Max stopped midpace and turned the full attention of his bright blue gaze on Violet, then Cassidy in turn. "You tell us."

Violet kept her tone level but Cassidy didn't miss the heat that threaded underneath the steel. "We know as much as you do. Before yesterday morning we ran a quiet business and kept to ourselves. Now we're convinced our landlady is hiding secrets and my partner's been cleaning up thousands of dollars' worth of damage to her work."

"What Captain Subtlety over here is telling you is that we have no better idea than you do." Tucker took a seat at a chair opposite the couch, the move a clear indication of his willingness to partner on the problem. "And it pisses us off."

"What I can't understand is what's prompted this." Cassidy took a sip of her coffee, willing the fear to subside so she could focus on the facts. "Until I walked up to the shop yesterday morning and found it broken into, there hasn't been a single problem. No strange phone calls. No strangers in off the street. Nothing."

Max took the seat opposite Tucker, his tone noticeably calmer when he spoke. "Same for you, Violet?"

She nodded before adding, "Lilah, as well. We spoke about it earlier and she said nothing seems out of the ordinary or abnormal. We've all just been working our tails off to build our reputation and take Elegance and Lace to the next level."

"What about the men Tucker chased? What made him go after them?"

Even as Cassidy asked the question, she knew what the answer would be. The men were suspicious and immediately aware of her and Tucker the moment the elevator doors swung open.

Cassidy still saw the men in her mind, the memory of their dark gazes and watchful eyes sending another lance of fear skittering up and down her back.

"I didn't like the look of them." Tucker shrugged, but Cassidy sensed the move was more forced than casual. "Nothing more, nothing less. But when I asked them to stop and they kept on going something popped."

"They peeled out of the parking lot like they had hell-hounds on their tails," Max added before two-pointing his coffee cup into a nearby wastebasket.

"I assumed muggers broke in yesterday but the suit-and-tie routine fits." Cassidy thought about the mystery of the alarm code and realized it fit a lot better than some thug looking for a quick score.

"How so?" Max spoke first, but his and Tucker's gazes were both sharp.

"The alarm never registered yesterday."

Cassidy saw the moment speculation turned to something else as Max's gaze collided with Tucker's. "You left that bit out, Buck."

"I've had a few things on my mind."

Cassidy caught Vi's unspoken message from the corner of her eye as they watched the two men circle around the issue. Violet spoke first. "Is there a problem, Mr. Baldwin?"

"You tell me, *Miss* Richardson." Max's disdain was evident even without the curled lip that preceded his words. "Why the hell didn't any of you mention we were looking at an inside job?"

"Because we're not." Cassidy settled her cup on the small, scarred coffee table at her knee.

"And what makes you so sure?" Max moved from his position at the door to stand beside Tucker. The simple move into alignment was a more effective reminder of these men's backgrounds than any dossier ever could be.

They had each other's backs.

Which made it that much more interesting, Cassidy noted, to see Tucker shift, ready to lay a hand on Max if the man moved another inch.

Whatever fear she might feel, the sight of these two protectors went a long way toward calming her nerves, and her tone was firm when she finally spoke. "Three people have that code. Lilah. Violet. Me. No one else."

"And in three years none of you have ever given it out?"

"No."

"No."

"Hell, no." Lilah's voice echoed from the doorway.

Tucker watched as Cassidy and Violet moved into position next to their friend. Warrior women, the two of them, protecting their third.

He might not know any of them well but he knew that stance. And he knew its underlying meaning.

Support.

Unconditional and absolutely unwavering.

"That's awfully unusual for a business that presumably has contractors coming in and out of it." Max took up the charge first, his alpha-dog tendencies obviously getting the best of him.

"That's how we run our business. We agreed before we even opened our doors, and it's an agreement we take seriously." Cassidy's graceful stance and calm voice brooked no arguments.

"And the contractors?" Max pressed, his focus drifting from the door.

"Contractors are scheduled so one of us is always there." Violet reinforced Cassidy's statement, even as Lilah remained silent.

Tucker assessed them once more. Knew his friend did the same.

Something was there. A darkness that was suddenly more than evident beneath the merry streak of pink that highlighted Lilah Castle's bright blond hair.

Were they dealing with a domestic issue?

Anger curled low in his gut at the thought. He'd executed his share of violence—he'd known it was an element of his commitment to his country and he'd done it willingly—but nothing excused a man who raised his fists to women.

Brushing it off to reconsider later, Tucker assessed each woman in turn. They were enticing, he'd give them that. Three gorgeous, hardworking women with a whole heap of trouble following them. It made a man reach inside himself and question the code he lived by.

He didn't leave a man behind.

He helped old ladies cross the street.

And he wouldn't let a woman who needed him go without his assistance.

None of it changed the fact that they had no idea what they were dealing with or why.

An image of their landlady lying in her hospital bed, her smile lighting up when Cassidy walked in, popped into his thoughts. Along with it, a question that had flirted through his mind since discovering Mrs. B. the day before on her kitchen floor.

"Let's take the alarm issue off the table for a minute. What connection do you have to Mrs. Beauregard besides the store?"

"Like I mentioned yesterday, she's a family friend." Cassidy spoke first. "My mother grew up knowing her, and she's always been a part of my life."

Max pounced. "If you know her, you've got to have an idea of what she might be hiding."

"Why do you assume she's hiding anything?" Violet took a step forward and despite the sleek navy suit she wore with sky-high pumps, Tucker saw the telling signs of protection in her fisted hands and arrow-straight stance.

"Why would you be naive enough to think she isn't?"

Cassidy laid her hand on Violet's arm. Tension settled

over all of them, thick as the summer heat, before Lilah's smile broke the moment. "I say we go find out who's right before one of them whips something out."

"Lilah!" A delightful blush pinked up Cassidy's cheeks. "Seriously?"

"Oh, lose that appalled face, Junior League. You know you were thinking the same."

"That's low." Despite their recent solidarity, Tucker was amused to see the Junior League comment stuck in Cassidy's craw. He made a note to file it away next time she jumped on her high horse with him suggesting she didn't need his help.

Before he could say anything, Lilah pushed on her friends once more. "Low, but effective. Come on. Let's have another go at that floor and figure out what's really going on."

Tucker considered the events at the hospital as he drove back toward the shop. They had left once the dinner hour began, requesting the hospital staff keep a sharp eye for anyone out of place. Satisfied they'd done what they could for Mrs. Beauregard, Tucker focused his thoughts on the mystery surrounding Elegance and Lace.

But he couldn't stop thinking about the two men in suits who'd given chase.

He'd seen them in the lobby when he and Max had walked into the hospital and something about them had bugged him at the time. But the very clear realization in their eyes when they spotted Cassidy through the open elevator doors had pushed him from wary suspicion straight into action.

Time in the Corps, moving all over the world, had given him a strong appreciation for the value of trusting his gut and it had jingled loud and clear from the elevator.

Of course, none of it changed the fact he'd nearly missed all of it fantasizing about Cassidy Tate's mouth. Or, more specifically, an image of having her in his arms, her back against the wall of the elevator, their mouths fused in a rush of heat and need and pent-up longing that took his breath away.

All while effectively removing any and all thoughts of a certain doctor.

Damn it.

His flight of fancy had nearly put her in danger. Between unwarranted jealousy over the damned physician and the actual threat of the two anonymous suits, he'd almost let her down.

Get out of your head, Buchanan. It leads to nothing good or productive.

The admonishment was a sore reminder of memories better left forgotten and he cursed himself once more as he swung down Riverfront toward her office.

He'd help her and then leave her the hell alone. His track record with personal relationships was already abominable and she deserved something better.

Like some damned toothy doctor with a tiny little... personality.

"You have exactly two minutes to fill us in before they get here." Lilah glanced out the front of Elegance and Lace like a furtive burglar. "It's not going to take them that long to get their demolition equipment."

"Fill you in on what?" Cassidy dropped into the plush velvet couch opposite the dressing rooms. Her gaze roamed over what was left of the cleanup. A broken plant that would need to go sat next to an open garbage bag holding the remains of scattered crystal beads, ripped lace and shattered glass.

Next to the pile was the small stool she sat on when working on a bride's hem. The stool had been her grandmother's—had been a family piece since Nana had been a small girl—and now it needed new fabric covering, its stuffing popping out between slash marks. Ignoring the equally harsh slash of pain, she focused on moving forward. She could run past the fabric store on the way home and select some new material. Maybe a royal purple...

"Yo. Cass! Come on, sweetie. I need details."

Cassidy keyed back into Lilah's waving hands six inches before her face. "I told you, there's nothing to tell."

"Yeah, right. Nothing." Lilah spied Violet from the back of the store and called her over. "Vi. Tell me you saw the same sparks I saw."

"Oh, I saw them." Vi's heels clicked over the treated concrete floor, a slight grimace on her face. "And while I'd like nothing more than to gossip about it, I think we have a bigger problem on our hands."

"What?" Cassidy let out a small breath at the shift in scrutiny but knew they weren't done with the topic. Getting Lilah off *any* topic before she was ready was nearly impossible.

Violet glanced toward the windows before dropping onto the couch next to hear. "The guys are suspicious and they're also involved. Despite Lilah's express invitation, are we sure we want that?"

"Sorry." Lilah wore the look of the contrite for a moment before she pressed on. "I should have asked first. But they're on their way now."

"So we tell them we had a change of heart." Cassidy shrugged. "In fact, maybe we *should* have a change of heart. This is still Mrs. B.'s place. I keep feeling it's wrong not to ask her first."

An image of their landlady lying pale in that hospital

bed struck her with blunt force. Was she hiding a secret? Josephine Beauregard had always been so sweet to them, and Cassidy genuinely believed the woman would never willingly put them in harm's way.

Maybe they'd both been the victims of random violence?

And even as she thought it, Cassidy knew better.

Someone with knowledge—secreted knowledge—of their alarm code got in or they had a sophisticated enough device to crack the eight-digit code. And either way she sliced it, both options left her sick.

The heavy knock on the front door pulled her attention from her friends. Without warning, a small flutter of excitement lit up her stomach, pushing that slightly nauseous feeling away as she thought of Tucker.

There were depths there, she mused. His demeanor was friendly. Jovial. Easy, even. But there were dark spots.

Time in the military would do it, Cassidy knew. Men and women had been asked to do and see some harsh things in the name of God and country. But it was more...

Tucker Buchanan had hidden depths. And the more time she spent with him, the more intrigued she was about uncovering them. About uncovering the man with the melt-me chocolate-brown eyes and the ugly dog.

"I'll let them in." Lilah jumped up like a jack-in-the-box.

Violet shifted to the end of the sofa, intent on getting up before she seemed to make a decision. Cassidy had known her friend far too long not to recognize when she wanted to say something.

"I'm fine, Vi."

"You sure? You found the problem and it was your work that was damaged. Are you sure you want to do this?"

She fought looking at the large men, traipsing through

their shop, heavy equipment in hand. "I don't think we have a choice."

"We always have a choice."

Cassidy caught a small smile from Tucker; she answered with one of her own before she could even think not to. "I'm not so sure about that."

He watched the men unload their truck from his position farther along Dragon. The street was quiet—few cars at this time of day—but he'd been careful, parking under a small stretch of trees offering shade. Add on the tinted windows and he was golden.

Although he couldn't see everything the guys carried, one had a demolition saw and another had a sledgehammer, so he was confident he knew what they were after.

The floor.

Settling in his seat, he viewed the scene through his binoculars. The blonde with the pink hair streak—Lilah, he remembered—opened the door, allowing the men to pass through.

The door closed and he didn't miss her hand at the lock, flipping it shut, before they all moved to stand in the large front window of the shop. Man, he loved the old warehouses here. So many of the storefronts had those huge viewing windows, and it was child's play to watch inside.

Although they all surrounded her, he could see the sweep of Cassidy's long red hair as she gestured toward Blondie. He also didn't miss the longing gaze stamped over her face as she stared at another one of the guys.

Damn. Charlie shook his head. "Hormones aplenty down there."

He loved a good roll as much as the next guy but this was like something off a freaking reality show. *Love and Crime in Big D* had a nice ring to it.

Laughing to himself, he quieted as he let that thought play out. The entire lot of them was young and attractive, but actual *attraction* was a whole different matter.

Attraction meant attachment.

And attachment was something he could use to his advantage.

He knew that trick better than most.

With deliberate movements, one of the guys—Tucker Buchanan, by his research—reached out and pulled the blinds closed, effectively blocking Charlie's view.

And that simple action gave him the last piece of information he needed.

Drills and sledgehammers. Locked doors. Shaded windows.

Yep. He knew just what they were after. And if he played his cards right, they'd do all the work and he could come in and sweep up the spoils.

Chapter 7

Tucker spread their tools out over a tarp on the floor as Max measured the poured concrete under the now removed carpet. Violet hovered around them, asking questions Tucker knew were driving Max crazy, and he couldn't help but smile.

"Are you sure you know what you're doing?"

Tucker tried—and failed miserably—to avoid staring at Cassidy's legs as his gaze traveled the long way up toward her face where she stood above him. "At the risk of painting us like a pair of twelve-year-old boys who enjoy breaking things, Max and I are quite accomplished in demolition."

"I'm not questioning your skills." She tapped a foot before frowning. "Okay. I am questioning your skills, but I'm mostly questioning if this is a good idea."

He didn't miss the obvious concern in her face or the very real questions that filled her eyes, troubling the clear blue to a darker shade bordering on gray. Sitting back on his haunches, he squared his focus on her face.

"Is this about Mrs. B. or what we might find when we open up the floor?"

"Isn't it all the same?"

"Not really."

Tucker saw her frown—and a small line that crinkled just above her left eyebrow—before she shook her head. "It has to be both."

Before he could say anything, she let out a small sigh. "Fine. You're right. It's the second one, but it's still sort of wrapped around the first. What if we find something horrible? And then what if we have to take action against Mrs. B.?"

Tucker knew full well this wasn't a laughing matter, but the sincerity that lined her face—and the very real fear he saw there—had a tease leaping to his lips. "What exactly do you think's under there? Some pagan sacrifice? A slaughtered goat maybe?"

He was encouraged by the small smile that softened that fear ever-so-slightly so he pressed on.

"Perhaps jars of pig's blood, just waiting for the proper prom to be dug up and put to good use?"

She did laugh at that, her smile going wide. "Now you're on to something. After Mrs. B. spills the blood, she'll then apply her telekinesis to cutting a swath through the Design District."

"An octogenarian horror movie come true."

Despite the dark conversation, Tucker was pleased to see the fear lifting from her eyes, determination taking its place.

"I suppose not knowing is the hardest part."

"It usually is."

That determination morphed into curiosity, and her voice was gentle when she spoke. "Was the military like that?"

Although he thought about his time in the Corps often— hell, who wouldn't think about the single biggest thing to shape them as an individual?—Tucker rarely thought about specific days or moments.

Instead, his memories were more often focused on how he'd felt—that rush of adrenaline before a major op or the long days of advance planning, or even those hours of boredom between major campaigns. He remembered them all, yet had left them to brew in a sort of memorialized soup in his mind since returning to civilian life.

"I'm sorry. I overstepped." Her body language matched her words, and Cassidy took a few steps back from him.

With quick motions, he was on his feet and moving toward her. "No, you didn't. But I'm not sure the best way to answer you."

"Oh?" She hesitated a moment and he saw her internal struggle, stamped in those expressive eyes. "It's hard to discuss that time?"

"Not hard to discuss, hard to describe." Tucker gestured her toward a small kitchenette they kept in the back of the office, suddenly thirsty for some coffee.

She said nothing, but did follow him toward the coffeemaker, which he took as a good sign.

Once he had a mug in hand, he turned to face her. "I certainly had my moments. You don't spend time on active duty and not come back with memories you'd prefer to leave behind. But it's more than that."

"Tell me."

How could he describe a moment? A day? A month?

And how could he explain how those months ran together into a series of instances of working and waiting, planning and plotting?

His gaze alighted on a small calendar affixed to the wall, a large black circle around next Saturday, and it suddenly all made sense.

"You go to a lot of weddings, right?"

"Sure." She nodded. "More and more since we've had the business."

"What do you remember about those days?"

"The dress, of course." She laughed at that, before her gaze narrowed, her mouth drawing into a serious line. "The cake. The first dance. The 'Macarena,' which is sort of this inevitable nightmare about two thirds of the way through every wedding."

Tucker mock-shuddered before lifting his eyebrows. "I do love a row of bridesmaids dancing in unison. Gotta love all that wiggling."

The light slap to his shoulder was well deserved, and he pressed on, barely repressing his smile to focus back on their conversation.

"So at this point, you've been to a steady stream of weddings for most of your life, even more since starting your business, yet you don't remember specifics. Just high points of each event."

"Yeah. Sure."

"That's how I remember my time in the military. Huge moments of great significance, wrapped around an endless number of days with my senses on high alert."

She nodded, and where he'd seen sorrow and the tinges of pity he now saw something else.

Understanding.

"Is that why you got Bailey?"

The question struck him as more profound than it should be. He loved the mutt but Bailey was still just a dog. But as he thought about that ugly face and the memories of bringing home a small puppy with oversize paws, he knew his feelings went far deeper.

He loved that damn dog. And he had memories—daily memories—of what it had been like to live with him. Train him. Run with him. Bailey and his business venture with Max had brought the spirit of everyday normalcy into his life.

Funny how it took one small, observant woman to show him that.

"I hadn't thought about it that way, but yeah. I guess it is why I got Bailey."

"You two make quite a pair."

He grinned at that, anxious to get them back to lighter territory. "We both have faces only a mother could love?"

"Nope." She reached for a mug of her own, tossing him a saucy look over her shoulder as she reached for the coffeepot. "You both have backsides that wiggle rather nicely when you run."

Cassidy stood in a circle with her two best friends and considered what they were about to do.

Or what they were about to allow the guys to do.

The concrete slab in question sat in a perfect square, set off by a grooved rim that outlined the area the men would cut.

"Once we do this, we can't undo it." Violet's voice was quiet, and Cassidy couldn't help the slight swell of amusement at her friend's tone.

Violet *always* cut to the chase.

She was their ringleader—whether self-appointed or simply a natural fit—and she always had been. Half cheerleader, half murmuring conscience, Violet Richardson kept them in line.

Lilah caught Cassidy's gaze before she spoke. All traces of mischief from earlier in the hospital waiting room had vanished. "You're thinking we shouldn't?"

"No. I'm just saying we can't undo this."

"We need to know." Cassidy allowed her gaze to roam

over the men who now stood before the narrow entryway to the kitchen, deep in whispered conversation of their own.

The galley kitchen left little room for them, so they'd taken up positions against the long wall that abutted the space. Bright, vivid photos framed the walls, setting an odd backdrop to the stern, tense picture the two of them made.

A blushing bride was framed behind Max, her smile into her bouquet of roses level with the top of his head, while Tucker set off a wall of bridesmaids in a vibrant mix of peach silk.

Pausing, she let her gaze drift past the vivid wash of peach. To Tucker's right was a matched frame of a groom in a tailored tuxedo. Despite herself, an image of what he'd look like dressed in the same crossed her mind, and her mouth went dry at the impressive picture her subconscious managed to create.

Long and tall, his shoulders framed by the black silk of a tuxedo, platinum squares winking at his cuffs. Tom Ford, maybe Gucci, for the design. No, she quickly amended, Brioni would be even better. She'd just helped a groom find the perfect fit in one of the designer's suits and knew Tucker would take the beautiful cut straight into perfection territory.

Violet pulled Cassidy from the image of a tuxedo-clad Tucker. If her friend knew the direction of Cassidy's thoughts, her calm, direct tone gave nothing away. "We do need to know, especially since someone else already appears to have knowledge we're sorely lacking."

"There's that, but I think there's a bigger question we need to ask ourselves." Lilah shoved a swath of hair behind her ear, the pink streak setting off the subtle rose of her cheek. "Do we trust them? Especially pending what we find."

The question was a fair one, and Cassidy heard the ghosts that lay under Lilah's words.

Her friend had walked through hell. Cassidy and Violet had walked next to her the entire time, but no matter how many steps they'd taken with Lilah, neither of them had lived it.

Nor had they had their trust shattered, nearly broken beyond repair.

So Cassidy stopped, considered for another moment, before she pressed on. "I trust the men. Tucker found me yesterday morning. He could have taken advantage of the situation and instead, he's been the first to help."

"True." Violet nodded her agreement. "Add on they're ex-military with stellar reputations. *And* they're building a business, just like us. A well-respected business if their recent deals are any indication."

Cassidy ignored how it was possible Violet knew the details of Dragon Designs's business transactions—there was little Violet didn't keep herself apprised of—and focused on the truth that lay under the comment. "We also can't discount that Max's grandfather has sung his grandson's praises for as long as we've been here. My gut says we can trust them."

"But what?" Lilah probed.

Cassidy hesitated, her gaze drawn once more to the men. They were impressive, with their large bodies, strong jawlines and their not-so-subtle air of confidence. They were leaders. Warriors. Protectors.

And one had captured her attention and thoughts far more than he ought to.

She didn't need entanglements and complications. And she certainly didn't need a white knight with a big dog and a ready smile. But most of all, she didn't need a relationship born out of the seeds of a volatile situation that heightened the senses and played with one's ability to think rationally.

Been there, done that, still owned a closet full of T-shirts.

So why did she find Tucker Buchanan, with his long, rangy build and dark chocolate eyes, so detrimental to her peace of mind?

"*And*, Cass?"

Cassidy gave her friends her full attention. "And it still doesn't change the fact that we don't know them. That other than Violet's passing introductions to Max, we really only met them yesterday."

"I trust them. And we all know that's saying something." Lilah took a deep breath, her pixie's face set in stern lines. "But I think we need to know what we're dealing with here. I love Mrs. B. but the circumstances are too strange and it's far too coincidental that the shop was broken into and she was attacked on the same day. We need to know. Then we can decide what comes next."

"Agreed." Violet nodded.

"Me, too." Cassidy added her voice to the vote, then turned toward the wall of testosterone that somehow managed to fit despite the photos of blushing brides, elated grooms and well-heeled bridal parties that haloed around their heads.

Maybe it was because the men fit so neatly into these odd circumstances that Cassidy knew she and her partners were making the right decision. Their neighborhood warriors had taken on the current problem facing Elegance and Lace. They would be fools to turn down their help. "You ready to get started?"

Tucker and Max pushed off the wall at her words and it was impossible to miss the electricity and anticipation that suddenly thrummed in the air.

Violet walked the short distance to the back door that led out to their loading dock and flipped the lock. "Now we're ready."

Cassidy marveled at the easy rhythm they fell into as they went to work with the various tools. Max ran the saw while Tucker measured and evaluated weaker points in the floor, marking various sections with a grease pencil.

"They look like they've done this before," Lilah whispered.

"I guess it takes as much understanding of how to take something apart as it does to build it."

Lilah turned, her eyes wide. "That's rather profound."

Cassidy smiled and shrugged. "What can I say? I'm a deep thinker."

With a quick hip nudge, Lilah pointed toward the hole. "What do you think's in there?"

"Tucker thinks it's Mrs. B.'s hidden teenage stash of pig's blood."

"Ooh. Creepy." Lilah nodded. "I like it."

"I'm hoping for jewels," Violet said as she rejoined them at a safe distance.

Suddenly nervous, Cassidy couldn't hold back the need to joke. "We're women. Don't we always hope for jewels?"

"Of course. But I'm thinking the sort that wind up in museums or adorn Fabergé eggs."

"You think there's a Fabergé egg in there?" Lilah gestured, suddenly getting into the game. "From Russia?"

As her friends played out various scenarios, from remnants of the Hope Diamond to enormous gems smuggled into Texas from a maharajah, Cassidy kept her gaze on Tucker.

His back was to her, and she took the stolen moment to look her fill. His thick black hair was damp with sweat, and a sheen of moisture covered his neck. His broad shoulders swiveled under the material of his T-shirt, and she allowed her gaze to drift lower, toward the play of triceps muscles where they peeked out from under the short-sleeved cotton.

Oh, how she loved a man's triceps muscles. That arch of defined muscle that flexed when a man was hard at work had always captivated her.

Entranced her.

Her gaze grew languid, and she moved on past that enticing show of strength, over his back and toward his hips. The derriere she'd teased him about earlier made an impressive picture under the worn denim of his jeans and the thought of Tucker Buchanan in a tuxedo drifted through her thoughts once more.

He'd be devastating clad head to toe in silky black.

Without warning, he turned toward her and shot her a wink as he sat back on his haunches. Even through the protective goggles he wore, she didn't miss the very clear interest stamped in his gaze. Cassidy nearly stumbled from her standing position, mortified to realize she'd been caught midstare.

Oh, who the hell was she kidding?

She'd been caught red-handed, smack in the middle of a rather delightful fantasy.

Tucker stood and pointed toward the hole, his grin wicked. "She's all yours, Max."

As the insistent whine of the demolition saw filled the echoing space, Cassidy took solace in the ear-splitting noise. She couldn't hide from Tucker's knowing gaze, but at least she could fantasize about throwing herself into the big, gaping hole they were about to cut into the floor of her business.

Josephine Beauregard flipped through her dismal choices playing on late-afternoon TV and fought a snort of disgust when she came upon a judge show. A landlord was demanding back payment from a tenant for painting his apartment walls without permission and claimed— with a series of fist pumps and red-faced rants—that he was in the right.

She knew the show meant the display as entertainment, but as she watched the theatrics she couldn't summon much past a decidedly sour taste in her mouth.

She knew she was particularly lucky with the tenants she had. Between the property she'd inherited from her father and the acquisitions she and her husband had made years ago, she had a roster of profitable homes and buildings full up and well paid for.

Yes, she maintained contracts on each and every one, but she endeavored to ensure she treated all fairly and allowed them the leeway to make those environments comfortable. Her father had been the first to teach her that people would quickly renew if they felt a place had become their home.

Thinking of her tenants immediately brought her back to her girls. She was so proud of Cassidy, Violet and Lilah—so excited for what they were building with Elegance and Lace—and had enjoyed watching from the sidelines as the young women worked toward their goals.

And boy, did they work hard.

Although she avoided being nosy, she'd seen Lilah's hot-pink delivery truck at all hours of the day making deliveries. Had heard more than one tale from a satisfied bride of how attentive and available Violet was for anything and everything. And Cassidy.

Jo held back the light sigh that floated up from her throat. Oh, the creations the girl could make. Gorgeous yards of silk and tulle, specially fashioned for the brides, who were destined to wear the most amazing dresses on their most amazing of days.

As the volume rose on the TV with another red-faced rant, she snapped it off, suddenly irritated at the display. She wasn't some burly curmudgeon, badgering her tenants and making their lives miserable. She cared about them and wanted to see them succeed. And yes, she wasn't ashamed to admit it, she took pride that they succeeded in a place *she* owned. A place—

A thick, menacing change in the atmosphere pulled her from her musings and a loud beep echoed from the monitor next to her head.

Had she drifted off?

She pulled herself from the imagined haze of white silk that always made her smile and tried to focus on her surroundings. Mere moments before she'd taken comfort in the large bed and warm stack of blankets that kept her cozy, but now she dragged at them, suddenly suffocated by the layers.

Was someone there?

Her nurse had pulled the blinds closed earlier when she'd urged Josephine to rest but the room was still lit in the golden hue of late afternoon.

The monitor beeped once more, a reminder that she needed to take it easy, and she took a deep breath.

And nearly screamed as a thin man in a dark suit slipped into her room.

He wagged a finger back and forth with the precision of a metronome. "Say nothing."

The scream still lingered in her throat—she was a Texan, after all, and she did what she wanted, others be damned—but something held her back. Something big and large that had settled on her chest years ago. She might have gotten used to carrying the burden, but it didn't alter the fact that it was a great and terrible weight.

And like a life preserver pressed beneath the water, it desperately wanted to surface from the depths.

"Excellent. I can see we understand each other."

Jo kept her gaze on the man, refusing to be intimidated, but couldn't stop the racing of her heart.

Good! Let it race and draw the attention of the nurses.

As if sensing the direction of her thoughts, he slipped something from his pocket. His moves were lightning-quick, and before she could scream he injected something directly into her IV.

Panic and something akin to living fire coursed through her like hot lava, seemingly heating her blood to the point of boiling.

"That should keep your heart rate at a nice, steady level, no matter how badly you wish to scream." He shoved the syringe back into his pocket and used his other hand to cover hers where they lay folded over her body.

Despite his long, slender build, he was strong, his fingers like iron bands around hers. "I'm not going to kill you. But I do expect you to listen to what I have to say."

Another wave of panic coursed through her, magnified in her head like a million buzzing bees.

Yet her machine—her lifeline to the nurses' station—stayed quiet.

His dark, reptilian gaze hadn't left hers since he'd entered the room, but she gave herself a moment to really look at him. To memorize his face and to understand what she was up against.

His eyes were a pale, practically colorless shade between hazel and green that really did remind her of a snake's. His skin was equally pale, yet he had a shock of black hair at odds with his fair coloring.

"You have something I want."

She shook her head, her gaze locked with his hypnotic one. "I have nothing."

"Come now, Josephine." The use of her name added another layer of fear to the moment—how did he know her?—and that swarm of bees buzzed louder in her head. "Of course you do. In fact, you have quite a large something. And if you persist in this ridiculous notion of lying to me I'm going to hurt those beautiful young women who make that old warehouse their home."

"No!" The word ripped from her throat, tearing at the edges of her vocal cords like razors.

"Then we're agreed."

Defeated, she nodded. No matter how badly she wished to keep her secret, she couldn't hurt the girls.

"Excellent. Now, since your young women have gotten nosy and managed to bring in reinforcements, we need to remove them. All of them. For their own good, of course."

When she said nothing, he squeezed her hands. "Nod for me like a good girl."

Every muscle locked in hatred, but she nodded, unwilling to put her girls at risk. At her acquiescence, he continued. "Excellent. Now, here's what I'd like you to do."

She listened as he detailed a sudden problem with some nonexistent bureau of the city, and a series of inspections they were tossing at her that she needed to see to or risk losing her own right to lease the building. How she'd pay her lovely young tenants to vacate their business for a few days. And how she'd add a fresh paint and carpet job to the mix so they would come back to a business that was even better than new.

"You can do this for me, right?"

"Yes." Although she'd attempted to snap the word, it came out sluggish and weak to her own ears.

"My men and I will be in and out before anyone's the wiser. And your girls will have a fresh new store so they can keep making dreams come true."

His hands tightened over hers to the point of pain and he shifted over her so that he filled her vision. An ocean of pain and misery swam behind his pale eyes, and she knew he meant every word.

Knew even more certainly that he'd enjoy inflicting pain if given the opportunity.

"Do we understand each other?"

"I understand perfectly."

This time her words were clean and clear, no emotion clogging her throat, and she took that as a small victory.

He must have sensed it, too, because his grip tightened yet another notch, a vise—worse, a python—squeezing ever harder, before he let go. "I want them out by tomorrow night."

He slid from the room once more, leaving as fast as he'd arrived. Although the light from outside had remained steady through the edges of the closed blinds, the room appeared lighter.

More airy.

And now devoid of that pervasive sense of evil that hovered around the slender man like a shroud.

She was still, willing her blood to cool and her mind to slow with the ramifications of what he asked.

Her father had given her a task. Had prepared her for it and told her of her legacy. She wouldn't fail him.

But she couldn't fail Cassidy, Violet or Lilah.

Nor could she fail Max.

Ideas whirled through her mind on swift feet, and she reviewed each of them, twisting, considering and then discarding nearly every one. And as one bad idea piled on top of the next, that swarm of bees in her mind grew louder.

More insistent.

Until, finally, the machine next to her began to buzz in time with the endless ringing in her mind.

Tucker hefted the sledgehammer and felt the satisfying break of concrete shiver up his arms. Max had finished up with the saw, and he took on the finer precision aspects of the job in between each of Tucker's rounds of demolition work, ensuring they didn't ruin whatever lay beneath the surface.

They worked well together—they always had—and he normally let his mind drift as they measured, forced and hammered their way through a demolition job.

But not this time. His thoughts were focused in one place.

Cassidy.

She intoxicated him. Her scent. The beautiful porcelain of her skin. And the hue of indigo that filled her eyes and telegraphed her interest.

Damn, but that shade of blue absolutely destroyed him.

He was interested in her. Hell, he'd have to be an idiot not to be. But it was something more. His reaction to her was so visceral. So intense.

And he was rapidly losing any interest in what lay beneath the floor.

Instead, the only thing that filled his mind's eye was *her*. More precious than jewels and more fascinating than any historical treasure. Cassidy Tate was a vision.

And she grew more precious to him by the hour.

The real question, to his mind, was if she felt the same way. None of the women had said anything directly, but he hadn't missed their little powwow earlier. They had their concerns about whether or not to allow him and Max into their current situation. And while they needed help, Tucker knew damn well they all struggled with how much to trust their burgeoning friendship.

He could hardly blame them, but it chafed all the same.

Aside from their not knowing each other, whatever surprise lay beneath the floor—and he'd be equally *unsurprised* if the answer was nothing—had drawn some rather nasty interest.

The women of Elegance and Lace needed help. And he'd be damned if he was walking away now.

"I'm trying not to hover but it's hard."

The voice echoed behind him, the low register grabbing him way down deep in his gut. As if he'd conjured her, Cassidy stood behind him, her gaze speculative as she stared at the mess they'd created.

"We're close." They'd been at it for a while now and were finally beginning to see the benefit of their labor. "Maybe another ten or fifteen minutes?"

The saw had churned up a thick layer of dust that coated everything. As soon as she'd realized the possible damage, Cassidy had charged off, hunting up a series of blankets to throw over her stock. She now had a light mist of white covering her shoulders, the dark blouse she wore a chalky gray.

"You get everything taken care of?"

"Everything's covered, and Violet and I moved some of the more delicate pieces into the storeroom and covered them there."

Max sat back on his heels and pointed toward a thick fracture line. "Shouldn't be too much more. I can feel the pieces giving way here."

The sharp ring of a phone echoed off the bared surface of the floor, and Max dragged his phone out of his back pocket. "Be right back."

Cassidy poked a large piece of concrete he and Max had hefted out earlier. "I had no idea it would take so long."

"Concrete's a messy job." Tucker reached for a fresh bottle of water and chugged deeply. The urge to brush some of the white chalky mist off Cassidy's cheeks was strong, but he held back.

Was it the presence of Max and Violet? Or something more?

He'd spent most of his life perfectly content to reach out and take what he wanted. After a childhood with very little, he'd always had ambition in spades. His supervisors in the Corps had seen that trait in a matter of weeks and leveraged it into active duty. Max had the same core qualities and they'd used that drive and determination to start a business after exiting the military.

He knew what he wanted and he went after it. So why was he so reticent to reach for what was so obviously between him and Cassidy?

No closer to an answer, Tucker stretched his back and shifted into position under one of the loft's overhead vents. Someone had amped the air, and he reveled in the cool breeze that floated over his neck and shoulders.

The water added a refreshing complement to the air-conditioning, and he took the moment to himself, washing away the grit in his throat. The tension in the loft space had risen with each piece of concrete they broke and now looking at Cassidy, he saw the worry that lay underneath the excitement.

Another tug pulled at his midsection and he ignored it, focused instead on her obvious concern. "It's going to be okay, you know."

"How can you be sure?"

"Because whatever's under here hasn't been your focus.

In fact, if I'm not mistaken I get the feeling you don't care all that much what's under here."

Tucker saw the moment his comment registered. The thin layer of tension that had stiffened her shoulders softened as her gaze drifted back to the ever-widening hole in the floor. "I hadn't thought about it that way."

"You're not in this for a quick score. And you've been concerned about Mrs. Beauregard every step of the way. We'll find what's here and then we'll handle it."

Violet and Lilah came up behind her, support that flanked her from both sides. Although they'd kept their distance throughout his exchange with Cassidy, he knew the women hadn't missed the discussion.

"Whatever's here isn't about us." Lilah wrapped her arm around Cassidy's shoulders. "Yeah, it's fun to talk about, but it's not ours, nor was it meant to be."

"We'll deal like we always do and move on," Violet said. "And then we're going to go back to creating Dallas's best weddings."

Max walked out of the kitchen, his face grim.

"What is it?" Violet spoke first, her concerned tone in opposition to the usual animosity that sparked between the two of them.

"That was my grandfather. We need to get to the hospital right now."

Chapter 8

Cassidy walked the same antiseptic halls they'd left a few hours before, fear and anxiety tying her stomach up in a tight knot.

Just like before. Just like before. Just like before.

The words had played a litany in her mind from the moment Max had told them of his grandfather's call.

She'd worked so hard to actively put that time out of her mind, yet it had found her once more.

Was a person supposed to experience that sort of grief twice in one lifetime? Watching those they cared about become victims of senseless violence?

A whirl of voices surrounded her as she and Tucker stepped off the elevator with Max. Although it had killed Lilah and Violet to stay behind, the half-deconstructed floor needed tending.

And though she'd developed a fear of guns long ago, when Cassidy had seen the Glock Max had left behind for added protection, she'd taken her first easy breath since they'd made the decision to dig up the floor.

"Do you know if Mrs. Beauregard has anyone to look after her?"

She smiled immediately, recalling images of the endless parade of individuals celebrating holidays, summer picnics and major college football games at Josephine Beauregard's house. "Only about half the city of Dallas."

As the reality of her surroundings struck, pain radiated from her chest, quelling the smile as hot tears pricked the backs of her eyes. She'd stayed strong since the day before, but the sudden realization Mrs. B. might no longer be with them hit harder than she could have ever imagined.

When Tucker's arms came around her, she turned into his chest, grateful for the warmth and support.

His large hand rolled circles over her back, and she clung to his waist, desperate to shake the memories that had suddenly risen up with fierce claws.

"Shh. It's okay."

Cassidy registered the murmured voices above her head as Tucker and Max exchanged words. With a gentle pat, he shifted to stare at her. "Max is going to go check in on Mrs. B. Why don't you and I go outside to get some air?"

"I need to see her."

"You obviously need a minute. They will only let a few into ICU at a time anyway so let him get the lay of the land. His grandfather's already up there."

"Okay." She whispered the word and couldn't quite stop the relief that filled her. While she wanted to see Mrs. B. for herself, the extra time to prepare was welcome. They'd rushed out of Elegance and Lace so quickly, it wasn't until they'd walked through the doors of the hospital that it had occurred to her what Mrs. B. might look like lying in a bed designed for critical care.

And Cassidy didn't care for the images currently crowding her overactive mind.

They took the quick trip back down the elevators before Tucker walked them toward a small garden outside the front of the hospital. Benches and small tables were strategically positioned to give people both privacy and a space to escape and enjoy the air.

The evening sun hadn't yet set and the air had a hot, tight feel that she'd never felt anywhere else but Texas. A light breeze whipped her hair, and she let the accumulated warmth of day seep into her bones.

The garden was quiet, the late-afternoon heat keeping most away, and she and Tucker took the first bench they found. Once they settled, his previous words tugged a string she'd wondered about earlier. "What was Max Senior doing here?"

"I don't know. I think he and your Mrs. B. are tight."

"Violet's persisted since we moved into the space that the two of them had a fling once upon a time."

"Maybe they're still flinging."

Although the thought filled her with happiness for her dear friend, she wasn't quite sure someone as infatuated with love as Mrs. Beauregard could have kept a secret like that to herself.

"Vi is sure, but why keep it a secret? It's not like there's anyone hanging around to disapprove."

"Not everyone loves putting their personal life on display."

"Yes, but…" A protest sprang to her lips, but she let it drop. The past few days had proven she didn't know everything about her landlady. Truth be told, she was fast coming to suspect she knew very little at all.

And hadn't that been a running theme of her life?

Cassidy knew the thought was maudlin—and horribly self-involved—but try as she might, she couldn't fully shake it off. Her entire life she'd underestimated others. Had taken them at face value even while they held all their cards behind their backs.

Her family. Robert. Now Mrs. B.

And her sister, most of all.

Which only took her right back to where she started with that dull panic that had assailed her the moment she walked into the emergency room.

Would the guilt ever go away?

She hadn't known—or tried to understand—the horrors of her sister's life. Hadn't understood that all wasn't right with Leah Tate McCallum's seemingly perfect world until it was too late.

And with those memories flashing through her mind, a hot wave of tears spilled over almost immediately.

"Cassidy?"

Her name floated on the evening breeze, whisper soft. The urge to trust him—and tell him of the grief that never subsided—rose up nearly as fast as the tears, but did she dare?

She didn't know him. They were complete strangers, beyond sharing a few moments of pulse-pounding adrenaline and a soul-crushing kiss. So why did it feel like they'd known each other forever?

"What is it?"

"It's too horrible." Fear pulsed in a rapid counterpoint to the heavy thuds of her heartbeat, the thought of rehashing the events of three years ago filling her with dread.

"You can tell me." He hesitated, and she didn't miss the hard catch in his throat when he finally spoke. "I understand horrible."

Tucker watched the play of emotions cross Cassidy's face and marveled once again at how strong she was. Pain radiated off her in waves, yet a core of strength shone from her vivid, water-filled blue gaze. And in that moment, he knew.

She was a survivor.

Wondering what she'd survived, however, had gripped him with a cold fist at the base of his spine.

What had she lived through?

"You can tell me. I hope you know that. Whatever happened to you, you can tell me."

"Nothing happened to me."

"Cassidy—"

She held up a hand. "Something happened to someone I loved."

"It's still something that happened to you."

A fresh wave of tears filled her eyes, their thick wetness heavy on her cheeks. Helpless, he pulled her close once more, at a loss for any other way to comfort her. She went willingly, her slim frame fitting tight against his shoulder.

Although a crying female terrified him far more than mudslides, sniper bullets or demolition equipment that wouldn't detonate, he vowed to himself he'd stay there as long as she needed.

The storm passed almost as quickly as it had started and he felt the tremors subside a few minutes later. What he couldn't disregard was the heavy wash of grief that had settled over her.

"I'm sorry if I churned up bad memories. Or asked you something you weren't ready to share." She wiped at tears before reaching into her massive purse for a tissue. Although he wanted to know who or what had hurt her, when he saw the opportunity to lighten the moment, he took it.

"You could hide Bailey in that bag."

The joke did its job, and he was rewarded by a soft, throaty laugh. "It's not that big."

"Oh, I don't know." Tucker poked at the purse, making a show of it, pleased when he was rewarded with another laugh *and* a smile. "If I laid off the bones I think he'd fit."

"He's not fat!"

The immediate defense of his crazy mutt warmed his heart, and he couldn't resist pulling her close in a tight hug. "I'll be sure to pass on the compliment."

"Thank you." She hesitated a moment, her watery gaze reflecting the late-afternoon light. "Really. Thank you."

The sun had nearly completed its day's journey, and the last layers of golden light framed the rich red of her hair in a vivid halo.

Halos?

The thoughts that had haunted him while working the concrete came tumbling back stronger than before, and the urge to shake his head like a befuddled cartoon character gripped him. Although he might have tried it to break the tension, he found himself unable to look away, his gaze locked with hers.

Once again, Tucker was reminded of the strength that lived inside her. Saw that steely core forged in those depths of blue.

That gaze drew him in—pulled him closer—but Cassidy was the one to close the distance between them. Her lips pressed to his, and in moments the late-afternoon heat that surrounded them was nothing compared to the heat that raged between them.

His tongue slipped between her lips, and she opened more fully to him on a dark gasp of pleasure. Obviously unwilling to play the passive miss, she sucked him into her mouth, her tongue tangling with his. A growl of need echoed low in his throat as he wrapped his arms around her and pulled her more tightly against his body.

Her hands lay flat against his chest, twin brands that nearly melted through the cotton of his shirt. The need to cradle her and devour her raged like a fever in his blood and he couldn't imagine how this small slip of a woman had come to mean so much in such a short period of time.

A loud eruption of giggles broke the moment, and Tucker pulled away from Cassidy to find two teenagers standing at the far edge of the garden. Balloons and stuffed animals filled their hands, and he saw the mix of shock and titillation in their eager faces.

"Excuse us." Tucker offered up a small smile before patting Cassidy on the arm. "We should probably get inside and see to Mrs. B."

"I think you're right."

He kept his arm firmly wrapped around her shoulders as they walked the short garden path back to the hospital lobby but Tucker didn't miss the whispered "he's hot"—or the creeping heat that traveled up his neck—before another round of giggles echoed behind their backs.

Cassidy fell against him in a heap of her own laughter the moment the sliding doors closed behind them.

"It's not funny."

"Yes, it is."

"That's the first time my kissing skills have been met with a rash of giggles."

"Take it as a compliment."

"A compliment?"

"Of course. I'm sure George Clooney, for instance, elicits giggles everywhere he goes."

Another round of laughter escaped her, and she clutched at his arm as they walked back into the hospital lobby. Tucker felt another wave of heat flame up his neck and was grateful for the cool air. "I'm quite sure George Clooney doesn't have to deal with evaluation of his technique."

"Oh, I don't know. I've done plenty of evaluating sitting in darkened movie theaters watching George."

He turned toward her as they reached the elevator,

pleased to see the smile had returned to her eyes. Although their impending visit to the ICU ensured it would be short-lived, it was good to see her enjoying a light-hearted moment.

He brushed a thumb over the ridge of her cheekbone and captured a last, lingering tear. The urge to wrap her in his arms and keep her from what inevitably came next was strong, but he knew the path wasn't his to walk.

The elevator doors swooshed open as if reinforcing his thoughts and her smile faded, along with her lingering laughter. "It's time to go up."

"You'll feel better once you see Josephine with your own eyes."

"Max would have told us if it was bad. Would have texted you or come to find us or something."

"I'm sure he would have." For all his friend's curmudgeonly ways, Tucker knew with certainty Max would have found a way to soften the blow if Josephine Beauregard was doing worse than they expected.

On a hard nod, Cassidy stepped through the door, then turned and extended her hand. "Let's go."

It was several minutes later before Tucker realized he'd never found out what secret she was running from.

Charlie placed the call, even as an epic battle waged within his conscience. Technically, he had no real information to share beyond some pulled shades and demolition equipment. But it didn't take a genius to make a connection between what they all suspected lay in the old warehouse on Dragon Street and those demolition tools.

Of course, he'd already been read the riot act by the boss over the goons the man had sent to investigate at the hospital.

Like it was his fault they didn't know how to be discreet. He had made it perfectly clear the old woman hadn't seen his face and he'd made it equally clear that his sister-in-law was completely clueless to his involvement. Did they listen?

Nope.

Instead, they thought it was a good idea to look like a pack of MIB agents scoping out the hospital on advance recon.

Charlie shook his head and downed the last of his latte. He'd picked it up at a local place around the corner from Cassidy's shop and it wasn't nearly as good as the frothy chocolate he got at Starbucks every morning. He glanced at the cup before tossing it out his window. Why had he even bothered? You couldn't beat perfection.

You also couldn't beat biding your time while you held a handful of aces.

He'd sat on this one for a while, waiting until the time was right. Until he had the right partners. And, most important, until he knew for a fact his sister-in-law would have no idea he was involved.

The bitch barely tolerated him, and her view of him was about two notches below gum on her shoe. She had no idea he'd broken into that crappy cottage she lived in with the equally crappy locks on the doors. As far as she knew, he'd made himself scarce since her sister went and offed herself three years ago and he was just fine with that.

"Yes?"

That single word snapped through the phone, and a distinct chill ran in waves over his spine. Charlie wondered—not for the first time—if he'd made a mistake pairing up with the Duke. The man had power, connections and *belief*, which, as far as Charlie was concerned, was essential for this op.

But there were times he wondered if the man had too

much belief. He treated the damn op like a freaking quest as opposed to what it really was: a nice score that would hold him over until his next scam.

"I have some news I think you'll be interested in."

"I doubt it."

Cool disdain wrapped around each word, and Charlie fought to hold back his temper. "You haven't heard what I have to say yet."

"I listened to you yesterday, didn't I? I'm not interested in incomplete missions."

"But the old woman didn't see me."

"You claim that, but I'm not so sure. But don't worry yourself. I've already handled your mess from yesterday afternoon."

Handled?

A short burst of panic bloomed in Charlie's chest. While he had no lingering love for the Saint of Swiss Avenue, as he thought of Mrs. Beauregard, he also knew the power the woman wielded. Her death would slow things down, and while it might distract Cassidy from her shop, it would also generate questions for anyone paying attention.

The old bat might be old, but she was spry and well cared for. The moment anyone made a connection between her house break-in and her dying, there'd be a race for answers.

"What do you mean, handled? Did you kill her already?"

"Not yet." After a beat of silence, the Duke spoke once more. "What did you learn?"

Another slow slide of nerves stamped themselves on his spine with icy fingers, and Charlie rushed through the information he'd gleaned on his late-afternoon stakeout. He kept his voice level, just like he had three years ago with the police, and answered question after question.

Don't think, just answer. Calm. Cool. Rational.

Yes, the women had help.

Yes, the men appeared to carry demolition equipment.

Yes, he saw them leave a short while ago.

It was several moments later, long after he'd hung up, that he realized he'd just given away his whole hand.

Exhausted by the day, Cassidy let the quiet beeping of machines fill her thoughts. She'd kept watch on both Mrs. B. and Max Senior for the past few hours and her surreptitious glances at Max's grandfather confirmed he was as worn-out as her dear friend.

She'd avoided pressing too hard but curiosity finally got the best of her. They'd already talked about how hot the summer was, a cute new restaurant in the Design District and how long the man had made Dallas his home.

He was sweet and congenial—with a formidable air that still surrounded him at eighty—and she finally felt comfortable enough to ask her burning question.

"How do you know Mrs. Beauregard?"

When silence was all that greeted her, Cassidy suspected she'd overstepped, so she was surprised when a gentle wash of memories lit the bright blue eyes that were a mirror image of his grandson's. "I've known Jo since we were kids. We grew up together."

"Oh." The word fell from her lips but none followed. If they'd grown up together—and the man obviously cared about Josephine to be here—why didn't they spend more time together? In all the years she'd spent in Mrs. B.'s company, she'd never met the man.

"We—" He hesitated, obviously searching for the right words. "We had to make a clean break a long time ago."

"I'm sorry."

"There are days I regret it." His voice lowered to a whisper. "More and more over the past few years."

"So why have you stayed away?"

"She found someone. I found someone. We had separate lives. My Mary gave me two sons and they gave me six grandchildren, so I have no complaints."

Cassidy let his words flow over her.

No complaints.

Was that even possible?

And was it a complaint if you felt like you were living a half life? Like all you did was watch others get their chances while you stayed in a sort of stasis? Alive, but never going anywhere?

It hadn't been lost on her that as her business took off her personal life grew increasingly uninteresting. She made wedding dresses, for Pete's sake. She created an integral part of other people's happy ever afters.

Even as her own was sorely lacking.

She hadn't had a date in over a year. Hadn't had something more since before…

The usual pain filled her heart at the memories of her sister, her life snuffed out much too quickly. She and Leah had never seen eye to eye, but Cassidy had loved her sister. And she'd always believed the sentiment was returned in Leah's own way.

Loss left holes, Cassidy knew. But when bad memories accompanied that loss, the holes were like craters on the soul. Vast pockets of emptiness that refused to fill.

A light moan from Mrs. B. pulled Cassidy from her maudlin musings and she leaned forward, her voice gentle. "Hey there."

Josephine's tissue-thin eyelids fluttered open, then widened as she took in Cassidy first, then Max Senior. "Where am I?"

"You're being cared for, Jo." Max patted her hand before taking it in his own. "You're safe."

Terror filled Mrs. B.'s face, and Cassidy tried to find the right words to comfort her. Where she'd have thought the sight of familiar faces and Max Senior's warm touch would have soothed, Mrs. B. only looked more agitated.

A hard beep of the machine near her head added to the sly fingers of discord that began to fill the room, and Cassidy hurried to calm her friend. "Come on, now. Shh. It's all right."

"No. No, it's not. You need to leave." Mrs. B. tugged her hand from Max's, the move surprisingly strong for a woman who had suffered a heart attack a few hours earlier.

"Jo. Calm down." Max reached for her hand but she batted it away again, her agitation telegraphing off her in waves.

Cassidy reached for Mrs. B.'s other hand and hoped a woman's touch would soothe. When that hand was snatched back even faster a slithery sort of panic pooled in Cassidy's stomach.

What had happened since early afternoon?

She'd been here and had seen the woman's progress with her own eyes. She was jovial and happy, teasing about her cute doctor.

And now?

The bright red of the room's panic button drew her eye but an ICU nurse ran in before Cassidy could push it. Her words brooked no arguments. "I need you both to please step outside."

"But she's—"

The nurse shook her head, effectively cutting Cassidy off. "I'm sorry but you need to go."

The events of the past days coalesced into a panicky

ball of fury, and Cassidy struggled to stay calm. What was going on?

Her gaze settled on Max Senior, his own panic telegraphing off him in thick waves. He kept murmuring the same words as the nurse ushered them toward the door—"Jo, it'll be fine"—before Cassidy heard him say something else.

"They need to know."

Chapter 9

Cassidy took the seat next to Max Senior in the ICU waiting room and kept her hand firmly over his. The older man hadn't stopped shaking, but his fingers stayed tight in her grasp. Cool air circulated around them, the air-conditioning cranked up against the unrelenting heat outside, and Cassidy fought her own shiver as the rush of adrenaline began to fade.

A nurse had stopped in briefly to provide an update—and the confirmation they'd settled Mrs. B. comfortably—before she departed.

"Mr. Baldwin?" When his rheumy eyes met hers, Cassidy saw the shockingly distinct notes of terror dulling that bright blue. "What do we need to know?"

His gaze shifted around the room, skipping across Tucker and Max before settling firmly on Cassidy. "I can't tell you. I made a promise."

"I know. But you have to know we'll help you. Whatever it is, we'll find a way to help you and Mrs. Beauregard."

"We swore. It would just be us and we swore never to tell."

"Pops." Max took the seat on the other side of his grandfather. "We know something's buried in the floor."

The hand in hers shook harder, and Cassidy sought to offer comfort and strength. She settled her free hand on top of their joined ones, willing as much as she could into the gentle touch.

Whatever the problem was—whether big or small—Cassidy had to wonder if it had grown over time. The fact that he and Josephine hadn't seen each other in years would have to have had an impact.

Had he made the problem out to be something monumental in his mind?

Regardless of what Max Senior believed, she, Violet and Lilah had been in that space for almost three years. Three peaceful years of running a business and entertaining a vast array of clients who came and went without a single moment of suspicious behavior.

"We want to help, Mr. Baldwin." Tucker took the seat opposite them across a scarred particleboard coffee table. "But we need to know what we're up against."

Tucker's gaze shifted from Max Senior to her, understanding lighting those dark depths. The older man was scared. And now his added fear for Josephine had him hunkering down instead of opening up.

"It's not your battle, young man." The quaver vanished from the older man's voice, replaced with ever-growing resolve.

"Pops." Max's voice was harsh, and he took a deep breath before he spoke again, his tone noticeably softer. "We're in this now. I know that wasn't your intention, but we are. And we need to know what we're up against."

"No, you don't."

"Pops—"

Max Senior pulled his hand free, that resolve morphing with distinct notes of frustration and anger. "It's bigger than Jo and me. Bigger than all of us. And I won't be saying anything else on this matter."

Tucker respected the ability to keep a secret. Respected even more an individual's refusal to break a confidence. But he struggled to understand how a man nearing the end of his life could sit on a secret that held an increasing threat by keeping others in the dark.

"I can't believe he won't tell us." Cassidy's voice carried on the evening breeze as they walked through the parking lot.

"He's scared." Tucker opened the car door for Cassidy and waited for her to climb up into his SUV. "And whatever it is, I think it's more Jo's secret than his."

"You think he'd have told us otherwise?"

Tucker considered, then nodded. "I do."

In moments they were navigating out of the hospital parking lot, the streets empty with the late hour. "I can't imagine what she'd be involved with. The woman's a pillar of the community. And she's a good person."

"So good people can't have secrets?"

He'd asked the question more out of curiosity than anything else, but when Cassidy grew quiet Tucker suspected he'd hit a nerve. "Everyone's entitled to the things they would prefer to keep close to the vest."

He slowed for a light, then turned toward Cassidy. "And if that secret has the power to harm?"

"I guess…" Her words tapered off.

"What?"

"You know, we're not far from Mrs. B.'s. You still have the keys from the locksmith, right?"

"Yes."

"Why don't we go nose around. See if we can find anything."

Tucker considered, common sense warring with the promise of getting underneath whatever it was they were dealing with. "It's not right."

"No, it's not right at all." Cassidy shook her head. "I hate the idea of going behind her back. And I equally hate that she and Max Senior feel they can't tell us. But we need to know what we're dealing with."

The light was still red, but a decision beckoned the moment it turned over. Straight would take them back to the Design District. A right would take them to Josephine Beauregard's.

A subtle hum erupted in the car, anticipation winging between both of them like the whiff of a potent drug. He kept his gaze level on Cassidy's, his focus absolute.

"Turn or go straight?"

A wash of green filtered through the windshield as the light changed. Cassidy nodded, her voice firm with commitment. "Make the right."

The house looked much as they'd left it after Mrs. B.'s accident. Max had righted a few things in the kitchen that had been overturned in her attack, but other than that, the quiet house reflected Tucker's impression from his earlier visit.

The weight of a life hovered in the hallways. Framed photos. Well-worn furniture. And a regal sense of quiet that spoke of age and wisdom.

Tucker followed behind Cassidy, her slim form moving quickly through the darkened hallway. "I think it'll either be in her study or her bedroom."

"This is a big house. Whatever it is we're looking for could be anywhere."

"Yes, but for some reason I can't imagine her wanting whatever it is too far away."

"Fair point, Nancy Drew."

Cassidy hip bumped him at that. "So does that make you Ned Nickerson?"

"I have absolutely no idea what you just said."

Moonlight filtered into the hallway from the open entrance to the living room as she stilled. "You can rattle off the names of the Three Musketeers but you don't know Nancy Drew's boyfriend?"

Tucker stilled, the unconscious comparison striking him like a blunt object. "That's how you see me?"

"I— Well— I mean—" Cassidy stopped. "You've been an admirable sidekick, I'll give you that."

He moved into her space, the sudden quiet awkwardness between them spurring him on. "Do sidekicks do this?"

Without giving her time to respond, he had her against the hallway wall, his hands wrapping tight around hers where they still lay at her side. The moment was a surprise, and he took full advantage, pressing his mouth to hers, delighting in the sizzling tension that erupted between them.

He pushed against the firm press of her lips, slipping his tongue past that tender barrier. She welcomed him in and he squeezed her hands, unwilling to reach for her body for fear they'd never get to what they came for.

A light moan drifted from her throat, and Tucker deepened the kiss, satisfied when she rose up to meet the challenge. Her tongue tangled with his, drawing him deep into her mouth.

The urge to take—to plunder and seduce—nearly pulled him under when she pulled back slightly, her voice thick with passion. "I don't quite remember reading about Nancy and Ned doing that on an investigation."

He squeezed her hands once more, desperate to return to some sort of equilibrium. "Bummer."

"Definitely." She nipped a quick kiss along his jaw. "I might have read more as a child if they had."

Lilah flipped on her industrial mixer and watched the mesmerizing play of blades in the thick yellow cake batter. She allowed the rich scents of vanilla and sugar to transport her for a few minutes as she worked through the current problem at hand.

Secrets.

Her life had been full of them up to now and it looked like no matter how hard she attempted to shake him, the monkey was still on her back.

Who the hell would believe they'd been sitting on something underneath the floor of their shop?

While she knew they'd technically not found anything yet—their demolition mission aborted in favor of tending to Mrs. B.—she knew they would.

Knew, as well as she knew she had a perfect batter, that something dangerous lay underneath the floor.

A swift knock echoed off the back door and she jumped, the hard sound jarring her from her thoughts. Who the hell was at her back door at ten o'clock at night?

Lilah had her phone out of her apron pocket and in her hand, 9-1-1 nearly dialed when she heard a man's voice muted by the heavy door. "It's Detective Reed Graystone. Remember me? I stopped by this morning to discuss the break-in and the attack on Mrs. Beauregard."

The hard knot in her belly uncurled while a wave of electricity zinged in its place. What was he doing here?

She flipped open the lock but stood in the doorway and tried diligently not to notice the way the back lights reflected off his dark hair, or how his eyes flashed with barely veiled humor. "What are you doing here?"

"I could ask you the same."

"This is my business. I can be here whenever I want."

"And this is my city. I'm entitled to do the same."

She stared at him, her perch at the door about three steps above him. Although he had knocked, she didn't miss the fact that he'd retreated down the steps as he waited for her to invite him in.

"That still doesn't explain why you're here."

"I wanted to check on you."

"Oh." A momentary flash of the shop's current state filled her mind's eye, and Lilah couldn't help but be grateful she and Violet had set the floor to rights after Max and Tucker and Cassidy had left. The still-unopened concrete had been re-covered, the carpet firmly in place.

"Can I come in?"

"Of course."

She gestured him in, again relieved when he kept his distance, his hands firmly behind his back. Did he sense her nerves? Or was it just the good cop routine, which would vanish once he was inside and had the advantage?

Been there, done that, her conscience taunted.

Yet even as that muscle memory stretched with familiarity, she couldn't muster any sense of a threat.

"What are you making?"

"Hmm?"

"Here." He pointed to the mixing bowl. "It smells good."

A naughty, little-boy grin suffused his face as he dipped a finger onto the edge of the spatula she'd settled next to the bowl. "Damn, that's good."

As his hand snuck toward the spatula for another taste she slapped his hand away. "You'll contaminate it."

He only grinned broader, and she fought more of that puzzling electricity that sent shock waves through her midsection. "I don't have cooties."

"Well, the Board of Health might have something to say about that."

She lifted the paddles from the batter and disengaged them, then handed him one. "Might as well take a good taste then."

His gaze drifted over her as he took the mixing paddle. "You're not having the other one?"

"I don't—" She glanced at the thick, golden batter and considered where it coated the other paddle. A protest sprang to her lips—how bakers shouldn't gain weight off their own creations—but she tamped down the well-remembered criticism. "Maybe I will."

The batter was rich and perfect as she ran her tongue over the thick blade. She nodded once in satisfaction, and was surprised to see his gray eyes steady on hers.

She'd never seen eyes quite that shade. A gunmetal-gray that reminded her of the Texas skies when a storm was whipping up. The color should have put her off—and she'd already wondered why it didn't—but those mercurial eyes were anything but bleak or cold.

"This is amazing." He licked off the last of his treat, and Lilah fought the hard rush of air that welled in her chest at the sight of his tongue, coated in her work.

"It should be. Customers are funny, you know. They don't want to buy bad cakes."

"This is for a customer?"

"Why do you think I wigged out about the Board of Health?" When he only smiled, she added, "I've never seen eyes quite the same shade as yours."

"They were my grandfather's eyes."

"They match your last name."

The words were out before she even realized it, and she didn't miss the flare of interest that blazed high in return. "I'm impressed you made the connection."

"I notice things."

"I do, too. Part of the job description." He never moved—never even shifted from his position on the counter—but she sensed the interest there all the same. "Although I wouldn't have pegged a baker as having the same skills."

"Not every skill comes from a classroom."

Reed stared at her a moment longer before he broke eye contact and began to move around the kitchen. "This is quite a workspace."

"It's my dream space. The moment I saw this kitchen I knew."

"Knew what?"

"That I could rebuild my life here."

Lilah had no idea why she'd chosen those words—or why she'd even consider telling them to a stranger—but they were out.

Was it self-preservation?

Or a warning, shot over the bow so he would know in advance she was damaged and broken.

"Why are you here again?"

"I saw the light on and wanted to make sure you were all right." When she said nothing and simply stared at him, he nodded, seemingly satisfied. "Since I can see that you are, I'll leave you to finish up."

He turned on his heel and headed out. Despite her better judgment, Lilah watched his swift, efficient movements as he walked away. She'd *thought* her vanilla batter delicious, but as her gaze drifted over his sculpted buttocks, she amended the notion.

The man was delicious. Every inch of him was in prime condition, and without warning or conscious effort, urges she'd repressed a long time ago sprang back to vivid life.

No doubt about it, she'd like to eat the man with a spoon.

"Good night, Lilah. Don't forget to lock up after me."

"Good night, Detective."

It was a long while later when she realized the detective's visit was the first time she'd been alone with a man in years and hadn't felt a single moment of fear.

Cassidy ran her index finger over her lower lip as she rifled through Mrs. B.'s desk drawer. She could still taste him there, that intriguing mix of masculine perfection that was Tucker Buchanan. Their kiss in the hallway had been unexpected—and that only made it that much more enticing.

How had he managed to sneak under her defenses?

She'd known him for only a short while, and yet here they were, breaking and entering and adding stolen kisses to the mix.

At the thought of breaking and entering—or unlocking and entering, as it were—Cassidy sobered, memories of that kiss fading as she remembered the reason they were here. She closed the desk drawer and stood up, her gaze drifting around the study.

"You okay?"

She focused on Tucker where he stood at a bookshelf, inspecting a long row of spines, pulling each book out one by one. "Yes."

"But?"

"But what?"

"But you're having second thoughts."

Cassidy shrugged, the truth of his words pulling at her like lead weights. She'd known Josephine Beauregard her entire life. She loved the woman like a grandmother. Yet here she was, throwing that history to the wind in favor of satisfying her curiosity. "Yeah, maybe."

"Me, too."

The admission was sweet—and wholly unexpected—and it only reinforced every thought she'd already had about Tucker. He was special. Different.

And a gentleman.

"I'm not even sure what we're looking for."

"Something we'll know when we see it?"

"I guess." Her gaze followed his movements, and she shrugged. She might feel bad now that they were here, rifling through things, but something had carried them from the hospital and into Mrs. B.'s house.

And that something was still proving elusive.

"What could they be hiding? By all accounts, they haven't seen each other in years."

"How do you know that?"

"Max Senior told me when we were sitting in the hospital room. He and Jo went their own ways and got married to other people. They haven't seen each other."

"How long ago was that?"

"It's got to be well over fifty years ago."

Tucker stopped his search. "They hid something that long ago?"

"They must have. When else would they have done it?"

His gaze skipped around the room before landing on a Louis XIV table that held a variety of photos. "Maybe we're looking in the wrong place."

"I know Mrs. B. If she's got evidence of something, it would be here in the house. It would have to be. She doesn't have an office or anything like that."

"No, I mean we're looking for some sort of evidence, but maybe what we need is something broader. Something that doesn't look like a clue." Tucker moved over to the photos, lifting each one in turn. "Do you recognize anyone in these?"

When they'd arrived, a small desk lamp was already

on, its cord attached to a timer. The soft light filtered through the room, and she moved in to review the various photos. Several were filled with people she didn't recognize, flanking Josephine in various poses, but several more were familiar. "That's her late husband, Tom. And that's a cousin who visited every year from England. And those are her parents."

Tucker pointed toward the friend. "Did she have family in England?"

"She's from there. She moved here when she was small before she'd acquired the accent but her father's was quite proper as I've been told. I never knew him but my mother did as a young girl."

"How did a British family end up in Dallas?"

"How does anyone end up anywhere?" Cassidy shrugged. "I think her parents settled here after World War II."

"That's interesting."

"I guess." She struggled to understand where Tucker was going with all his questions when he picked up the frame of Jo's parents again. He turned it over in his hands before tugging on the stand attached to the backing.

"What are you doing?"

And old yellowed paper dropped to the table as the frame sprung free of the backing.

"Tucker!"

He set the pieces of the frame on the desk and lifted the paper, gently unfolding the thick, yellowed sheets.

"Take a look at this."

Chapter 10

"What does it say?"

Tucker shook his head, his hands gentle on the old paper as he turned it over in the dim light. "Let's find out."

"What made you even think to do that?" Cassidy pointed at the photo. "To pull out the back of the frame? That's not something you just do."

How had he known?

He'd never considered himself a particularly intuitive person, but between years of observation and training in the service and a distinct love of straight lines and angles as an architect, he'd sensed something was off.

"I'm not sure. All I know was that the frame felt different. Heavier somehow, and the back bowed out slightly under my fingers."

The paper was thick, the sort of thing that might come as a personal note from someone, and even with its age he sensed the richness of the vellum.

"Open it."

Tucker handed it to her. "You do the honors."

Excitement quivered around her shoulders in subtle waves, and Tucker hadn't missed the breathless notes in her voice.

Sort of like how she'd sounded after they'd kissed.

A swift pump of excitement kicked in his stomach at the memory of their kiss in the hallway and he caught himself, forcing his attention back to the matter at hand.

They were here on a job. The stolen moments had simply been that—stolen. He'd do well to remember that, especially since they were currently standing in an old, victimized woman's house, searching for evidence of why she and her property had suddenly been targeted with violence.

"It's from Buckingham Palace." Those breathless notes were back, and the awe veiled beneath was unmistakable.

"What?" Thoughts of Mrs. B. fled as Cassidy's comment registered. Whatever Tucker might have expected in the brief moments since they'd found the paper, a missive from royalty certainly wasn't it.

"Look." She shifted the page in the light, the thick ink stamped in the header marking the sender.

"You've got to be kidding me."

"Look here."

Cassidy held the paper out and they both scanned the short note.

Mister Brown. It is with gratitude that my wife and I express our appreciation for your continued duty to your country. Your continued possession of the materials we've discussed and your willingness to dispose of these items is of continued importance. It is with sadness we accept the news of your departure to Texas but wish you and your family continued health and prosperity.

"It's signed by King George."

"Which one's he?" Tucker scanned the date—after

World War II—and then turned the paper over to see if there was anything further. He understood global politics quite well but was admittedly rusty on his royalty.

"Queen Elizabeth's father."

"The current queen?"

"One and the same."

"So why hide it in the back of a picture frame?" Tucker picked up the now separated photo of Mrs. B.'s parents. "This is the sort of thing you frame all on its own."

"This has to have something to do with whatever's secreted in our floor."

He wanted to dismiss it—wanted to believe it was simple coincidence that they'd found such an intriguing piece of communication—but he knew better.

Kings didn't simply send notes out to their fellow countrymen.

And they didn't ask them to hide things.

Your continued possession of the materials we've discussed and your willingness to dispose of these items is of continued importance.

"This is unbelievable." Tucker scanned the missive once more, the richness of the vellum and the royal seal seemingly real.

"It was her father who took the jewels. Like it was a favor."

"This was more than a favor. Her father came here on a mission."

Cassidy locked up Mrs. Beauregard's home and did a quick scan of the quiet street as they walked toward Tucker's SUV. She held her large purse tight against her body, the contents still more of a fanciful notion than something real she could wrap her mind around.

Yet they were real.

They'd agreed to take both the paper and the photo as evidence to share with Violet, Lilah and Max. The details were hard to imagine—secret letters from the royal family—and it would help to have additional eyes on the materials to see if they seemed as ominous to them as they did to Cassidy and Tucker.

And then they'd confront Jo.

Although it pained her to have rifled through Mrs. B.'s house, she refused to lie about it. They'd confront her the next day with what they'd found, and Cassidy knew she'd take her lumps for going through the woman's personal things.

But she refused to be sorry.

She'd missed an opportunity once before to do what was right. There was no way she was repeating the mistake.

"You're quiet."

Cassidy hesitated, the need to keep her personal life buried warring with the need to keep someone she cared about safe. "I'm sad. I know I shouldn't be and I know we don't have all the answers, but I can't help being sad over Mrs. B. She looked so scared."

Tucker shook his head as he opened the door for her. "And panicked. Like someone got to her."

"She's been in the hospital since the accident. How could someone have gotten into such a secured area?"

"What about those goons I chased into the parking lot?"

How had she forgotten about that?

Her own sense of panic lit up her nerve endings before slithering through her stomach with all the force of a live wire. "We have to tell Detective Graystone. He's got to be able to look at footage from the hospital. There's no way they don't have surveillance."

Tucker's gaze was assessing before he stepped away and

closed her door. She'd seen the questions in those warm brown depths and wondered how she'd answer them.

In moments, he was in the passenger seat, pulling away from the curb. "We'll call Graystone in the morning."

She supposed it would keep. If Mrs. B. had been under strong care before, she was absolutely under watch in ICU. Even so, something in waiting didn't sit well.

She'd waited once before…

"What's bothering you?"

The urgency to get home—to get in bed and simply pull the covers over her head—was strong, but Cassidy remained resolute. She refused to let the panic win. "I hate being helpless."

"You're not helpless. And you're not alone."

"I wish that were true."

Oh, how she wished it were true.

How she wished some sense of normalcy would return instead of the constant memories, hovering just beneath the surface, always waiting to break through.

"You're not alone." Tucker's voice remained firm, his face set in hard lines as streetlights washed over his features.

She took in the hard line of his jaw and the warmth and strength that emanated off him as naturally as he took each breath. And without warning, a hard sob rose up in her throat, choking in its intensity.

"My sister. It was my sister." She exhaled again on a heavy breath that was half moan, half sigh at finally saying the words. "I know it's not the same but every time I stop and think about what's happening I feel so helpless. Like it's happening all over again."

"What happened?"

The memories she worked so hard to keep at bay broke

through, warring with the images of what she could only suspect had happened. Danger and desolation and death.

Each jockeyed for position as she imagined the last days and months of her sister's life.

"Leah. My sister. She died. Overdosed on booze and pills. She left a note."

"I'm sorry—" He broke off when she raised her hand, and stopped, clearly waiting for her to continue. She had to get through this. In one great big rush of information, she had to get through.

"I knew she wasn't happy in her marriage, but I had no idea she was so unhappy. Or that she felt so alone. She's my sister. I should have known. Should have sensed something was wrong."

"You can't blame yourself for that."

Violet and Lilah had tried the same arguments but nothing could assuage the guilt. "If not me, then who? She's my family."

"And as your family, she chose to keep things from you. How is that your fault?"

She shook her head, rubbing her hands over her arms in an effort to stay warm, even with the ambient heat that still surrounded them like a thick blanket, even with the car's air-conditioning on full blast.

"I won't make excuses, Tucker. I wasn't there for her. And that's on me. It will always be on me."

Grief was something Tucker understood. He'd steeped himself in it at a young age with loss of his own. But this sense of responsibility Cassidy held herself accountable to was a puzzle. Everything he'd observed up to now had indicated she was a strong-willed woman with a mind of her own.

So how could someone so confident—so full of life—

think that she held such a deep degree of responsibility for the actions of another?

Yes, it hurt to lose a loved one. But mind reading was a tall order for anyone.

The normally crowded streets were empty as he drove through downtown toward the Design District. Although the city wasn't devoid of a homeless problem, the heat had forced many into shelters and there were few stragglers out and about on the streets.

"I'll drop you at the store to get your car and then follow you home."

"You don't—"

"We'll swing by and get Bailey and then we'll follow you home. I'd like to check your house, too."

Any additional protest died on her lips. "Thank you."

The absence of traffic gave him additional time to look at her. She was already slim but up until now he'd seen those slender shoulders were able to carry great burdens. Hell, the woman had moved around her store like a whirling dervish, setting things to rights with precision and focus.

But in this moment, that same build simply looked small.

And completely overwhelmed with grief.

"I see you looking at me."

"And?"

"And I keep hearing your words." She hesitated, then pressed on. "About not being at fault."

"I don't get the feeling you believe them."

"It's not that simple. I chose not to have an active relationship with her. My own sister."

"You have a relationship with Violet and Lilah that's sisterlike. It seems as if you're capable of one."

He thought of the camaraderie between the three

women—and the fierce devotion—and knew the thought to be completely accurate. They were a support system and they were a family. One created instead of born to, but a family all the same.

"I should have had one with Leah, too."

"Yet you didn't. Why not?"

She grew quiet again, and Tucker sensed he'd over-stepped. So it was with some surprise when she spoke once more. "I told you the other night about my father. And how he wasn't crazy about what I was doing."

"Yes."

"Leah wasn't, either. My parents should have supported me and they didn't. To have my sister side with them—" Her light sigh seemed to fill the confines of the car. "It hurt. And it still does. Mrs. B. was actually a rock during that time. To both of us. She managed to straddle both sides—see both our perspectives."

"You and your sister were close to her?"

"She was Leah's godmother so there was a bond there. Always. But she's also been supportive of me. It's the rest of my family who couldn't make that same effort."

Tucker knew that pain. Knew the continued frustration at those around you who were supposed to be your biggest allies and who were instead steeped in the role of enemy. He'd lived with that pain—and the anger born of that pain—for a long time.

Until anger had turned to indifference.

His voice was strangled when he finally spoke, understanding choking the words. "Our loved ones don't always know what we need."

"No. They don't. I loved my sister, but we had little in common beyond blood and shared childhoods. So we grew into adults who shared quick, perfunctory visits at the holidays or an occasional drink during the workweek."

"A mutual decision."

"Or an unwillingness to try harder."

Frustration rose up. Whether it was the raw open wounds of his own childhood or his inability to help her see that she wasn't responsible for her sister, Tucker didn't know.

All he did know was that her normally vivid eyes had faded to a dull, leaden blue and his heart ached for the burden she carried.

But it shattered at the realization she believed herself responsible for her sister's broken life.

Tucker followed Cassidy's car through the streets of East Dallas, Bailey panting heavily from the backseat. She'd followed him to his apartment a few blocks from the office to pick up the mutt, then man and dog had followed her home. Bailey had settled himself in the backseat, but his heavy panting was a dead giveaway of just how excited he was to be along on the adventure.

"Damn crazy situation." Tucker muttered it, even as his own wave of excitement pulsed through his veins. He and a reluctant Max had taken on helping the women with varying degrees of commitment, but tonight had changed everything.

They were *in*. The no-turning-back, see-it-through-to-the-end sort of in.

And he was more excited than he'd have believed possible.

Was this what happened when you went back into civilian life? He'd never completely connected with the concept of the adrenaline junkie—he valued his life, thank you very much—but he did appreciate the heightened awareness and razor-sharp reflexes that came to bear on an op. Neither of them had had that in a long time, their roles as gentleman business owners not providing quite the same adrenaline highs day in and day out.

The thought lingered at the back of his mind as he pulled up behind Cassidy in her driveway. After letting Bailey out—his puppylike excitement over exploring new ground sending him off like a shot—Tucker grabbed his own bag from the trunk.

"I'm sorry to put you through all this trouble."

"It's no trouble, Cassidy."

"Of course it is, and I'm sorry you're stuck dealing with it."

She'd said the same when he'd left to get Bailey. Said it again as they were climbing into their cars. Since he had no interest in hearing it yet again, he turned toward her and dragged her against him, her loud *oompf* the only sound before he clamped his mouth on hers.

The tension of the past few hours fell away as the moment overtook them both. The sweet scent of honeysuckle filled his senses—was that her or her yard?—but when her even sweeter tongue slipped between his lips he forgot to question anything.

Hell, he damn near forgot to breathe.

With gentle motions, at odds with the heat that raged between them, he ran his fingers in long lines over her body, grazing his fingertips up and down her rib cage in one long, sinuous caress. When Cassidy pressed herself closer to his chest, her hands exploratory across his shoulders, he slipped a hand over the sensitive skin of her stomach.

His actions were greeted with a small mewl, and he kept up the gentle stroking even as his mouth dueled with hers.

A loud bark pulled him from the mindless passion, but still he kept his mouth fused with Cassidy's until a heavy set of paws landed dead center on his back.

"Damn mutt," he muttered against her lips. The smile

that greeted him went a long way toward assuaging his annoyance.

But it did nothing for the raging needs of his body, and his blood pounded in hard, choppy waves as he disengaged himself from her embrace.

"Bailey." Although he intended to be stern, his voice came out on a harsh exhale and it was only when Bailey barked again—this time more agitated—that Tucker keyed in to the dog's distress. Lean muscle quivered under coarse, brindled fur, and Tucker followed the direction of Bailey's gaze.

"Damn it."

Something flashed in the dark across the street—if he hadn't been watching so closely he'd have missed it—and Tucker moved into action. With a soft but firm hand on Bailey's head, he ordered him to stay before he took off after his quarry.

Cassidy's holler echoed behind him, along with another bark from Bailey, but Tucker kept on moving, unwilling to waste another moment.

The guy knew he'd been made and had a hell of a head start, but Tucker pressed himself on.

"Four freaking miles a day better be good for something." The words fell from his lips like gunshots and as the man passed under an unavoidable streetlamp Tucker caught his profile in sharp relief.

He couldn't make out specific features but the guy was blond, of medium height and wore a suit. Cycling through his memories of the men he'd chased out of the hospital, Tucker recollected the blond hair of the second of the two goons.

Bingo.

The distance and the ambient heat were his ally, and Tucker noted how the man's pace slowed. A head start gave the bastard a mighty advantage, but Tucker pushed himself harder and maintained a grueling pace in pursuit of his prey.

As he pounded over the distance, a slow, simmering rage began to build. This guy was watching Cassidy's house. Had watched the two of them together, in the midst of a stolen moment.

Although he'd been momentarily frustrated at Bailey's interruption, Tucker was suddenly grateful. His dog's awareness had not only trumped his own, but it had gone a long way toward stopping the passion-filled display on Cassidy's front lawn.

The heat of her mouth and the flavor of her still lingered on his tongue like a rich wine, and he clenched his fists at the remembered softness of her skin. A renewed wave of anger fueled him even harder now that their private moment had been observed, then subsequently ruined.

The gap between them narrowed farther, and Tucker knew he was close. He'd nearly cleared the distance—only about fifteen yards separated them—when a large SUV squealed off the main road and barreled toward them on the quiet neighborhood street. Shots rang out, their heavy thunder drawing him up short.

What the *hell*?

Tucker threw his body backward, reversing both his momentum and direction. He nearly stumbled as his foot lost its grip on asphalt before windmilling his arms to right himself.

He *had* to get out of range.

The driver was managing a car as well as a gun, but his screeching halt to pick up his passenger was going to give him time to get off another round of shots, likely not as haywire as the last.

And other than attracting the notice of the neighbors, the driver had nothing to lose.

As he maneuvered himself into the shadows of a nearby house, Tucker recognized the underlying strategy. The blond goon had zigzagged his way through the neighborhood as he gave chase, moving ever closer to the main thoroughfare that buttressed Cassidy's street. He'd efficiently positioned himself to grab his getaway car.

Tucker saw the pattern perfectly in his mind now. Blondie didn't need to win the footrace, he just needed to keep his lead until he had backup.

His desire for answers was strong, and the thought flitted through his mind to take his chances by storming the SUV to at least read the license plate, but his innate sense of self-preservation ultimately won out.

That decision was reinforced as one last gunshot rang out, the bullet exploding in the bushes mere inches from his feet, before the black SUV peeled off the curb, Tucker's quarry now ensconced in the passenger seat.

Whether it was an errant shot or a deliberate warning, Tucker wasn't sure.

All he did know was that he needed to get back to Cassidy.

Cassidy stood on her front porch, Bailey's heavy, reassuring form crossing a path back and forth in front of her. She'd tried to go down the steps when she heard what sounded like a gunshot, but he'd begun barking, his agitation enough to keep her in place.

Damn fool man. Was Tucker Buchanan insane?

Although she had no desire to take off after a stalker, she had no interest in having *him* take off after a stalker, either. An armed stalker, no less.

And when had Tucker's safety begun to trump her own?

She dropped to one knee next to Bailey and wrapped her arms around his neck. Although she sought to calm

him, she quickly realized the move was really about soothing herself. Hard muscle quivered under her hands and she
pressed her head to his, holding him close.

Although she knew his big, protective body was still no
match for a bullet, Bailey radiated protection and a self-
less courage that was surprisingly similar to his owner's.

On a loud yip and whiny, impatient cry, he stood at
tighter attention, and within moments Tucker appeared
across the street, loping though her neighbor's yard.

"Go ahead." She stood up and patted Bailey on his rump
to get him moving, but the dog stayed, just as he'd been
told. His excitement was palpable, but he never moved
from her side.

Tucker crossed the yard, and relief had her taking her
first easy breath since they'd left the hospital a few hours
earlier. He picked up the duffel he'd dropped earlier, then
kept on toward the porch.

"What happened?"

Jaw set in a firm line, Tucker said nothing, just dropped his
bag on the porch and pulled her close. She went willingly, not
caring if her question was unanswered. Or if the neighbors
saw them. She didn't even care if anyone was still out there.

He was safe. Whole.

She took another deep breath, then hugged him tighter.
"You're all right."

"I'm fine." His large hands ran soothing circles over
her back, but she didn't miss that his hold on her was as
tight as her own.

On a hard sob, she dragged him toward the door. "Let's
get inside."

Charlie cursed as he drove determinedly toward LBJ
Freeway, his only goal to get distance between his sister-in-

law's neighborhood and the freaking wannabe hero who'd nearly caught up with Alex.

The one-sided conversation had begun before he'd even hit the highway, and he listened as Alex gave the same series of answers over and over.

No, I'm sure he didn't make me.

Yes, I understand.

No, I won't be late in the morning.

He waited until the man had stowed his phone firmly in his suit jacket pocket before speaking. "Boss is pissed."

"As he should be."

Charlie hadn't been able to make the underlying accent—Russian? German?—but he knew Alex was a man of few words. But since he'd just pulled his ass from a very uncomfortable sling, Charlie figured he'd earned the right to a few questions.

"The Duke's a hard man to please."

Alex shrugged, the move casual in the reflected glow of the highway's streetlamps. "That's why he's the Duke."

"None of us could control the fact that the girls met up with the cavalry the moment we started this op."

"We've been lazy. Undisciplined." The words spilled forth, full of disdain and self-loathing. "The men of Dragon Designs are an inconvenience, nothing more."

"They're ex-military, man. I did a bit of research about them on their website. They were part of the Army Corps of Engineers. That means they know how to divert rivers and build dams and blow stuff up."

"Excuses are immaterial. We must do better."

"Speak for yourself. I've been doing my part already. I found this gig for the Duke."

"No." Alex was quiet for a long moment, the pause growing eerie as Charlie waited for him to continue. "The Duke found you."

"Hell, no." Charlie fought to hold back the rising anger but damn, the good-little-soldier routine was wearing thin. "I set this up. I'm the one who figured out what the girls are sitting on while they play bridal boutique."

"You think you're in control but you know nothing." Alex turned to face him, his gaze starkly empty in the reflected lights. "The Duke found you. Only a fool would believe otherwise."

Cassidy handed Tucker a mug of coffee before taking a seat on her couch. He sat on the opposite end with Bailey at his feet, the dog happily munching on a rawhide bone that looked about the width of a football field. And if his contented little grunts were any indication, the dog wasn't stopping until he hit the end zone.

"Start at the beginning."

Although it had driven her crazy with curiosity to wait until the coffee brewed, Cassidy and Tucker had both used the time to call their friends and confirm everyone was safe.

Of course, once they'd both shared the details on the stalker and Tucker's subsequent chase through the neighborhood, the calls had unleashed a torrent of concerned gasps, adding time to the calls.

Cassidy had reassured Violet and Lilah that they needed to stay put and make a plan to call Detective Graystone in the morning. While she'd have preferred the afternoon, she had two fittings the next day and knew she needed to get to him early to stay on schedule.

As a business, they'd already lost too many days to whatever the heck was going on around them—or under them, as the case might be—and she couldn't afford to skip the planned fittings and still stay on track for everything she had due this month.

"All the way at the beginning?"

His comment pulled her from her musings, his heated gaze pulling her firmly back to the here and now. She swallowed hard but did manage to get out a weak "yes" in response.

"Then I'd say it started with a rather inspiring kiss in your front yard."

Images slammed themselves back into her mind. While they hadn't strayed far from her thoughts, concerns over Tucker's late-night run had jockeyed for first place. Now that she *did* remember—and could still feel the brand of his lips and the light caress of his fingertips over the sensitive skin of her stomach—Cassidy struggled with how to play the moment.

Cool and collected? Or honest about how he affected her?

She opted for honesty and hoped he'd appreciate the gesture. "While I enjoy having my brains leak out of my head as much as the next woman, I'm talking about your race through my neighborhood like the hounds of hell were at your feet."

"I'd rather talk about the kissing."

Desire flashed in her belly—hard and hot—and she took a sip of her coffee in an attempt to regain her equilibrium.

Was that even possible? She'd had no equilibrium since meeting Tucker Buchanan and she was fast coming to think it had very little to do with the fact that people were following her with loaded guns.

Again, her thoughts dragged her where her hormones had no fear of treading, and images of doing a lot more than some kissing in her front yard filled her mind.

Hot, heated caresses while early-evening light played over both their bodies.

Slow, carnal kisses where they explored every inch of each other.

Long, luscious strokes of his body entering hers...

Cassidy pulled herself from the powerful images and attempted, once more, to focus on their conversation.

Even if it was becoming more and more evident that all her normal arguments against getting involved with him, like the fact they'd met the morning before, seemed increasingly less convincing.

Her only defense was the reminder she clung to like a lifeline. They were two people who'd met and who had turned to each other in a moment of crisis. Relationships forged in *that* fire weren't destined for a very long run.

She knew that one from firsthand experience.

"And there you've gone away from me again." Tucker ran a finger over the shell of her ear, sending delicious shivers down her spine and pulling her back from her thoughts. "Or did your brain really leak out? Come on, sweetheart, talk."

The endearment twisted her heart before hardening it in firm lines of regret. She wasn't his sweetheart and she'd do well to remember that.

"Tell me about the guy you chased."

Tucker considered her for another moment, his gaze as dark as his black coffee as he searched her face, before he continued. "I'm pretty sure it was one of the guys from the hospital."

"The ones in suits?"

"Yep."

"Who goes around shooting at people in three-piece suits?"

"Someone with backing and support."

Tucker's assessment pulled her up short and she nearly

fumbled her mug, righting it at the last moment before ending up with a lap full of hot coffee. "Backing?"

"A lot of it."

Whatever she'd imagined this was all about suddenly took on an entirely new meaning as she evaluated his comments. "You think someone has a lot more knowledge than we do? Knowledge of Mrs. B. and what's hidden in her floor?"

"Yes, I do. I think someone knows exactly what's under that floor, or at least believes they do. Our only chance is to get to it first."

She thought over the decisions they'd made. "We need to finish digging up that floor."

"Opening up a huge hole isn't the way to keep Detective Graystone's curiosity at bay."

"I suppose not. I can't imagine he misses much."

"I think we have to open the floor ourselves. Without the detective's involvement."

"He needs to know."

"Does he? We don't even know. Only now we're sitting on a half-dug hole in the floor and a mysterious letter."

Cassidy knew involvement from the police was to their benefit, but curiosity and her lifelong relationship with Jo Beauregard held her back.

There could be anything in that floor. And whatever was there was obviously valuable, or those after it wouldn't be so ruthless. Of course, heading down that path—and the belief that the concrete veiled something of value—brought her thinking back full circle.

They should get help from the police and go back to their lives.

Tucker took another sip of his coffee, quiet as he waited for her to continue, and in that moment something that had been nagging at her finally surfaced. "You said something to me earlier but I'd say it's doubly true of you."

"What's that?"

"You don't seem at all interested in what's under the floor."

"I'm far more interested in the woman who walks and works above it."

Again, that rush of desire threatened to swamp her like a wave in a hurricane, only this time, she was helpless to move away or resist. Helpless to resist the arguments her subconscious was intent on serving up.

Temporary passion.

Heightened tension.

Adrenaline high.

Every argument that whispered through her mind grew more and more faint as she allowed her gaze to roam over Tucker's kind, understanding face.

He reached out and took her mug from her hands, settling it along with his on a table beside him. Turning back, he pulled her close, draping his arm across her shoulders and snuggling her against his warm, solid chest.

His gaze never left her face and his words were earnest when he finally spoke. "I'm not going to let anything happen to you. Or to your friends. You have my word on that. Max's, too."

"I know."

"Do you?"

In that simple question Cassidy knew absolutely that he understood her.

Her hesitance to trust anyone. Her struggles to be open to new people in her life. And her desire to stop fighting the horrible sense of loneliness that had replaced her family in her life.

He understood.

She had work to do. Things she had to get done before she finally headed off to sleep. But for a few moments, she allowed herself to give in and take the comfort he offered. As they sat there in her small living room, she rested her head against his chest and let the quiet moment surround her.

She took solace in Bailey's gentle snores, the toll of his earlier adventure obviously trumping the hard work of devouring his bone. And as she gave herself up to the quiet, Cassidy reveled in the presence of the large man who sat, ever watchful, beside her.

Chapter 11

Still groggy from sleep, Tucker followed the smell of coffee through her small house toward the kitchen. He'd fallen asleep on Cassidy's living-room couch, at some point stretching out when she'd murmured she had to finish something in her office.

Next thing he knew he was blinking away the early-morning sun that blazed through her front bay windows, announcing the new day.

He'd slept hard, no doubt about it, but he usually maintained a base level of awareness, even when tired. He'd learned in the Corps to sleep light, and his last year with Bailey had helped him continue the practice. Although Bailey had trained well, he wasn't so far past puppyhood that Tucker could fully relax his guard. A late-night chew session with a new pair of running shoes the previous month had only reinforced the point.

But he'd hit it hard last night.

He padded into Cassidy's kitchen and came to a stop at the sight that greeted him.

Bailey lay at Cassidy's feet, his bone between his paws, while she ate a slice of toast with peanut butter and scratched at an image in a sketch pad with a pencil. Both seemed oblivious to him so he took a moment to look his fill.

The sun was softer in here, less direct, and it highlighted the magnificent array of reds in her hair. From deep auburn to a soft ginger and a multitude of shades in between, he wanted to reach out and fist his hands in all those lush strands.

His gaze had already moved on toward her lips when Bailey let out a short yip, giving him away.

"Good morning." She laid her pencil down, a soft smile playing about her lips. "Coffee's ready, and I can make you toast, eggs, cereal or all of the above."

"You don't need to cook. I'll get some toast."

"Oh, and I have bananas, too."

"Breakfast of champions."

"I bet you've had less."

He thought about her statement—heard the question lying underneath—and turned to face her after depressing the tab on the toaster. "You seem curious about my time in the Corps."

"Does that bother you?"

"No." He paused, wanting to get it right. "It doesn't bother me at all. Consider my comment observation more than censure."

"I know we should be focused on the issue at hand—" She broke off, and once again he sensed there was something bigger lying underneath her words.

The toaster popped, and he busied himself with the butter and jelly she'd already set out, giving her a moment to think through what she wanted to say.

In his experience, once someone got up the courage to broach a subject, they wanted to get it out. Some well-placed silence often gave that needed push to get them over the hump.

Toast in one hand and a fresh mug of coffee in the other, he took a seat opposite her.

He didn't have to wait long.

"You seem to have a healthy attitude about whatever you saw while in the service. But it's a big part of your life and you don't say much."

"I have the occasional nightmare from time to time, but I consider myself fortunately exempt from some more destructive memories." He thought about some of the men he knew who weren't so lucky and paused a moment to take a sip of his coffee. "Our first project after starting Dragon Designs was doing some pro bono work for a new veteran's facility in Dallas."

"The one that's going up just north of downtown."

"One and the same."

"That's yours?"

He saw that spark—recognized the compliment of another creator—and nodded. "Top to bottom."

"You've created something wonderful with your talent. A haven for others."

"You do the same." He reached out and tapped his finger against the top of her sketchpad. "That's a pretty amazing drawing. Even now, as only some quick pencils over breakfast, I can see the design and workmanship. The woman who ends up with that dress will benefit from your talent."

"It's our job at Elegance and Lace to create a beautiful day for others."

"Something you've created out of the ashes of tragedy."

She paused and the same pain he'd seen the night before when she spoke of her sister flashed once more before fading. "I hadn't thought about it that way."

"Maybe you should. It's an accomplishment. To take

difficulty and make something out of it. Something strong and good."

He took a big bite of his toast and tapped the sketch pad again. "So. Where are we headed today? You said you had fittings."

"*I'm* headed to a couple of my brides' homes. I assumed you were headed back to work. I already spoke to Detective Graystone. He wants to talk to both of us."

"He can wait until later. I'm not leaving you on your own."

"Tucker, I'll be fine."

Bailey whined at his side for some toast and he tossed over the last piece of his crust before reaching for his coffee. "I'm not sure what part of 'I'm with you until we get the floor uncovered and taken care of' you don't get yet."

"You can't go with me to a fitting."

"I'm not coming into the woman's bedroom while she tries things on." He shot her a big grin before standing to make another round of toast. "Unless you're in need of my dress-zipping services."

"Um, no." She came up behind him to fill her coffee mug. "How will I explain you?"

"Designer in training? Bodyguard? New boyfriend? Take your pick."

"It's unprofessional."

"It's the deal if you want to keep your appointments today."

She set her mug down, then whirled on him. "When did you get so bossy?"

"When someone decided to ransack your business, then stalk us to your home and then shoot at me when I wanted answers."

The dark reminder of the threat that hung over her head

stopped her, her pale skin going even paler and highlighting the circles under her eyes.

He wanted to apologize—knew he should—but held his tongue as her gaze brightened, like blue sky opening up behind a mass of storm clouds. "Then I think I have just the job for you."

"Oh? What's that?"

"Lackey."

Cassidy looked over her shoulder, tossing out orders as she hauled two oversize cases full of her supplies. "Don't let that dress drop on the ground. In fact, don't even think about the ground."

"I'm not thinking about anything."

"I believe you're thinking something that includes the *B* word but I promise not to hold it against you. Vi and Lilah often think the same things when I'm knee-deep in a fitting."

She heard the hard bark of laughter and knew they were back on even ground. It had been a close call, she mused, as she rang Bridget Talloway's doorbell.

Tucker had been determined to help, but he clearly had had no idea what went into the production of a wedding dress. An hour in her company and now he knew.

"You do this for every dress you make?" The thick layers of silk crinkled in his hands, but Cassidy was pleased to note he held the wrapped material high and across both arms.

"We usually do it at the shop, but yes, several times per dress."

"How many times does it take?"

"As many as it takes to get it right." When he said nothing, she added, "I'm sure you don't get every sketch right the first time."

"Hell, no."

"This is the same."

"But you already have her measurements."

"It doesn't mean there aren't adjustments. Modifications. A tuck here or letting out a seam there."

"I respect what you're saying but still don't quite get it." He hefted the swath in his arms a bit higher. "There's enough material here to cover a rhino."

"Tucker!" She hip-bumped him because her hands were full of her own supplies. "You never say that to a bride."

"I didn't say she was one."

"Nothing that remotely suggests weight is ever to be uttered around a bride." At the sound of footsteps on the other side of the doorway, she added in a lower voice, "Or to any woman, for that matter. Did you just crawl out from under a rock?"

His scowl was deep when the door opened but he said nothing as her blushing—and slender—bride greeted them from the other side of the door.

"Cassidy!" The loud screech and big hug pulled her through the door on a whirlwind, the woman's excitement so extreme she didn't even register Tucker's presence. "You're here!"

"Good morning, Bridget. I hope you don't mind I brought my assistant along."

"Of course not."

Tucker lifted the material high. "Where do you want me to set this?"

"Go ahead and put it on my bed." Bridget pointed toward a door on the first floor. She waited until Tucker disappeared into the room before she whirled. "Tell me he's yours."

"My assistant?" Cassidy ignored the flutter in her belly at the lie. "Yes, he works for me."

"That's all?"

"Yeah. Why?"

"I don't know." Bridget shrugged. "I just thought there was something more. Like you can't stand to be away from him for a single moment and he feels the same so he had to come with you."

"That would be horribly unprofessional."

"Oh, bull." Bridget crossed to the fridge and pulled out three waters. "You, Violet and Lilah are some of the most professional professionals I know. That doesn't mean you're not human. Besides, I think a group of women who run an awesome bridal company should all be lucky enough to be wild and crazy in love."

It wasn't the first time someone had pointed out that she and her partners were still single, running a boutique that specialized in the most love-struck part of love. Either together or in individual consultations with brides, each of them had dealt with it. They'd cultivated thick skins and a litany of polite remarks to deflect the questions or excited comments. She and her friends all knew the comments were shared in excitement and in the spirit of happiness, love and sisterhood.

So why did this one stick a bit harder than usual?

Bridget handed her a water. "So what's wrong with the shop? Not that I'm sorry you came to me, but what happened?"

Cassidy shared the practiced excuse—some unavoidable work on the floor that was churning up too much dust—and quickly gestured toward the woman's bedroom.

Tucker came back from the bedroom, his face set in grim lines. Cassidy nearly laughed at his somber demeanor but instead pointed toward Bridget. "Bridget and her fiancé, Cole, are getting married at the end of next month at the Arboretum."

He might not be happy in his surroundings or with playing delivery boy, but she had to give him credit.

Tucker Buchanan knew how to handle a woman.

A bright smile lit his face and he moved into animated conversation, full of the right balance of subtle flirtation and interest as he peppered Bridget with questions about her big day.

At the point where they moved into a discussion of her fiancé's decision to do a morning coat versus a standard tuxedo Cassidy figured he'd suffered enough.

"Why don't we get started?"

At Bridget's excited nod and Tucker's raised eyebrows behind her bride's head, Cassidy pointed toward the living room. "Tucker. I believe you needed to call our contractor and light a fire under him. I'll take Bridget to the bedroom."

"I'll be here if you need me. Have fun."

Bridget waved at him as she practically danced down the hall. "We will."

Cassidy didn't miss his words—meant just for her—before she followed her happy bride.

"I really am great with zippers."

Unwilling to give him the last laugh, she took a few steps back and moved into his chest. Lifting to her tiptoes, she pressed her lips near his ear. "Funny. So am I."

Max stood over an oversize card table Violet had set up for him in the front of the shop. They'd decided to hold off breaking through the concrete till after hours when they could all concentrate on the situation. For now, they had several blueprints spread out and he reviewed each of them, making notes on a large legal pad.

For her part, she couldn't make sense of any of them

but hadn't yet found a reason to move away from the large, capable man filling the front of her shop.

That's because you don't want to.

While she prided herself on being a smart, sensible woman who could tackle any task put in front of her, the blueprints were like reading Greek. She also prided herself on being a woman who could handle her hormones, so why the hell did her gaze keep straying to the corded muscles of his forearms or the thick biceps that flexed beneath the sleeves of his T-shirt?

"This was a good idea." Max pointed toward the layout of Dragon Designs. "Nearly all these warehouses were built around the same time after World War II. We might find something in our blueprints that help us figure out the lay of the land. I'm glad you thought of this."

She stumbled over the compliment—they hadn't exactly been civil to each other up until now, but she left that thought unspoken. "It's amazing your grandfather's got the originals."

"The man throws nothing away. He's got a copy at home of these, too."

"So anal-retentive tendencies really are hereditary."

Max shot her a dark look before it was replaced with a smile and a hard laugh. She couldn't hold back her own, the stress of the past few days more tiring than she'd realized.

It was good to laugh. Good to find something to break up the tension. And it was even better to laugh with him.

"I keep thinking about your observations from last night. About how closed up your grandfather and Mrs. B. are. Is it possible you got some small detail from the discussion you've maybe overlooked?"

"I don't think so." Max tossed his pencil on the blueprints and stepped away. "Old man's closed up tighter than an oil drum."

Violet's gaze shifted to the back of the shop. "You think he knows what's in here?"

"I think he knows something."

"And we're smack in the middle of it all."

The interest she always saw in his deep blue gaze flickered once more before something more somber took its place.

Honesty.

"I think you, Lilah and Cassidy are in this. Deep in this. And I think we need to take a more direct approach with the detective. Get the police down here watching the store."

A light shiver worked its way along her back, at odds with the warm sun that streamed in the windows. "But we don't know anything. And the police can't protect us indefinitely. Whoever did this had to have known for a while, yet they bided their time. A few more days won't be much in the scheme of things overall."

"No, I suppose not."

"That was fun."

"Liar." Cassidy's response was immediate as she eyed him sideways from the passenger seat.

"It was. After I tuned out the wedding mania and began plotting some moves with my fantasy football team."

Tucker kept his eyes on the road but didn't miss the light sniff before she added, "I certainly hope you didn't pick that new rookie the Cowboys drafted for your team. He might be a fantasy someday but that boy needs some serious seasoning."

"What do you take me for?" He'd been burned by rookies before and wasn't inclined to repeat the performance unless forced.

"Just making sure you don't have an inflated sense of excitement for your new hometown team."

"So noted." He risked a glance at her, the same satisfaction he'd seen leaving Bridget's house still painted across her face. "You had fun this morning."

"It's fun to see someone so excited and know I had a small part in that happiness. I do enjoy it."

"Yet you've never had the urge to say 'I do' yourself?"

Tucker wasn't sure why he felt the need to ask *that* particular question, but now that it was out he was curious to hear her answer.

"Am I wearing a sign today?"

A sign?

She pressed on before he could question her. "Sorry. But Bridget made a similar comment when you were putting her dress in her room. It comes with the territory but it gets old sometimes."

"Questions we don't want to answer usually do." Her gaze was thoughtful as he turned off into a fast-food parking lot. "You hungry?"

"Now that's a question I always have an answer to. Yes."

"What do you want?"

"Burger. Fries. Vanilla shake."

"A woman after my own heart."

He ordered a double, changing only the vanilla for chocolate on his order, then settled behind the two cars waiting before them. He reached out to stroke her hand. "My question might be one you don't want to answer, but I'm still curious."

Her fingers closed over his, the move so unexpected it cratered straight through his stomach before he could catch his breath.

"I came close. Once in college and again a few years ago."

Although the words weren't what he was expecting,

they went down surprisingly better with her hand locked with his. "Not the right guys?"

"Not by a long shot. First one was too young. We're just lucky we both figured it out before he bought much more than a ring."

"You didn't get into the wedding mania?"

Her grip never lessened but her gaze stayed steady on a carwash across the parking lot. "We thought graduating first was important and we focused on buying a house. The day I stood next to him to sign the papers on a contract for our brand-new home in the suburbs, I panicked and ran out of the model home."

"It's a big moment."

"And one-hundred-percent right when it's something you want. When it's not something you want, it's big, stifling and cuts off all your air."

"Did you hyperventilate when you bought your current house?"

"Nope. I danced into the mortgage office the same way Bridget danced down her hallway today."

"While prancing isn't in my repertoire, I was pretty light-footed the day I got Bailey."

"Dancing, not prancing, smart aleck." She squeezed his hand before letting it go so he could pull up to the window. "You love that dog."

"It's sick, I know, but yes, I love that damn dog like a brother."

"I think it's nice. I heard it said once that our pets are the only chance we get to pick a family member. From those loyal brown eyes to that silly tail, it's clear you picked well."

Tucker paid the cashier and took the milk shakes, then the bag, Cassidy's words bringing a smile to his face. He had chosen Bailey and the pup was the best family he'd ever had.

Family...

The word stuck as he navigated the rest of the drive-through and into the parking lot.

Family.

Excitement replaced the crazy nerves in his stomach, and he pulled into a parking space and turned toward her.

"That's it."

"What?" She looked up from pulling a wrapped burger out of the bag, the scent of fried potatoes following on its heels. "What's it?"

"Family. This whole thing." When she only stared at him, Tucker pressed on, urgent now to get out the words. "Everything happening. It's all connected. The knowledge someone has. The connections between all of you. Even the break-in to your shop the other morning. The person had the alarm code. You know who's doing this."

"I don't know anyone who would do this."

"Then Violet or Lilah do. It's connected, Cassidy. Don't you see it?"

He saw her work through it—saw the ideas racing through her eyes as she pondered, then discarded each—before she shook her head. "No one I know would do this. My immediate family certainly wouldn't. And even my extended family just doesn't fit. They ask me about the shop at the occasional family gathering, but then the subject fades and we move on to something else."

"It's someone you know. We need to get back to the shop."

"We have to go see bride number two."

"Can you reschedule her?"

"Do you want me to break her heart?"

He wanted to argue but thought once more of Bridget

Talloway's dance down her hallway and Cassidy's reaction to that pure, unadulterated joy.

It's fun to see someone so excited and know I had a small part in that happiness.

"Fine. We go there and then we head back to find your partners. The three of you know who's doing this. We just need to follow the connections and we'll find him, too."

Chapter 12

Cassidy dragged her supplies from the back of Tucker's SUV and blew out a hard breath. If her morning appointment was the height of joy and pleasure, her afternoon bridezilla nearly had her throwing in the towel.

The hem wasn't right.

The train was too long to be chapel and too short to be cathedral.

The bodice gave the bride slut boobs, not church boobs.

On and on it had gone, despite the fact this should have been their last fitting before the big day.

Tucker had been a trouper, and Cassidy figured she owed him big-time since she'd been adamant about not canceling the appointment. For herself, she already envisioned a large glass of wine after she got her supplies unloaded inside.

Her gaze caught on the overflowing garbage container at the back of the building and she stopped short. Something cold and dark slithered through her, despite the oppressive afternoon heat, and she stared at the evidence of their shop break-in—black plastic bags of garbage piled so high they spilled from the lip of the industrial bin.

"What's wrong?" Tucker rustled behind her, both wrapped gowns piled high in his hands. His oversize bundle was so large, she felt the press of frothy material at her back even though he stood several inches behind her.

She turned toward him, reassured by his large form even as she tried to process the small yet dangerous example of what they were up against.

Someone had broken into Elegance and Lace.

His eyes crinkled at the corners, his concern more than evident as he tried to juggle the heavy material. "Cass? Tell me what's wrong?"

"I just noticed the garbage can. That's all."

She saw his attention shift, then swing back to her. "I can call the city to come make a special pickup."

It was sweet, she thought, his willingness to remove something she found distasteful. On a small smile, she shook her head. "It's not a snake, Tucker. It can keep."

"It upsets you."

"No, what it means upsets me."

Vanilla hung heavy in the air as the smell of Lilah's latest creation greeted them. Cassidy pushed through the door with her hip, giving Tucker an easier entry with his load of dresses, and tried to put what she'd seen out of her mind.

They were all safe. And once she confronted Mrs. B. with the note, they'd get to the bottom of things and then begin to move on.

She had to focus on that simple fact or she'd drive herself crazy.

"Let's take those back to my workspace."

The familiar space in the large oversize office next to Violet's went a long way toward offering some measure of comfort. Although still covered against the risk of dust, several dress dummies held gowns in various stages of completion, and a wall of sketches held the patterns of her work. Another wall held photos of completed creations, their owners immortalized forever, their special days stamped in her workplace.

Her dreams were on that wall and in that room.

Free of his burden, Tucker came up behind her and wrapped his arms around her from behind. "We're going to get to the bottom of this."

"I know."

He rested his head against hers as his hands roamed along her arms, soothing and enticing all at the same time. She felt alive in his arms. Safe, yes, but alive in ways she'd never felt before.

They'd shared so much already. Dangerous moments, but more than that. In less than seventy-two hours, she'd shared her past. Her family issues. Even the misery and anguish that filled her over the loss of her sister.

He hadn't flinched through a bit of it.

Such a contrast to her second fiancé.

Images of Robert Barrington's perfect features filled her mind's eye. In the two years they'd been together, Lilah had teased her often about how she and Robert were one of Dallas's power couples, her with her up-and-coming business and him with his third-generation, family-based antiques business.

They were a pair who had their picture captured for the society pages at nearly every event they attended and who were considered the next generation of the city's crème de la crème.

What a mirage.

She'd known it, of course. Sensed the distance that had grown stronger and stronger over the months after Robert had proposed.

And then Leah had died and her world had shattered,

and Robert had showed no interest in helping her build it up again.

She might have concerns about entering a relationship with Tucker that was forged in the fires of adrenaline and danger, but she also knew damn well she wasn't the best judge, even of so-called "normal" relationships.

Her experience with Robert had been the antithesis of adrenaline-fueled and it hadn't ended up successful.

They'd had a slow and steady courtship. The "right" group of friends and acquaintances. An appropriately planned and well-timed engagement. Basically, nothing out of the ordinary or unexpected until the very end when it all fell apart.

The worst part was that after a few months, she'd realized that the only thing she missed was the idea of him. The actual man was far from her thoughts and she hadn't missed a beat pining for him.

Tucker, on the other hand…

She turned into his arms and reveled in the solid strength to be found there. Sure of herself and what she wanted, she pulled his head to hers, capturing his lips with her own.

Thoughts of imminent danger and crazy brides vanished as she took this for herself. Long, lush moments erupted between them, full of passion and promise. His hands played over her lower back, his fingers caressing the skin of her spine as his mouth moved over hers with masterful precision.

Moments as delicate as the sugar Lilah spun over her creations captured them both, only his lips were more satisfying than anything she'd ever tasted.

The gentle stroking over her spine grew more urgent, and she felt his hand slip lower, covering her derriere and pressing her more fully against his body. Heat crawled over her skin, a demanding taskmaster that pushed her on, desperate to take more.

To take all.

She ran her hands over the short hair at his nape. The soft strands tickled her fingers and provided another sensual exploration as their mouths continued their carnal mating dance.

She wanted him.

She'd known it, of course. Had felt the tug of instant attraction from their first moments, but this was something more.

The idea of having any choice in this—the mere thought of walking away from him—was fast fading due to the needs of her body and the joy of being in his arms.

"You had fast foo—"

Lilah's words were cut off midcensure as her voice echoed from the doorway of Cassidy's office.

"Oops. Sorry." Lilah had the grace to look contrite, but Cassidy didn't miss the clear enjoyment that covered her face.

"No, you're not." Cassidy slipped from Tucker's arms and attempted to right the folds of her blouse.

"You're right. I'm not." Lilah waved the empty fast-food bag she'd carried into the office. "And clearly this wasn't your biggest sin today."

"Put that away."

"You're the one who tossed it in the kitchen. You know if Violet sees this you're looking at a lecture, and she'll drag me into it just for fun."

Tucker's face was drawn in a sober expression but Cassidy didn't miss the laughter that crinkled the edges of his dark eyes. "I'm the one to blame. I had no idea tossing away trash from lunch could incite such a riot."

"Then you don't know Violet." Lilah shuddered before

wadding up the bag into a small ball and tossing it into Cassidy's wastebasket. "The woman can go on for hours about the evils of trans fats and sodium."

Tucker clutched his chest. "The horror."

"Exactly."

"Since I've thoroughly interrupted your moment and made you feel guilty for lunch, come on out and keep me company as I put that cake together for the Butler-Parker engagement party."

Cassidy shot Tucker a light shrug but his answering smile indicated he'd taken this in stride.

"Where's Max?"

"He was set up in front looking at blueprints with Violet until she ran out for a bridal emergency at the Anatole about fifteen minutes ago."

"I'll just go hunt up Max." Tucker pulled her close for one last kiss, his lips firm and possessive as he laid one on her. Cassidy didn't miss Lilah's sharp exhale of breath or the fact that her already weak knees got a little more rubbery at the touch of Tucker's lips.

"For the record." He shot a wink at Lilah. "I don't feel guilty at all."

Cassidy knew she should keep her cool and turn and follow Lilah to the kitchen, but for the moment, she was unable to move.

His very attractive posterior held her attention, but it was the smile he tossed over his shoulder as he walked— half cocky and half full of longing—that wrapped her heart in a tight fist that refused to let go.

"Tell me all about Tucker the hottie."

Cassidy settled herself on a stool near Lilah's workstation, her wine reward for managing her bridezilla firmly in hand.

"First let me tell you about today's fitting. I need to get it out."

Lilah's disappointment was palpable, but she nodded. "Vent away."

Cassidy walked her friend through the afternoon and was pouring her second glass when Lilah veered the conversation straight back to their neighbor. "Sounds like Tucker was a champ through the entire thing. Most men would have run for the hills. Or the nearest set of razor blades."

"He hung in there and he actually made it fun, shooting me faces behind her back. The bride was insistent on getting his input, so she stood in her living room for about an hour preening for him, all the while bitching at me."

"Some women don't know how to be anything but catty to another woman when a good-looking man's around."

Lilah's gaze never moved off the delicate piping she worked around the base of a three-tiered cake but Cassidy felt the gravitas of her statement as clearly as a gunshot.

"You think that was it?"

"Come on, Cass. She's been a pain, but what you're describing is off the charts. Natasha, aka bridezilla, enjoyed the male attention. And I bet she enjoyed making you look like her personal servant even more."

"I suppose."

"You know I'm right. And you also know she recognized competition."

"What competition? She's getting married. There's only one place she should be looking. At her fiancé." Even as she said the words, Cassidy knew Lilah had a point. The air had changed the moment she and Tucker had walked into Natasha's home. She'd chalked it up to being off her own turf, but it was something more.

Something destructive and mistrustful and selfish.

"It used to be like that at my sister's house. Leah and Charlie had a weird energy about them when you were in their company."

Lilah set down her piping bag and reached for her wineglass. "You haven't said much about her lately."

"The memories are all churned up with what's going on. I sort of broke down over it to Tucker. I know it's not the same but it feels the same, you know?"

"It's not the same." Lilah reached out to cover her hand. "But I can see how the feelings could be. Destruction, disorder and chaos. The hallmarks of bad situations."

Cassidy squeezed back. She knew Lilah's words were anything but casual, having been forged in the fires of her own chaos from her first marriage. "You okay?"

"We're talking about you and Mr. Yummy. And Leah if you need to. But yes, I'm fine." Lilah took another sip of her wine before picking up a new bag filled with a soft lilac-colored frosting. "Tell me more about this weird energy. You always mentioned how much you hated going to your sister's for holidays but nothing this specific."

"It was always tense, especially after they got married. He was a little off when they were dating but I was in college and dealing with my own stuff and hated how my family didn't like my work, so I had tuned out for a few years. And then boom, they're married and I'm seeing them for family events and I realize my brother-in-law is a jerk."

"Of the first order. But she loved him, right?"

"I always thought so. In fact, there were times I envied her, being so in love with someone and so crazy about him. But now that I think back on it—" Cassidy broke off, a memory of their Christmas before Leah died filling her mind's eye.

They were at Christmas Eve dinner, all play-acting at the sweet happy family routine when a loud crash had come from the kitchen. The swinging door had been closed but the yelling had been more than evident.

"Now what?"

"Just something I remembered." She filled Lilah in on the long-forgotten fight. "It got so loud Robert finally went in to calm things down. Leah had burned herself getting a pan of lasagna out of the oven and Charlie had gone after her about it when she dropped it."

"Jerk."

"Yeah." Lilah nodded, her anxious feelings from that long-ago night resettling themselves in her stomach. "He was. Still is, I'm sure. I just don't have to see him anymore."

"What did happen to him?"

"Last I heard he was bumming around in between jobs. He hasn't worked steadily since she died."

"That's a long time to grieve." Lilah looked up from her careful work. "A long time."

"Probably his latest way to excuse himself and gain some sympathy in the process. The loss of my young wife and all that."

"You sure don't have any lingering feelings there."

"None." Cassidy shook her head, trying to shake off the memories. "And there's something awfully sad about that."

The man they called the Duke was reclined out by an Olympic-size pool behind one of the largest homes in one of Dallas's most exclusive neighborhoods. Charlie took in the lush green lawn—an anomaly this time of year when the summer heat was at its zenith—and admired what the man had.

When he pictured his future, he envisioned himself in something similar, his every whim satisfied the moment he had them.

Something burned low in his gut to think this man had access to the very thing he wanted. The very thing he'd worked so hard on his own to have.

He'd masterminded this plot. So why was he now stuck bowing and scraping because the man had a bug up his bum about his stupid, inept henchmen?

"Take a seat, Mr. McCallum."

Alex sat in the last seat on the patio, a fresh bruise on his eye that hadn't been there last night when Charlie had driven him home. Alex's usual partner in crime, a bruiser of a guy named Trey, had moved up and now flanked Charlie's side.

"You got a problem?"

"Take a seat and see that I don't." Trey never cracked a smile, and Charlie felt the first stirring of panic swirl low in his stomach, replacing the ocean of envy that had opened up upon his arrival.

"It's cool." He took the indicated seat and was greeted by the Duke's chilling stare. It was freaky, since the guy hadn't removed his sunglasses, but Charlie felt the stare keenly despite not being able to see the guy's eyes.

"Your intel's been something of a disappointment, Mr. McCallum."

"How's that?"

The Duke smiled, his pale skin a creepy contrast to the dark color of his goatee. His whiskers were as black as midnight, the contrast so stark it made you want to stare. In fact, it made him wonder why the guy even kept a beard it made him look so damn weird.

As his former mother-in-law would have said, there's no accounting for taste.

Charlie dragged his gaze away and focused on the matter at hand. What the hell did he care about the guy's grooming choices anyway?

"First you suggest you will be able to find the exact location of the item inside the bridal store. However, you got a late start, then bumbled and fumbled so long daylight came."

"But—"

The Duke held up his hand. "I'm not finished. You then suggested the girls were busy digging up the hole themselves, and when Alex and Trey returned to the location, they were met with policemen patrolling the neighborhood and no evidence of anything amiss through the windows."

"I never said they were alone. In fact, I specified—"

"Enough, Mr. McCallum."

The words were low—so low he had to lean forward to hear—and that was all it took.

The Duke struck, his seemingly lazy pose on the lounge chair all for show. The man moved so fast, Charlie had no time to react, and before he knew it the slender man had him facedown on the pool patio, his cheek scraped against concrete.

"You then allow Alex to nearly get made by your former sister-in-law in her front yard. A woman you assured me repeatedly was a docile sort of miss."

"She's a coward." Charlie heaved and bucked backward but the man's grip was relentless. "She sits in her damn shop and sews all day. How was I supposed to know she'd start screwing the neighbor?"

"I've already punished Alex and he's been appropriately sorry for his actions."

Charlie felt the weight lessen slightly and shifted. It was only as he turned onto his back, his arm banging into the deck chair he'd been sitting on, that he registered the gun pointed in his face.

Where the *hell* had that come from?

The survivor's instinct he'd honed since birth reared up.

There was no way he was going down for this. No way he was taking the fall. This was his op. His...

The shock of pain was immense as it hit his throat. Immediately, air whooshed from him in a great, gurgling gasp.

On swift feet, the Duke stood. His bare chest had a large spatter of blood and he wiped it away with a white towel.

Charlie wondered at the strange thoughts that moved through his mind. Such a white towel, now ruined with streaks of red. Bright red on a body of such pale white. Red blood...his blood...

His head lolled back onto the patio and it was only when the Duke snapped out an order that he was aware of another figure. The man came to stand next to the Duke, his looming form blocking out the late-afternoon sun.

Was it Trey again? Maybe Alex? Maybe—

Charlie squinted, desperate to focus on the face he saw, and choked on the blood that filled his throat. And even as he tried to make out the one word that echoed in his mind, nothing but a loud gurgle spilled from his lips.

Robert.

Chapter 13

Tucker swiped his hands over a rag and muttered under his breath. First the bridal fittings, full of endless gossip that made his eyes want to cross, and now an hour digging in the dirt like he was ten.

"You mind telling me why we're doing this now?"

Max had already filled him in on the blueprints he'd reviewed earlier before he'd shifted to digging out a bed of dirt around the front of Elegance and Lace. The two of them had been methodically filling in a combination of bushes and perennials since Tucker had walked outside.

At least there was beer.

"Keeps us busy. Gives us a reason to keep watch." Max hefted a thick shovelful of mulch from a nearby wheelbarrow—where the hell had he gotten that?—and tossed it underneath the compact cherry laurel Tucker had just centered and secured with compacted dirt. "And it doesn't look suspicious that we're spending so much time here to anyone watching."

As excuses went it was a fair one but it still didn't change the fact it was a billion freaking degrees out with shade nowhere to be found.

"Next time I'm knocking down walls and demoing a site you're coming with me."

Max grinned, his smile carefree as he cracked open a fresh beer. "That's hardly a threat, Buck. You know I love to knock stuff down. Remember that dam we demolished our first year in the Corps?"

Since his thoughts had been traveling similar paths, Tucker gave himself a moment to sit back on his heels and take a large swallow of his own beer. "I remember. That was a fun op. Made even better, as I recall, was when you were nearly called on to marry a villager's daughter."

"She came after me, man."

"And then proceeded to strip naked in front of you."

"I was taking a shower and she snuck in. I never touched her. I swear."

"An excuse that fell on her father's very deaf ears."

The memory had them both laughing now, although Max hadn't found it quite so humorous at the time. But the situation had righted itself, especially once a video feed ended up corroborating Max's claims of innocence.

Tucker's thoughts drifted from that poor village girl with little prospects and an American soldier she thought could take her away from it all to the women who ran Elegance and Lace.

Here were three women who had opportunity in abundance and they were taking the utmost advantage of their fortunate position. In the short time he'd known them, he'd seen each of them work hard—had observed their diligence and focus—and admired the heck out of them for it.

"You hear from your grandfather?"

"I tried him a few times. Got a text back that he'd call me later."

Tucker wiped the sweat from his eyes as he stared at his friend. "You buying it?"

"Nah, but I'm giving him his space. From that letter you described, sounds like we've got enough to confront him and Jo later."

They were interrupted by a slow-moving car that bore the city seal and pulled up beside them. "Are you the current residents of this property?"

"No, ma'am." Tucker put his best Southern-boy imitation on display and hoped it worked on the severely dressed woman in the small white car.

"Are the current renters inside?"

"Yes." Tucker dropped the aw-shucks routine. "What do you need?"

"I need to speak with them."

The woman pulled up and found a spot next to the beater of a truck Max used to go out to construction sites and stepped from the car. Her only nod to the heat was a pair of open-toed sandals. When she made no move to wait for them, Tucker dropped his shovel and followed her inside.

"What is this about, Miss—"

Tucker let the word hang and waited for her to offer up her name. When she didn't respond he revised his initial opinion of how to approach the salty woman who seemed impervious to heat.

She also seemed impervious to charm or politeness of any sort.

"I repeat my earlier question. Are you the renter of this business?"

"No."

"Then what I'm doing here is none of *your* business."

Tucker caught Max's raised eyebrows and hard cough that did nothing to cover his friend's outburst of laughter.

Cassidy walked out from the back entrance to Lilah's kitchen, her friend on her heels. "What's going on?"

"City has something they want to discuss with you."

"We had a health inspection two weeks ago." Lilah piped up from behind, her dark voice leaving no doubt about what she thought of a surprise visit.

"I'm not from the Board of Health."

The woman repeated her request to speak to the business owners, and when Cassidy and Lilah confirmed their rights, she launched in.

"Was this building renovated upon your move in?"

"This portion of the building was left mostly intact." Cassidy gestured toward Lilah before pointing toward the back of the building. "We did extensive remodeling of the kitchen."

"The kitchen doesn't meet current fire-code requirements."

"Of course it does," Lilah snapped, her usual congeniality nowhere in evidence. "I saw the plans myself."

"Can you produce those plans?"

Cassidy and Violet stared at each other before both spoke at once.

"Our business partner manages those pieces—"

"She'll be back shortly—"

Tucker stepped forward. "What's this about?"

"Violation of fire codes is cause for removal from the premises." The woman dragged some forms from a slim folder. "You have one hour to vacate the premises."

"This is absurd. We're not going anywhere." Lilah moved another step closer, her stance as battle worthy as any general's Tucker had ever seen.

Cassidy's phone rang, the sound interrupting the fight that was clearly brewing between Lilah and the Queen of Fire Codes.

"Mrs. Beauregard. Hello." The unmistakable sound of relief filled Cassidy's voice before she turned away to take the call. Attuned to her, Tucker heard the moment her voice dropped, growing darker as the conversation continued. He couldn't hear all that was said, but knew she wasn't happy.

"That was Mrs. B." Cassidy shoved her phone in her back pocket a few moments later. "She apologized but said that we need to leave for a few days."

"Laxatives in their cupcakes. That'll do it. One per city council member. Oh. And a dozen for the fire chief." Lilah's rantings had grown increasingly inventive since they'd headed to Dragon Designs for pizza, wine and complaints.

"That's gross." Violet huffed out her distaste as she reached for her third piece of pizza.

Violet's usual subsistence of raw vegetables, whole grains and high fiber meant pizza was usually off the table and she normally took only one piece when they ordered it in, if any. But when Max handed her another beer— her second—Cassidy couldn't hold her tongue. "You like beer? Since when?"

"Since I was kicked out of my business like some vagrant squatter."

"So what did Mrs. B. say again?"

Cassidy had been over it too many times to count in the past few hours but she walked through it again. Her landlady's flat voice, simple instructions and admonition that they needed to leave quickly.

Lilah was philosophical as she dipped her pizza crust in ranch dressing. "At least she said she'd pay for the inconvenience."

"Why?" Tucker had been unusually quiet since he'd arrived back at the office from picking up Bailey and his question jarred all of them.

"Because she's good to us and knows it's her fault?"

Lilah shrugged. "I mean, I like Mrs. B. and all, but it's her building."

"But they're your renovations. You're responsible for meeting code along with the contractor you hire."

"Why didn't you say this before, Tucker?" Violet wiped her mouth with her napkin. "We could have saved a heck of a lot of time dragging stuff in and out of the shop."

"You're out because someone wants you out," Tucker said.

Violet nodded, which was complemented by a light twitch of her lips. "And it was easier to leave and pretend like we were following orders so we can go back on our own terms."

"Go back?" Cassidy didn't miss the glances between Violet and Lilah and gestured them both with her head into a small kitchen alcove for more soda. She waited until the three of them were alone before she spoke. "Care to tell me what's going on?"

"Um, well…" Lilah brushed her bright pink streak back behind her ear.

"We did a little more work on the floor this afternoon." Ever the voice of reason, Violet filled her in quickly. "When Max was outside."

"It wasn't hard. We sort of did a Shawshank on it with some of the smaller tools." Lilah gestured toward the men. "They'd already done the tough stuff and we just did a bit of fine tuning."

"What'd you do with the mess? And how'd you cover the hole?" Cassidy knew her friends were always up for the unexpected, but this was big even for them.

"I tapped away while Vi kept up with the hand vac. That thing's better than we realized." Lilah hurried on when Cassidy waved a hand. "And then we stuffed it with some of your material."

"Not the silk." Violet jumped in quickly. "I used some of the tulle that was in the garbage that you had to throw away because it was damaged."

As she listened to their tale, Cassidy had to admit to being a bit jealous to have missed the fun. "Why not just pull up what was under there?"

"Because it's still stuck in there. We needed the guys to help us get it out and then I got the call to head over to help out my own bridezilla today."

Cassidy processed Violet's words. "You didn't see anything at all?"

"Just a thick black box."

"Which we've just made a hell of a lot more accessible to anyone who breaks in."

"She had to pick pink." Tucker muttered the words as Lilah's van turned off the far end of Dragon Street.

"It's her signature." Cassidy pulled at the neck of the long-sleeved black T-shirt that covered her to her knees. Whatever else this evening brought, she had a new appreciation for those who ran special ops. Even her clothing had been decided upon before they left Dragon Designs.

"That van's like a flashing neon sign."

"We talked her out of the neon, actually."

"You're making jokes?" Tucker turned toward her, his dark eyes wide.

"I'm nervous. And it's true," she muttered.

She knew Tucker was still mad at her for her insistence on coming and the urgency surrounding the retrieval of the box was her only saving grace. If Tucker's assessment was correct, whoever had them removed from the premises under the guise of code violations was going to make their move tonight. Which meant they had to act fast and had to do it with minimal risk.

They'd already mapped out how they were going to use some of her dress samples. They could wrap the box inside a frothy layer of material and sneak the box out of the building. If they were being watched, it would look like she'd forgotten something.

And if they were caught by the city for truly being in violation?

Then she could use the dress as her excuse for violating the order to vacate the premises.

"We can't keep waiting. We need to move."

"I'm waiting for Max's signal that he's in position." Tucker reached for his phone. "And there he is."

They'd already agreed they weren't going in the front door, but she and Tucker had spent the past hour staking out the building from a vantage point that gave them eyes on the front and back doors. The security additions Max had procured that morning also provided an extra pair of eyes, and Violet and Lilah were keeping watch at Dragon Designs with Bailey, their faithful companion.

"You can still go back."

"I'm in this."

"You're in danger, and I'm the worst sort of fool for ignoring that."

With a hard tug on his arm she pulled him close. "I'm in this, Tucker." She pressed a hard kiss to his lips. "All the way."

His hand gripped the back of her head before she could get away, and he whispered against her lips, "If it gets out of hand, promise me you'll run. There are apartments not far from here. Vi and Lilah can come get you if—" He broke off, and she heard what he was going to say as clearly as if he'd spoken the words.

"We're all walking away from here. Free and clear."

She kissed him once more for luck, then pointed toward the building. "Let's go."

Max had stowed Lilah's delivery van in the service bay and was already waiting at the back door. "You ready for this, Cassidy?"

She nodded and couldn't hold back the smile. Whether it was the adrenaline rush or the sheer relief of finally trying to get ahead of some of this madness, she didn't know.

With one glance at Tucker, she realized she didn't care.

He and Max had jumped in and given their all, without thought to their personal safety. She could do no less. Whatever had found its way to her door needed to be stopped and she was going to be a part of fixing the problem.

Tucker patted her back. "Okay. In and out, just like we planned."

Cassidy nodded as she disarmed the entrance to the kitchen. She diligently avoided looking around—Tucker was keeping watch for her—and focused on the new set of security codes updated just that morning.

And took solace that no matter how badly their enemy wanted to get in, they hadn't gotten in yet. No one had set off the alarm or tripped the perimeter cameras.

As she tapped in the last number, the alarm flipped to green, and she breathed a sigh of relief. Step one down.

Max stayed at the back, waiting near the door until he got an all-clear from Cassidy and Tucker. On their signal—indicating that they had checked the interior and then set up the needed tools—he'd then close and lock the door, resetting the alarm.

Cassidy moved to her workroom and selected the sample stock that had been sent to her the previous week by a distributor who was hoping for her business. Although she hated to waste the two gowns by possibly dragging them through the dirt and gravel outside, she knew she needed to be prepared with an excuse should they need one.

A hard curse from the area in front of Violet's desk filtered toward her and she made quick work of the two dresses, wrapping them over her arms.

Tucker stood over the hole, a thick shovel poised under the now visible black box. Max chiseled at the concrete still crowding the sides of the metal container, instructing Tucker to lift every few minutes.

"Damn, this is wedged tight," Tucker muttered as he put more weight under the shovel.

Cassidy knew the need for speed trumped a more delicate approach to whatever was buried in the floor, but she hoped they didn't damage whatever was inside the box.

Her phone vibrated in her back pocket, and Cassidy fumbled the dresses under one arm as she pulled out the device. "It's from Violet."

GET OUT OF THERE. NOW.

The fear they'd ruin the box was nothing compared to the fear of discovery. "Guys. We need to leave."

"We almost have it." Tucker gritted the words, his arms straining as he and Max alternated pressure on either side of the box.

Her phone buzzed once more, and Cassidy pulled her attention from the push-pull taking place over the hole in her floor.

NOW!

She typed a quick got it back to Violet and ran to the guys. "We have to go."

Heat rolled off Tucker's body in a wave as she reached

for him. Her goal was to get through to him about the need to leave, but instead she found herself thrown off balance when he lost his footing, the heavy box coming loose in a hard burst from the ground.

They both tumbled, the concrete floor rising up to meet her in a rush. She moved at the last minute, dropping the gossamer fluff in her arms to cushion their fall, but it didn't change the fact she'd just hit a layer of concrete with a grown man on top of her.

He rolled off her quickly, cursing as he went, before pulling her close. "Did I hurt you?"

"I'm good." His weight had knocked the air from her lungs, but the dresses had provided a little cushioning for both of them as they tumbled. She shifted, struggling to a seated position, and screamed when a gunshot punctured the front window.

"Get down!"

Tucker covered her once more. He cradled her head with his hands while he matched his body to hers. They both flinched as another shot rang out, and he fitted himself more tightly against her.

The phone in her pocket rang at the same time the office phone kicked in, in time with the whining alarm. Max was closest and grabbed the receiver off Violet's desk, hollering for help as he rattled off the address before slamming down the phone.

Head down, Max then snatched the dresses and wrapped the box in the thick layers of material while Tucker fired several rounds at the front windows. They all heard a loud grunt, followed by a shout, from the direction of the shattered window.

"Let's go!" Tucker pulled her to her feet, pressing her forward as soon as she was upright. He kept his body between her and the front windows, pushing them both toward the kitchen and the freedom that awaited them with Lilah's pink van.

They'd cleared the door that divided the showroom from the kitchen when Max's shout rang out. "Buck! Down!"

Tucker's heavy body fell over hers once more, and she struggled to breathe as her face was pressed close to the floor.

"I'm sorry, Cassidy," he whispered into her ear. "You have to stay down."

"I won't move."

Tucker eased off her, belly-crawling toward the back door. Max stood back, his aim steady on the entryway, ready to lay down a round of protective fire, when it slowly slid open. Tucker let off a round of shots, low through the door, but all any of them saw beyond it was empty air.

"What the hell?" Tucker inched closer to the door, his back to the wall. Cassidy watched each step and prayed nothing stood outside, out of his frame of view.

A wave of nausea threatened her stomach as she imagined any number of horrors waiting for Tucker in the loading dock, but she fought it back.

He'd be okay.

The police were on their way. She, Vi and Lilah had already agreed—if Violet or Lilah saw something on the security feeds they weren't comfortable with, they would call. And the tripped alarm would provide backup. To hell with whatever was in the floor, their collective safety came first.

"Buck." Max kept his voice low. "You see anything?"

"Not one damn—" Tucker broke off, the air around him going silent.

Was he hurt?

Was someone there?

Without waiting to find out, Cassidy leaped. Shoving

off the floor, she threw herself toward him, dragging him back from the doorway as hard as she could.

It was only when he moved back, his eyes wide, that Cassidy saw what had stopped him midsentence.

Her former brother-in-law lay on the back steps, his sightless eyes staring up at the night sky.

Chapter 14

Blue and red lights flashed endlessly outside the front of Elegance and Lace as dawn fought its way free, minute by minute, to brighten the early-morning sky.

Tucker stared at those mesmerizing lights through the shattered front window of Elegance and Lace and cursed himself yet again for their suicide mission.

What the hell had they been thinking? And why did any of them think attempting to beat their enemies here was even possible?

He'd sensed from the start they were playing against someone well out of their league but had ignored his gut. Instead, he'd pushed the idea of someone the women knew being the culprit and downgraded the possible threat to all of them.

But the night's events proved they were battling someone who was not only determined, but who gave no thought to the value of human life.

He was an architect and a former serviceman. And while he had a more-than-passing knowledge of firearms and weaponry, he was no hit man. But what was left on the back steps of Elegance and Lace…

Tucker shuddered.

He'd seen the bodies of enemies and innocents in war. Seen soldiers become the victims of any number of violent atrocities. But the dead body only recently removed by the police had been the victim of a brutal murder.

A *deliberate* and brutal murder.

"Are you okay?" Cassidy sat next to him and took his hand in hers.

"I'm fine."

"I can't get over it." She squeezed his hand once more, and he let her talk. "It's Leah's husband. My former brother-in-law. I mean, we were just talking about him. And you kept pressing that it was a family member who'd broken in. He's got to be the one."

Words continued to spill from her lips, and he listened, but had no response. All he could picture was Cassidy in place of her brother-in-law. And no matter how he tried to dismiss it, all he saw was her face, those gorgeous, lively blue eyes staring sightlessly ahead, the delicate arch of her neck, covered in blood.

"Mr. Buchanan." Detective Graystone had arrived an hour before, his competent air only slightly marred by the dark hair that stuck up in tufts over his head.

"Yes?"

"I understand you were the first to see the body."

"Yes."

"Did you know it was a relative of Miss Tate?"

"No, I didn't."

"Please tell me how you found the body."

Although he'd taken the detective through it, as had Max and Cassidy, Tucker walked through the moments again with the detective. The concerns they felt about whatever was hidden in the floor. The strange request to vacate the property.

"And during any of that time did it cross your mind to call me?"

The detective had maintained his equilibrium fairly well, but it was clear he'd had enough.

So it was no small surprise when Cassidy spoke up next to him, her voice clear and strong. "Then you're not going to like what else we have to tell you."

Cassidy pointed out the hole in the floor near Violet's desk and walked the detective through the events of the past several days. From the slightly distended carpet they'd noticed after the initial break-in to the final removal of the thick black box the night before, Cassidy shared everything.

"What's inside the box?"

"We don't know. We didn't get that far."

"So where is it?"

Max spoke up. "I stowed it in the van."

Although she knew he'd done his best to protect whatever they'd found, Cassidy didn't recall seeing Max leave the room. "You had it in hand when we discovered…" She stopped, unsure of the correct term to use, but decided to finish her thought. "The body."

"I stowed it after. When the police were on their way."

"What were you intending to do with the box, Mr. Baldwin?" The detective's gaze was cold as he stared down all six feet four inches of Max Baldwin. They were well matched, the detective only an inch or two shorter than Max's thick frame.

Although she got the distinct sensation the two men were merely sizing each other up, the act held a strange sense of ceremony. It was only when Max took a step back, his posture seeming to deflate, that some of the tension in the room evaporated. "I didn't know what the women wanted to do with the box and I didn't feel it was my place to decide."

"Well, now it's my place to decide. Show me the van."

They led the detective through the back door, and Cassidy avoided staring at the dried blood on the stoop.

Would she ever *not* see it?

"We parked the van here last night."

"Getaway car?"

Graystone's voice was dry but honest, and Cassidy vowed to give him the same in return. "Cover. If the city really was holding us in violation, we needed to make it look like we'd come back for a job."

"I'll be looking into that, by the way. Did the woman who showed up claiming to be a city worker leave any paperwork?"

"She left something."

"I'd like a copy."

Cassidy nodded as they filed down the back driveway and toward the loading area where Lilah filled up her van for runs. She turned toward Max. "Where'd you put it?"

"In the back." He pulled on the back doors, tugging them open, only to find the space empty.

"I'm not amused, Baldwin."

"I put it right here."

Max climbed up into the van, crossing through the cavernous space as if somehow looking hard enough would conjure the black box. "It was here. I swear it."

Robert Barrington let himself into his apartment overlooking all of downtown and went straight for the kale juice he'd left chilling in the fridge overnight. He laid the twenty-five-thousand-dollar check that had been handed to him upon delivery of the black box and congratulated himself on a job well done.

Although he wouldn't deny the squeamish factor of Charlie's body, he had to admit using the body as a distraction was brilliant.

Just like the Duke.

The man knew how to get things *done*. It was a trait he admired. Respected. And, if things worked out like he hoped, something he'd emulate on his own road to success.

The amazing part was how it had all come together. He'd stayed in touch with Charlie off and on since he'd ditched Cassidy. The guy was a pain most of the time but he had his uses, and Robert had found him worthwhile to keep around.

And then late one night, after way too many martinis downed in the Cliff, Charlie started in on a fantastical tale about hidden jewels from World War II. Apparently Leah, his late wife, had gotten some hazy details from a family friend when she was a teenager. When he started talking about Cassidy's beloved Josephine Beauregard, Robert had his connection.

Then a mutual friend connected him with the Duke, and bam. He had a very lucrative gig going.

The man threw money around like it was water. A hundred grand for the information. Twenty-five for last night's delivery. And a cool million if he stayed in this until the end, fencing what they undoubtedly had found in the box.

Robert laughed as he poured the thick liquid into a glass and took a sip. The cool, crisp taste slid down his throat like the finest of wines. Better, really, because this wasn't toxic to his liver.

He hated toxic things.

He drank socially because it was expected of him and because it got him information, his late-night bender with Charlie McCallum a prime example. But it wasn't his preferred drug of choice.

Clean living and a well-thought-out plan for his future beat any substance, any day.

His door buzzed and he wondered at it. No one in the lobby had called up and he paid well for the advance notice. Phone in hand, he called the lobby on speed dial before he even had the door open.

At the sight of the Duke, Alex and Trey on the other side of his front door, Robert lowered the phone. Before he could turn it off, Trey's hand snaked out and grabbed the phone. He flipped it off and shoved it into his pocket before barreling his way through the door.

"What's the matter?"

Images of the evening before at the Duke's home flashed through his mind. Charlie had been caught off guard and manhandled the moment he'd walked in. Of course, the idiot deserved it, his repeated fumbling having become an increasing liability.

But Robert had done nothing. Hell, he hadn't been out of their sight more than a half hour.

What was going on?

Alex shoved him, and Robert stumbled backward. The man was on him like a suit and had his back pressed against his high marble bar before Robert could even get his footing. The unmistakable sound of a switchblade met his ears moments before the knife flashed in his peripheral vision.

What the *hell*?

"I did what you asked!" Robert grunted the words, the hand at his windpipe making it hard to speak.

"I'm afraid not."

Robert saw the Duke move into the other side of his peripheral vision and risked a glance away from the knife and onto the man he'd come to admire and respect in so short a time.

"I didn't do anything." Alex squeezed harder on his Adam's apple, and Robert gasped for breath. "I. Didn't."

"Let him speak, Alex." The Duke waved a hand to indicate his wishes, but other than that small gesture, he didn't move from his position. His eyes were uncovered and Robert stared into the pale green orbs.

There was no warmth there. No humor. No humanity.

There was absolutely nothing.

And for the first time since the night Charlie had chewed his ear off in a noisy bar, Robert acknowledged he might have made a poor choice. He considered himself an enterprising businessman, but perhaps entering into a business arrangement with a man whose reputation in Dallas was legendary wasn't the best idea.

But damn it, he'd done all he was asked. Had delivered every step of the way.

"You have one opportunity to tell me the truth."

Robert nodded, mesmerized by the Duke's reptilian eyes.

"Where are the contents of the box?"

"I delivered them to you."

Alex ran the blade across the thin skin of his upper chest, and Robert screamed as the metal sliced flesh.

"I'm not a man of great patience, Mr. Barrington."

Robert shook his head, desperate to spill as much information as he could from a mouth that had gone dry as cotton. On a hard swallow, he kept his gaze level with the Duke's and hoped like hell he could make the man understand.

"I secured the box just as I told you. I grabbed it from the back of the pink van and ran. I came straight to your home. I never opened it."

"Not once?"

Tears rolled freely now, spilling over his cheeks with

the same cadence as the blood that rolled over his collarbone and dripped onto his pale marble countertop. "It wasn't mine to open."

Alex lifted the knife once more, and Robert screamed, now crying freely. "It wasn't mine to open!"

The Duke pushed Alex out of the way and replaced the goon's hand with his own. He was a slender man but his grip was surprisingly strong.

"There is a major piece of the collection missing. You have forty-eight hours to get it back. Nod if you understand."

Robert nodded, willing to agree to anything. "I understand."

The Duke's grip remained iron-tight, his gaze just as unyielding.

Although he feared any further reprisal, Robert pushed on. Ignorance had put him in this position and he'd be a fool not to get as much detail as he could. "What piece is it? What am I looking for?"

"Wrong question, Mr. Barrington."

The Duke never let up the pressure on his chest. Instead, he grabbed a fistful of shirt and rubbed it over the now gaping wound.

Fire erupted over his skin, and Robert screamed once more, unable to stop the noise that seemed to be dragged from the very depths of his body.

"I think it goes without saying, you'll know it when you see it."

Robert gulped for air, raw fire painted over his chest. As he fought to surface through the pain, one thought filled his mind.

"Cassidy?"

"Ah. Now, there's a question, Mr. Barrington. I think you might be catching on."

Robert reran the night before through his mind. He'd seen Cassidy and her group of boyfriends enter the building. Had followed up with Charlie's body while they did the hard work of digging up the floor.

He'd timed it perfectly, allowing Trey and Alex to hit the front door, pushing the lot of them out the back.

Cassidy had whatever piece it was that had gone missing. That had to be it. Someone had removed it before putting it in the van.

The Duke stepped back, the pristine white cuffs of his shirt still the same pure ivory as when he'd walked in. "I suggest you become reacquainted with your former fiancée. By any means necessary."

Cassidy stood in the center of Elegance and Lace, broom and dustpan in hand, and wondered how she could possibly be doing cleanup duty mere days after doing it for the first time. She'd already taken count of her stock, pleased to see it was blessedly untouched.

Other than the dresses she'd taken the previous evening from her office, everything was intact.

Under her breath, she muttered, "Not that anyone's going to want to buy a dress with the lingering smell of gunpowder clinging to the silk."

The tears that had threatened a few days before were nowhere in evidence as she took to the floor with a vengeance. Although the night before had been far more shocking than the initial break-in, she had more information this time.

More knowledge.

And knowledge was power.

Whatever was going on was clearly linked to her former brother-in-law. Cassidy knew it was unkind to think ill of the dead, but try as she might she couldn't conjure up too many sad feelings for Charlie McCallum. He'd made his decisions and bore the consequences.

Of course, none of it changed the fact that he'd left a mark on her business. Left the residue of his broken life that she, Violet and Lilah would now bear as they worked to move forward.

They'd clean up, of course. Fix the broken windows and scrub the blood off the back stairs. But none of it could remove the lingering smear on their business.

Tucker came through the door to Lilah's side of the business, their small hand vac in one hand and yet another trash bag full of garbage in another.

"Put me to work." Although his words suggested otherwise, she saw the tired lines that pulled at his face.

They'd all spelled each other at various intervals throughout the morning, moving back and forth between Dragon Designs and Elegance and Lace to catch a few hours of needed sleep. No one was quite ready to go home, but the rests were a welcome reprieve from the stress of the past few days.

But as she looked over his tired eyes and drawn mouth, she knew he hadn't bothered to take his fair share of rest.

"You've done so much already, I can hardly ask you to do this, too. Go on and get some rest."

A light frown creased his brows, but he said nothing as he went to work changing out the garbage bag she'd methodically filled with glass and debris.

She watched him, the stiff set of his shoulders telling an even bigger story than his silence.

"You're quiet."

"Nothing to say."

"Oh, I don't know. I'd say there's quite a bit to say." She focused on a swath of small shards scattered under one of the shop's oversize love seats. "I just can't seem to find the words."

"You seem to find two words often enough. 'I'm sorry.'"

Silence descended once again. "You don't think I'm appreciative of what you've done? Of what Max has done? You've both risked far more than a bit of your time."

"We knew what we were taking on."

"Oh, so now you need to play the silent, suffering hero."

He dragged the heavy bag out of the container and pulled at the ties, snapping the plastic together in harsh motions as he knotted it tight. "It's better than playing the martyred shop owner."

Her patience had long since frayed at the ends, and his outburst only managed to light those edges with swift sparks. "What the hell, Tucker?"

"I'll tell you what the hell." He tossed the garbage toward the front door, the bag making a heavy thunk as it fell. "I'm not here for your apologies. Or to be some hero. I'm here because I care. Because I give a freaking crap about what happens to you."

"I—"

His hands came around her shoulders, and he dragged her close, then pressed her head to his chest. "I see that body lying outside the door and all I can picture in its place is you. All I can see is you."

"I'm here. I'm fine." She wrapped her arms around him and rubbed her hands over his back. His muscles quivered, tension stamped in every sinew.

"I brought you into that. Something could have happened to you while Max and I were busy playing cowboy."

"I wanted to do this. It's my shop. My livelihood. I have a right to be here."

"I have a duty to protect you."

Duty?

Cassidy knew she was as tired as he was, but something in the word had her seeing red. Shoving back, she stared at him, all the unsaid fears of the past days spilling over in an explosion.

"I'm not your duty. Or your job. Or someone you have to keep an eye on. I'm a grown woman with a business and a responsibility to that business. What kind of person would I be if I'd let you come here to fight my battles?"

"You'd be just like everyone else!"

A lifetime of hurt painted itself across his face, and she knew they were no longer talking about cleanup or business risks or even the danger that currently dogged all of them.

"What happened to you?" The words fell from her lips, a match to his question from two nights before.

"Nothing."

She clenched her hands around the handle of the broom and fought to keep her voice level. "Tell me you don't want to talk about it but don't lie to me."

His gaze settled on a spot on the far side of the room, indecision hovering around him in what looked like a stormy swirl of emotions and memories.

She'd almost convinced herself he wasn't going to say anything—wasn't going to let her inside that roiling sea—when he began to speak.

"My brother died when I was ten."

Words of sympathy were nearly out when she pulled them back. There would be time for them later.

Time after he finally spilled whatever had been pent up inside for so very long.

"He was eighteen."

"That's a big age difference."

"Yeah. My parents had difficulty getting pregnant between us."

His gaze drifted to a different time and place and where she saw avoidance before, she now saw memories come alive in his eyes.

"Scott was the classic golden boy. Big and athletic, he was everything to our town." He shook his head. "It's cliché to say it like that, but it's true. And my parents adored him."

Cassidy braced herself for what came next.

"He was killed in a football accident in early fall. A freak tackle that just had too much strength in it. Came in at the wrong angle."

As someone who'd lived her life in the state where football was king, she cringed every year when she heard the inevitable news story or two about young men who lost their lives to the sport. "The game's dangerous. People want to dismiss that but it doesn't make it any less true."

When he continued to stare toward the windows, she pressed on. "What does that have to do with fighting other people's battles?"

"Losing Scott destroyed my parents. And it should have. I know why it did—" He broke off, and she saw the very real struggle of a lifetime of guilt and disappointment.

She'd sensed hidden depths in him. Had known the easygoing personality and quick, charming smile were a veneer, layered over something darker.

"I understand why they'd lose a part of themselves when they lost their child. I didn't understand it then but as an adult I do understand. But they gave me up in the process. Resented me for still being alive."

"So you just tried harder."

"For all the good it did me. No matter the grade I made or the activity I took an interest in, it was never good enough. *I* was never good enough. But when I refused to play football, that was the last straw."

Her sympathy had a new target and the words she'd tried so hard to hold back as he spoke exploded with raw, blinding anger. "Why the hell would anyone think you playing football was a good idea?"

"A way to recapture Scott's glory days? A way to restore hope? Who the hell knows."

"Hope for who? Your parents? It certainly couldn't have been for the town's crestfallen hopes. You said you moved around."

"My parents couldn't stand to see all the places that reminded them of my brother so we bummed around to different places where one of them managed to get work."

He turned to her then. "I'd already disappointed them enough with my focus on math and science and my desire to build things. Then I entered the military and my father had his final proof that his second son was a raging disappointment."

"A son at West Point is a disappointment?"

"It is when expectations lie somewhere else. Funny, though, he accepts the checks I send with righteous satisfaction."

Cassidy knew family dynamics were never easy. Hell, she'd spent a lifetime trying to figure hers out and never seemed to make much progress there.

But what his parents did to him was wrong.

No child should have to live in the shadowed pain of someone else's shattered dreams.

Instinctively, she knew words weren't the answer. So instead, she moved into his body, wrapping her arms tight around him.

The firestorm that blazed between them calmed, leaving only a few small embers in its wake. And when he wrapped his arms around her, Cassidy felt the last smoldering sparks wink out.

He still trembled but said nothing more as they stood there in the midst of the debris. But as she held that large, strong body against hers, Cassidy knew something had changed.

Her heart had been split wide-open and there was no closing it back up.

Chapter 15

Tucker settled into the red overstuffed cushions of Lilah's massive sectional with a plate of canapés in his hand and a beer chilling on the coffee table before him. Lilah had insisted they all come to her house so she could cook them dinner and give everyone a chance to unwind from the past few days. Her townhome was in Dallas's trendy Uptown neighborhood, and the moment he'd walked through the door he could see the setting fit her to a T.

Vivid walls splashed with color offset fluffy furniture and funky paintings. Add on the kitchen that would make Julia Child weep with envy and he couldn't have designed a house more perfect for her.

Cassidy and Violet had made themselves quickly at home in the kitchen, and he and Max had taken over the living room to watch a ballgame. All in all, an easy night with friends.

If you didn't count the lingering smell of gunfire and the memories of a dead body that haunted them all.

Oh, yeah, right. Or the fact he'd spilled his guts to Cassidy.

Damn, Buchanan. Shake it off.

Lilah had invited Bailey to join the party, and the mutt sat worshipfully at his feet, his soulful gaze on the plate in Tucker's hand. As food choices went he couldn't argue with small hot dogs wrapped in bacon and puff pastry. Or a home-cooked meal.

Evidently, neither could man's best friend.

He knew he needed to get his head in the game but even the excellent food and even-more-excellent company couldn't erase the ass he'd made of himself in front of Cassidy.

He'd never been one to second-guess himself—if he felt something he went with it—but ranting at her in the middle of her ruined shop like some love-struck school-boy wasn't the brightest idea he'd ever had. And telling her about his poor, pitiful past hadn't been on the day's agenda. Or on any day's agenda.

Ever.

"Did you see that?" Max hollered a choice obscenity at the umpire before loading up another plate of gourmet beanie weenies. "Damn, these are good."

Lilah floated in with another full tray. "Then have more."

"Marry me, Lilah, and make these every day. Please." Max slapped a hand to his heart and nearly wobbled his appetizer plate. The pup stood at the ready, and Tucker could have sworn Bailey already imagined the appetizers falling, like manna from heaven.

Before Lilah could answer, Violet's voice filtered from the direction of the kitchen. "If you knew how many calories are in those you'd rethink that request. She's a temptress of the worst kind."

"Hey." An affronted look covered Max's face. "I exercise."

Violet walked in and settled herself on the couch, a

glass of white wine in her hand. "Since you'd have to run to Fort Worth and back every day I'm not sure you're up for it, Baldwin."

"I don't think the devil wears pink streaks in his hair."

Lilah laughed at that before rubbing her hands together. "Then clearly you haven't tried my red velvet cupcakes."

The banter was easy and the game lively as dinner cooked in the kitchen. Whether it was the jovial atmosphere or a concerted attempt to relax, Tucker wasn't sure, but it all vanished a few minutes later when Cassidy drifted in from a small living room off the front hall.

"Cass?" Lilah moved first. "What is it?"

"Mrs. B. She was moved to a regular room and I tried calling her to see how she's doing."

"How is she?"

"I'm not sure. She mumbled something about being fine, told me to stay away and hung up."

Max was the first to speak. "Was my grandfather with her?"

"I don't know. The call was so short I didn't get much more than what I just told you."

Max was already up, his phone in hand. "I'll call him."

Lilah had barely lowered the volume on the TV when Max stomped back down the hall as fast as he left.

Tucker sat forward, disengaging himself from the deep cushions of the couch. "Was he there?"

"He's ignoring me."

"He could be busy." Although contrary, Violet's voice was gentle when she spoke. "He'll call back."

"I left him a message earlier, as well, and he hasn't called—" Max broke off as his phone buzzed with an incoming text. He muttered a low curse before turning to the rest of them as he read the text out loud. "I'm fine. Talk later."

"I'll lay you odds they're together," Violet said.

"Damn straight they are. They've been hiding something from the get-go." Max shook his head and stopped. Tucker had known his friend for a long time—had trusted the man to watch his back through more ops than he could count—which made the indecision he saw layered on Max's face that much more jarring.

"What is it?"

"I was going to give the old man the courtesy of a first look but now I don't know."

They all stared at him, no one saying anything until Tucker broke the silence. "First look at what?"

"This."

The room grew quiet and even Bailey was at full attention as Max dug into his back pocket. When he came up with a cloth-wrapped package, Tucker knew they were in trouble.

And as Max unwrapped three enormous rubies, Tucker felt the bottom drop out of his stomach.

Max dragged his phone out one more time, then shoved it back into his shirt pocket on a loud harrumph. Jo knew how upset he was—how worried for his grandson and his friends—and she wondered yet again if she'd made the right choice.

She had gone along with the charade to get the girls out of the building. Wanted them far gone when that evil man came for the jewels.

But what if it still wasn't enough?

What if he decided to go after them anyway?

Those cold green eyes still lived in her memory, flicking over her like she were nothing. Like the secret she'd spent her life protecting was simply there for the taking.

How could she have been so stupid?

They'd promised to take it to their graves. She and Max had sworn, all those years ago, yet she'd still failed. Through arrogance and some misbegotten sense of pride.

"They're in danger. And they don't even know why."

"We can't tell them." Max shook his head, stubborn as ever when he got a bit between his teeth.

"Why not? The secret's out. Keeping it any longer won't help them and it certainly won't keep them safe."

"The box was stolen. That bastard has what he came for. Now we just need to wait and let things die down. We can't tell, Jo."

She'd made the promise so long ago. Had sworn to her father she'd never share it, but what did it matter now? Those dark days were long gone and the need for secrecy—to keep a state secret for people who had long since stopped fighting for a cause—seemed pointless.

"What will we gain by revealing something long buried? Your father wanted all evidence removed of his involvement. He made a promise and willingly upheld his duties."

"My father's been gone for forty years. The war ended over sixty-five years ago. When does it stop mattering any longer?"

"The location of the jewels has never been revealed, even to this day. The location of the copies shouldn't, either. We promised."

The harsh light of the TV highlighted half of his face, leaving the rest in shadows. Even with the garish backwash of color, Josephine could still see the boy she fell in love with. The one she'd given her heart to so long ago.

She'd trusted him then. Had always trusted him, even when life took them in opposite directions. Even when her heart had broken in two.

Did she stop trusting him now?

Did she have a choice?

* * *

The rich scent of lasagna wafted around them but no one paid any attention as they stood around Lilah's kitchen table, three equally large jewels covering a small cotton cloth at the center.

"Take us through it again, Max." Tucker had already asked a few times, but Cassidy was grateful he asked again. The reality of what they had laid out before them was mind-boggling.

"When I put the box in the van I had a feeling whoever shot at us wasn't gone. The body was too convenient. So I opened it up to get a good look. Since everything was wrapped, I grabbed what I could fit in my pocket off the top and closed it back up." He shrugged. "I know it's not ideal, but I figured it would give us some sort of bargaining power if we needed it."

"Or get us all killed when whoever wants it figures out it's gone." Cassidy whispered the words, the images of her late brother-in-law filling her mind's eye.

This was what Charlie had involved himself with. Greed and avarice had been his downfall and it had gotten him killed.

Gems and murder. It was like something out of the TV movies she, Lilah and Violet loved curling up with for an afternoon of bad woman-in-jeopardy television.

Only it was real.

Rock-solid, shiny, sparkling reality.

And it lay on the scarred oak table that used to belong to Lilah Castle's grandmother.

"We have to talk to Mrs. B. about it," Violet said, ever the voice of reason. "Then we need to give it to the detectives."

"Right. Which eliminates any bargaining chip we have." Lilah's wan, pale face was drawn up, her mouth in a straight line, and Cassidy knew what she was thinking. Knew the pain she still lived with.

No matter how far her friend had come, she'd always live with the pain of her horrible first marriage. Would always carry that thin veneer of fear that she'd never truly be safe again.

"The only way we stay safe is if we each take one and hide it. It's the only way," Lilah said.

"Are you nuts?" Tucker's voice exploded across the table. Although the words were in response to Lilah, his gaze was firmly planted on Cassidy. "You can't make yourselves vulnerable like that. You need to get rid of those. Remove them and all traces they ever existed."

"No, Lilah's right." Max shook his head, all his normal bluster vanished in the stark light of his impulsive decision. "I took that choice away from them when I took these."

Violet lifted one, examined it under the light. "So we go public with them. Make a splash and show the world we're turning them over. Whoever killed Charlie sees that and knows we're not worth coming after."

"Unless he thinks you held a few back for yourselves." Tucker crossed his arms, his earlier reticence back in full force. "There's no way whoever got their hands on this knew a full count of what's in the box. Hell, do we even know what these are? Where they're from? How long they've been buried under the floor?"

"We need to see Mrs. B. She and Max's grandfather are at the center of this." Cassidy knew the strange phone call from earlier coupled with Max's lack of response from his grandfather basically confirmed their involvement. But still, they held out, keeping their own counsel. "They're scared. They think they're keeping us safe by keeping us in the dark."

"They're wrong." Tucker's voice was flat.

At the somber faces around the table, Cassidy knew the truth in Tucker's words. But she also knew how unwilling Mrs. B. could be when she set her mind to something.

The woman carried a secret—had lived with it most of her life, if Max Senior's involvement was any indication—and she wasn't ready to give it up.

"I need to get to him. They're vulnerable alone."

"No one goes anywhere by themselves or stays by themselves until we figure this out." Tucker issued the order and in that moment, Cassidy had a flash of the solider he used to be.

Strong. Forceful. Unyielding.

She'd thought Max the unspoken team lead, but the respect in his gaze told another story. They were partners. They took care of each other and depended on each other.

Just like she did with Lilah and Violet.

They were a family. Not of blood, but of the heart. And those bonds were as unbreakable as steel.

Tucker whistled for Bailey at Lilah's back door and watched the dog bound playfully over the small patch of backyard. It wasn't the larger space he had at his own home, but Bailey had proven himself highly adaptable the past few nights, going where he was told and keeping watch over his expanding human family.

That's what they were. Through some unspoken agreement, the five of them had managed to become a unit in an incredibly short period of time.

Bonds forged in the fires of hell.

He'd never been big on war stories. He'd always assumed the "war is hell" tales were a way of taking the horror, dusting it off and creating a more comforting story that gave that horror distance and meaning.

How wrong he'd been.

He felt like he'd lived a lifetime in the past week. From some of the most exquisite highs he'd ever experienced to the depths of shock at the depravity of his fellow humans.

Bailey trotted past him, and he closed the door, flipping the locks.

"You ready for me to set the alarm?" Lilah stood behind him in the kitchen, her blond pixie hair sticking up where she'd repeatedly run her fingers through it, twisting the strands.

He'd watched her since Max had made his big reveal. He'd already sensed she hid something, but the sheer grit she employed as they talked through what to do with the jewels told a different story. "You doing okay?"

"Yep." She busied herself at a keypad near the back door. He'd seen its twin at the front. "And I'll be even better in a minute."

She punched in a long code—that alone spoke volumes—before she gave a satisfied nod when the light flashed over to red.

"That's quite a system. I saw the perimeter cameras when I let Bailey out."

"A girl in the city can't be too careful."

"No. I guess not."

When she said nothing else, Tucker knew that was his cue to drop it. Whatever she'd survived was her journey. Her battle.

Yet something pressed him on.

Maybe it was the oddly cathartic exposure of his own demons earlier. Or, a small voice whispered through his mind, it might just be the simple kindness of offering help to a friend in need.

"I'm not going anywhere tonight."

"I know. Although—" she stopped, mischief twinkling

in her brown eyes, chasing away the dark clouds "—I think your time's about up to make a move on my best friend."

"It's not like that."

"I sure hope it's like that."

Before he could argue further—or suggest getting it on with her friend a floor below her was a bit of an obnoxious he-man move—she stepped up and pressed a kiss to his cheek.

"We don't get many chances for happiness. It'd be a real shame to waste one. Especially when you both need it so badly."

Lilah's words were still rolling around his head a half hour later as he lay staring up at the ceiling. Her townhome was three stories and he had the first-floor guest room. Bailey snored gently at his side, his occasional whimpering and motions of running in place suggesting he was in a deep sleep.

Lucky mutt.

Tucker slammed a hand into his pillow, fluffing it up before crossing his arms behind his head. Visions of Cassidy, a few floors above him, filled his mind's eye. He'd gotten a tour when they arrived, his architect's nosy nature expecting no less, and he'd seen her bag in a guest room on the third floor.

The urge to go to her kept beating at him, along with Lilah's words of encouragement.

And every time he shoved back the covers to go to her, his own beleaguered thoughts battered him with a round of arguments that had him lying back down again.

Don't take advantage of her.

She's in trouble. Only a complete jerk would try to get it on under the circumstances.

Give her space.

He'd rotated in a few other choice, expletive-filled comments in his mental battle, which was the only reason he could figure he didn't hear the door slide open.

"Hey." Cassidy's voice traveled the width of the room. "Are you up?"

"I'm up."

The movement and sliver of light from the hallway was enough to pull Bailey from his dream-induced puppy adventures and he sat up, his body instantly alert. As soon as he realized it was Cassidy, he settled down, a happy little sigh echoing from his throat.

First Lilah and now the dog?

Tucker shook off the odd thought and motioned Cassidy in. "I'm awake. What's the matter?"

"I can't sleep."

"It was a big day."

She moved closer to the bed, and his already tense body tightened painfully. An oversize gray T-shirt with the SMU logo emblazoned across her chest stopped midthigh, setting off her long, slender legs. That vibrant hair hung around her shoulders in curly waves and the urge to reach out and run his fingers through the silky strands nearly had him off the bed.

Don't take advantage.

He wanted to curse his conscience to hell and back but still, he stayed where he was.

"Tucker?" She moved against the bed, lifting one knee to lean against the mattress. He felt the light depression of her weight and nearly groaned at how close she was.

At how easy it would be to reach out and touch her.

"Cassidy."

"Why are you hiding in here?"

"I'm not hiding."

"Then please don't make me wait for you any longer."

Her smile was bright in the slivers of moonlight that

shone through the slats of the blinds. That smile was warmth. It was invitation.

And in that moment, he knew she welcomed him.

He reached for her, dragging her until she sprawled against his chest, his lips trailing a path against her throat as his hands played around the hem of her T-shirt. His fingers brushed over the soft skin of her lower back and he inched the cotton up before she shifted, slipping along his body like quicksilver.

Before he could stop her, she levered herself into a sitting position over his midsection and stared down at him. "This is for us. Let's forget what's outside and ignore what's waiting. This is ours."

"Ours."

The word came out on a husky whisper before he pulled her full against him, his mouth hot on hers. She went willingly, a partner in their midnight discovery of each other's secrets.

Tucker moved his fingers over the sensitive skin of her spine before drifting on a lazy path toward the sides of her breasts. She levered herself off his chest and reached for the hem of the T-shirt before his seeking hands stopped, gripping hers.

"Let me."

Her eyes had adjusted to the dim light in the room and she could see the wide pupils in his dark eyes as he looked up at her. She reveled in that look—the one that made her feel like a goddess—and dropped the hem to give him free access.

He lifted the material in one fell swoop, the neckline catching on her hair before he pulled it completely from her body. That dark, magnetic gaze never wavered but she watched, fascinated, as he clenched his jaw the moment his hands began to move over her skin.

Here was a man in control.

And in that instant, Cassidy acknowledged just how desperately she wanted to make him lose it.

Sharp darts of pleasure radiated from her nerves everywhere he touched. Her skin was on fire with the joy of being with him. With the joy of being worshipped.

He caressed her in lazy circles over her stomach as he worked his way, with exquisite slowness, to her breasts. By the time his hands covered the heavy globes, she pressed herself against him, whimpering as his fingers played over her aching nipples.

"Tucker."

His voice was a lazy whisper as her head fell back, the simple joy of being touched filling her with wonder.

When his hand drifted away she opened her eyes, captivated by the wicked grin that reflected back at her. With one hand he supported her lower back while he maintained that exquisite contact with her breasts the other.

And then he leaned forward, capturing her bare nipple between his teeth.

A hard moan fell from her lips as the warm suction drew her in, deeper and deeper, against the sexy ministrations of his tongue.

Over and over, he circled her body, the erotic heat driving her slowly mad. A hot, achy need centered in her core and she writhed against him, desperate for him to release the pent-up longing.

As that ache expanded, filling her limbs with restless energy, she focused on returning the pleasure. With sinuous motions designed to torment, she slid against his body. The thin scrap of silk that still covered her core added another layer of torture against her heated body as she explored the perfection that was Tucker Buchanan.

Long, ropey muscles corded his arms and shoulders, the latter thick and rounded and hard. As she traced a path along his chest, she gloried in the hard planes and angles, so firm to the touch.

Eager to mimic the same pleasure he'd given, she ran her tongue over the heat of his chest before circling the tight skin of his nipple. He exhaled on a harsh intake of breath, the motion spurring her on as she drifted, lazy as a Sunday afternoon, to reward his other nipple.

"You drive me crazy."

"Likewise, Ace." She grinned up at him, the glorious pleasure suffusing her in generous waves. "I also happen to still have a few tricks up my sleeve."

"That's funny. So do I."

He shifted, ready to capture her underneath him to continue the pleasure, but she beat him to the punch, her hand snaking quickly beneath the waistband of his briefs.

Tucker stilled at her touch, another hard exhale escaping his lips as she tightened her grip. "Told you I had a few tricks."

"So you did." He gritted his teeth and she watched—no, gloried—when his eyelids drooped to half-mast.

And then she added a few more, stroking his body and pushing him through his paces as he pressed himself into her hand.

He said her name again—the sound like a miracle to her ears—before his hand gripped her wrist, stemming her movements. "You have no idea what you're doing to me."

She leaned forward and pressed her lips to his ears. "Oh, but I think I do."

A harsh laugh escaped his throat, half need, half joy,

but he held her steady. "Much as I hate to have you stop, I have a few other plans for you."

"Tell me about them." She marveled at the rough whisper that seemed to emanate from the depths of her toes.

"I have an even better idea. Let me show you."

He rolled her onto her back, and she used the momentum to push his briefs down, cupping the firm lines of his buttocks in her palms. He twisted and finished the job, then returned his hands to her waist and the thin layer of silk that still separated their bodies. "Game foul. You're overdressed."

"What are you going to do about it?"

He had his hands at her waist, the material halfway down her thighs when he stilled, his forehead dropping to hers.

"What?" It took Cassidy a moment to see through the haze of passion and realize he'd stopped moving. "What is it?"

"I don't have anything…any protection."

A laugh bubbled up in her throat, the sound dark and dangerous. It stopped her for a moment… Was that really her? The carefree temptress with a secret?

"Why are you laughing?"

"Look in the end table."

Confusion stamped itself in his passion-glazed eyes, and Cassidy took pity on him and reached for the slim drawer herself. "Lilah to the rescue."

"She keeps condoms in her guest rooms?"

"Not as a general rule. Or I don't know, maybe she does, I've never looked before."

"So how do you know they're there?"

"Because she told me so before she said good-night and closed my bedroom door."

"The woman bakes small slices of heaven and she even

serves it up in her guest rooms. Remind me to buy her something." Tucker's hand closed over hers in the drawer as he snagged a foil packet. "Like a car."

She laughed hard at that, the unrefined giggle too care-free and happy to hold back. "I'll be sure to tell her."

His answering grin was as carefree as her own before he narrowed his gaze, the smile falling away. "You're amazing."

"Right back at ya, sexy."

"No. I mean it. You're truly something special."

She quieted, the compliment washing over her like sunshine on a spring day.

All her life, she'd battled the feeling of not being enough. Of never quite living up to expectations. How extraordinary, then, to look into this man's eyes and feel just right.

Absolutely, positively, 100-percent right.

She swallowed hard, the moment expanding in her chest like a warm flow of lava. He'd captured her heart, and she'd known it immediately. Had realized it the moment she'd seen at him from the front steps of her business, when he stood staring up at her with his ugly dog at his side.

But as he stared down at her now, his body poised over hers, she knew everything had changed.

She loved.

Reaching down, she guided him inside her body and braced herself for the onslaught of pleasure.

And as they both began to move—their rhythms matched and in tune with each other—Cassidy let herself fall.

Chapter 16

Tucker lifted his arms to stretch and came awake around an armful of woman instead. Memories of the night before flooded his mind as a gentle hum of satisfaction lit under his skin.

He ran a hand along her side, molding his fingers to the gentle swell of her hips. She stirred under his questing hands, and a light moan drifted from the depths of her throat. His already erect body stirred to life, anxious to pick up where they'd left off a few hours earlier.

She stirred next to him, a groggier moan spilling from her lips before she rolled into him on a dull "oof."

Her eyes shot open at the contact, sleep rapidly fading from those rich depths of blue.

"Morning."

"Well." A light blush filled her cheeks. "I think I've just proven I'm nothing if not graceful first thing in the morning."

The cute blush brought him up onto an elbow before he leaned down to press a lingering kiss to her lips. "I like clumsy." He trailed a line of kisses along her neck. "With a side of delightfully mussed."

"Um, Tucker."

"Hmm?" He ran his tongue over her collarbone and delighted in the sleepy taste of her.

"Before you explore too much farther I think someone else needs your attention."

Tucker felt the cold nose against his leg as Cassidy's words registered and reluctantly rolled over to stare at Bailey. "You've got great timing."

She patted his shoulder before pushing against him. "I'd say he's got great control considering he's not that far past puppyhood."

"Yeah." Tucker patted Bailey's soft head. "He's a good boy. But he's got lousy timing."

After one last lingering kiss, he got out of bed and tugged on a pair of running shorts and a T-shirt, then opened the bedroom door. Inspired, he turned back to stare at her. "Is it too much to ask you not to move an inch from that spot?"

"It wouldn't be if I didn't have an appointment this morning."

Visions of more bridezillas floated through his mind, and his face must have registered his horror because she quickly waved him off. "Vi, Lilah and I are looking at a new venue. We're evaluating it for our clients."

"Sounds…fun."

"It will be." She pushed a thick wave of hair behind her shoulder, and Tucker's mouth went as dry as the Sahara. "And since the three of us will be together you really are off the hook from coming with us."

"I thought we agreed last night. Out in groups."

"And mathematically Lilah, Violet and I make a group."

He saw the very neat corner she'd backed him into and kept his mouth shut. He'd make a better argument after he had a cup of coffee.

Or so he told himself.

"Look. Go get Bailey out and we can talk about it over breakfast. Lilah's making French toast to butter you up."

A hard snort rose up in his throat. "You can't think I'm that cheap and easy."

"Oh, I don't know." She winked before she slinked out of bed, naked as the day she was born, and headed toward the shower. "I think I've got your number."

Twenty minutes later Tucker was on his third piece of French toast and second side of bacon and had to admit he was feeling awfully cheap and way too easy.

Evidently, the man who'd taken pride in living off rations for a week while he plotted to blow up a major enemy thoroughfare was an easy mark when it came to gourmet fare and perfectly cooked pork products.

"The location is three miles from the office. We're driving together and we're meeting two event planners once we get there, one of whom is a former professional wrestler."

Tucker shot Cassidy the fish eye as he snagged another piece of bacon. "You're making that up."

Cassidy lifted up three fingers in the Girl Scout salute. "Honest as the day is long. He wrestled as Jungle Jim the Destroyer. Look him up. There's no way someone's taking a shot at us in broad daylight."

The three of them had made different versions of the same argument since Lilah had set down the first plate of French toast and he'd pretty much agreed to their plan when another thought hit him. "And what about the jewels?"

"I've got a safe upstairs. They're already locked in there and there's no reason to think they're going anywhere, especially after I set the house alarm," Lilah said.

"We need to get them in a safe-deposit box." Violet

eyed the plate of bacon before reaching past it for a bowl of mixed berries.

Cassidy spoke first. "That assumes we're keeping them. We'll know more once we talk to Mrs. B. We're headed there after the event meeting."

"Have you considered the fact she might not talk to you? Something's got her spooked, and if she thinks keeping quiet is for your own good, the likelihood of getting something out of her is slim."

"That's why we need to go there and see her. I've known her my whole life." Cassidy pushed a piece of toast around her syrup. "I just need some time with her to convince her to trust us with whatever this is."

Tucker wasn't so sure but he kept his thoughts to himself. He'd fielded a text from Max earlier and his grandfather still hadn't budged on whatever it was he knew.

"Max and I will join you at the hospital."

"We don't want to overwhelm them."

"Then you all can take Mrs. B. and we'll take Max Senior. I don't know about you, but I'm done being left in the dark."

In the end, Tucker accompanied the women to their appointment at a new high-rise hotel that had opened downtown. He told himself it was nothing more than curiosity over Jungle Jim, but one glance at Cassidy, her head bent close with Lilah's and Violet's, and Tucker knew he was deluding himself.

It was her.

She'd captivated him and he didn't want to let her out of his sight.

Add on the very real threat lurking, waiting to strike at her and her friends like a snake in the grass, and he decided his time was better spent tagging along.

"What do you think, Tucker?" As if she sensed he'd zoned out to another planet, Cassidy reeled him back in, a smug smile stamped across her face. "Do you like the silver drape for this sweetheart table or the soft mauve?"

"Neither. I would prefer a deep, dark red."

"A bold choice." Violet nodded before tilting her head to stare across the ballroom at a picture only she could imagine. "But a potential clash for a spring wedding."

"Why the red?" The teasing lightness had vanished, replaced by genuine curiosity as Cassidy lifted a swatch of tablecloth they'd each touched and discarded earlier.

"Because it's bold. It says look at me."

"Everyone's already looking at the bride."

"No." He shook his head, not sure why it mattered to him so much to reiterate his point. "Red says we're a couple. It says look at us, standing here boldly before you. It says we're having a party to kick off our forever."

The three women stared at him in various states of surprise, but it was Cassidy who moved up and slid her hand in his. "What a lovely sentiment."

"Is it sentiment if it's true?"

"I'd say so." She pressed a brief kiss to his lips. Although quick, it hinted at something more. Something permanent. And as Tucker followed them from the ballroom to the kitchen, he couldn't get the image of something more out of his mind.

An hour later Cassidy found him seated at one of the undressed table rounds back in the ballroom. Although he'd had every good intention when he followed the women into the kitchen, Lilah's in-depth questioning over how the hotel prep staff manned their warming stations, the number of available cook tops and proper ice-making equipment had finally forced him to throw in the towel.

He had a few phone calls to make and some follow-up

on an upcoming job, and the quiet of the ballroom gave him a chance to work through his ever-growing to-do list.

"That's an hour of my life I can't get back." She flopped into a chair opposite him and dropped her head into her hands.

"I thought you wanted to do this?"

"I did. Until I felt my brains leak out of my head over a discussion of cake-serving techniques. We need to learn to split these trips up." She winked. "Or ditch Lilah with the head chef the moment we walk in."

Tucker laid a hand over hers, grateful for the reassuring contact. He knew they were safe here. Had kept an eye on the perimeter as well as every strange face they passed.

But no matter how hard he tried, he couldn't seem to settle this morning.

She lifted her hand, palm-up, and laced their fingers. "Did one of us at least get some work done?"

Whether it was the gentle question—partnership filling each and every word—or the feel of her fingers wrapped in his, Tucker wasn't sure. But in that moment, something clicked.

Swift and immediate, with all the force of a bullet dropping into a chamber.

Or a stubborn, lonely man falling hard and fast into love.

"Tucker?"

Her smile remained gentle, but he saw the questions in her eyes. He wanted to answer them—all of them—but instead he swallowed hard around the dryness that coated his throat like powder. "I got some details on a job site I need to visit next week."

"That's good." She squeezed his fingers. "Good and *normal*."

"And I got an update from Max. His grandfather is still playing the stubborn mule card."

A small sigh left her lips. "Which means we're going to spend another afternoon at the hospital."

"Looks like it."

"Which also means I am not going to think about all the work I have to get done in the next two days before another round of fittings."

Her phone went off, echoing through the cavernous ballroom. Tucker dropped her hand as she reached for her purse and busied himself with his own phone, looking up when she gasped.

"What is it?"

Her eyes narrowed on her cell's glass face before she bypassed the call.

"That was an awfully coincidental blast from my past." The phone beeped as the voice mail notification popped up. "That was my ex-fiancé."

"Which one?" When she shot him the eye, he lifted his hands. "Come on. It's a valid question."

"Number two. And somehow I don't think he's calling so we can take a jaunt down memory lane."

Cassidy fought the swells of anger and forced herself to ride them like waves on the ocean. No matter how high they rose she pictured riding them out, then flowing gently back to shore.

But damn it all to hell.

The calm vanished as her mind worked through the realities of Robert's call.

She didn't believe in coincidence.

And she was fast coming to believe there was no way every horrifying thing that had happened in the past few years wasn't connected.

First her sister. Then her brother-in-law. Even the attack on Mrs. B.

There was no way they weren't connected in some way.

Of course, what did that say about her and what was shaping up to be her abominably poor judgment?

For days she'd fought the rising sensation that she didn't really know the people in her life. Was that their fault? Or had she created the distance all on her own?

"Play the voice mail again." The light, flirty teasing that had filled Tucker's voice as they'd walked through the hotel had vanished at the news that Robert Barrington had reappeared in her life.

"Absolutely not." Lilah interjected her sizeable opinion into the discussion. "I've heard that slimeball's voice enough times already. We know what that voice mail says and we all know damn well what it means."

"He's in on this."

The words fell from Cassidy's lips, and she was surprised by the sorrow she heard there.

She'd been engaged to the man. Had been on the verge of joining her life to his. Had things worked out, they'd have been married for over three years now. They'd likely have a child or one on the way. Maybe both.

And she'd be married to a criminal.

The accusations continued to fly through her thoughts, as unwelcome as they were true.

"Are you going to call him back?" Violet's question hovered over the table like a bubble everyone watched, waiting for it to burst.

"Nope."

"What if he's behind this?" Ever the diplomat, Violet leaped to the question of the hour.

Cassidy knew she was playing with fire. Knew that whatever was going on had its roots in something far more dangerous—and with people who played by a depraved set of rules.

But on the subject of Robert she refused to budge.

"Then he's got to come to me. On my turf. On my terms."

The man known as the Duke viewed the array of gemstones laid out on his desk, a full-scale replica of the one JFK used in the White House. He was still working on how to replace this desk with the one in Kennedy's presidential library and knew in time he'd figure out how.

In the meantime, he'd focus on the issue at hand.

He ran a finger over one of the stones.

He'd heard the rumors for years. That the replicas of the Crown Jewels created during World War II were later secreted out of Britain, still intact. And to think they'd been sitting in Texas ever since.

The owners of the jewels thought themselves so adept at keeping the secret, but those at home had talked.

Someone always talked.

He'd learned the lesson young. His father was a brutal taskmaster, schooled in the old ways. He was a man who understood the value of silence, secrecy and absolute dedication to one's task and he'd instilled it in his only son.

By honing those skills and taking advantage of the grand masses who didn't have the drive or the perseverance to do the same, the Duke had learned one could always find success.

And now he had.

Or nearly had.

For all the intel he'd managed to secure, he'd never been able to acquire a full accounting of the contents smuggled out of England. The most likely scenario was a set of replicas, fully matched to the largest stones in the collection, with the smaller stones unduplicated as they were considered less at risk.

Or less valuable. Only the very biggest and best for a monarch.

He ran a finger over the three largest pieces—the replicas of Cullinan I and II as well as the Koh-i-Nor. The most well-known of the Crown Jewels, the copies were extraordinarily well-done and would command a premium on their own.

If he chose to give them up.

He lifted the Koh-i-Nor, watching the light play over it, his eagerness at possessing it fading into the refracting glass. While he respected the work, the piece was fake. And no matter how well-done, it would never match the original.

Maybe he wouldn't keep it after all.

A wave of dissatisfaction curled through his belly with hungry claws as he tossed the copy on the desk.

He wanted what was missing.

"You do realize I have what appears to be three priceless jewels sitting in my safe. In my house." Lilah said the words around a half-chewed straw as it stuck up out of a green drink that had turned her mouth the same color.

Cassidy eyed her from the driver's seat and couldn't hold back a laugh. "Your tongue's green."

"Is it?" Lilah pulled down the visor mirror and stuck out her tongue. "So it is."

"Why do you drink that sludge?" Violet had a coffee— her insistence on getting one had taken them through a second drive-through before heading toward the hospital—and Cassidy only grinned harder.

Her friends.

The three of them were as different as could be yet they

knew each other. From their years-old jokes to finishing each other's sentences to the endless eye rolling at one another's quirks, they *knew* each other.

And loved each other.

These were her sisters. For a long time it had pained her to put them in the same category as Leah—to even think of them as more familylike than her own—until they'd been the ones to stand with her over her sister's grave.

In that moment, she'd known. The family she'd made had seen her through. They'd given her their loyalty and their love and she could never fully repay what they brought to her life.

In the making, they'd also given her a place to belong.

And in finding her place, the pain of her own family became manageable.

Lilah took another sip before letting out a small, disgusted sigh. "Come on, ladies, get with the program. Am I the only one who can't get my mind off the jewels? Where did they come from? I mean, Mrs. B. obviously, but before that?"

They'd worked through the puzzle over and over, not getting very far.

"Speaking of Mrs. B., we need to game-plan how we're going to tell her." Cassidy knew they needed to ask the questions, but between the woman's deteriorating health and the pure shock of what had happened to all of them, she knew they needed to tread lightly. "We can't just blurt it out that Lilah's got a bunch of priceless jewels in her safe."

Ever the diplomat, Violet launched in. "I know she's an old friend and I also know she's been incredibly good to us, but I think we need to agree we can't tell her where the jewels are."

Vi was right. Of course she was. But Cassidy couldn't

hold back the darts of pain at the idea she couldn't trust a woman she'd known since she was a small child. "You're absolutely right."

"So what should we say?" Lilah asked.

Cassidy turned toward her friend, her gaze catching on that green tongue, and she couldn't hold back the giggle that crept up her throat.

"Why are you laughing?" Lilah wiped her lips with a napkin.

"Because you look like you're seven. And because I'm with you guys. And despite the insane weirdness of the past week, I'm lucky to have you both."

Violet laid a hand on her shoulder and offered up a tight squeeze. "We're lucky, too."

Lilah added her hand to the pile. "And since we're your bestest of friends, it's about time you spilled about Tucker."

Cassidy had known it was coming but still winced at the evidence it was time for show-and-tell.

"You only need to tell us what you're comfortable telling us." Violet was the voice of wisdom. "Which we, of course, hope is everything."

"I'm not telling you everything."

Lilah let out a low grunt of disagreement. "Oh, give a girl a break. I need the juicy parts because I've had absolutely *no* juicy parts for a dismally long period of time."

"Sorry. I'm keeping the juicy parts to myself."

"Spoilsport." Lilah took another sip of her green concoction, a mulish expression on her face.

"But I will tell you what led up to the juicy parts."

Those brown eyes brightened as she pushed her pink streak behind her ear. "All's forgiven."

So Cassidy told her friends about the past week. The quiet moments, the protective moments and even the fun moments, with Tucker wagging his eyebrows behind crazy brides or teasing her about his skills with zippers.

She kept the deeper stuff to herself. His past was his business and it was enough that he'd shared it with her. But she did share a bit about his time in the Corps and his friendship with Max.

"He's a good guy. It nearly killed him to leave the three of us to drive to the hospital by ourselves." The words were high praise from Violet and not a compliment she gave out lightly. She was fiercely protective of her friends and it showed in who she was willing to let close.

"He is a good guy. They're both good guys." A heavy stirring filled her chest, the knowledge she had met a good man rushing through her in a flood of gratitude. "But yeah. Tucker's special."

"You're in love."

Lilah said it first but Violet was close on her heels. "You love him."

Cassidy shook her head as a low hum kicked in under her skin. The vibrations of change.

Sex was one thing, but love?

Sex was human need, and she didn't dismiss what had happened the night before—she could acknowledge it was something that had satisfied them both.

Love, on the other hand, was commitment and merged lives and *forever*.

And her track record at forever sucked.

Of course, Tucker Buchanan hadn't been a part of her life before.

Was that really all it took? The arrival of the right person for all the wrong ones to simply fade away?

Violet's quiet voice broke into her musings. "I know that look."

"What look? And how can you even see it since you're in the backseat and I'm facing the road?"

"Because I know you. I also know the set of your shoulders and that quiet place you go to when you're upset. It's totally different from your quiet, dreamy 'I'm designing' place."

A red light gave her the perfect opportunity, and Cassidy turned in her seat. "My dreamy 'I'm designing' place?"

"Oh, yeah." Lilah got into it. "We lose you for stretches at a time when you just go somewhere."

"I don't go anywhere."

"Sure you do. It's Cassidy time and we love you for it."

She mulled over the picture her friends painted. She did get lost in her work sometimes. And she'd been known not to come out of her studio except for short breaks for days on end.

But dreamy?

The light turned and she moved through the last intersection before the hospital entrance. "So how is it I look different now?"

"There's nothing floaty and dreamy about you right now." Lilah patted her arm. "You're just sort of squinty and tense."

"Lilah!"

Cassidy wanted to be mad—knew she should conjure up something in reaction—but all she could do was smile at the honest truth in her friends' words.

"I can't be in love with Tucker Buchanan. Can. Not. I've known him for, like, four days."

"Sometimes that's all it takes."

"And sometimes we can read too many novels and watch too many movies." Cassidy pulled into the parking lot, grateful the conversation would come to an end soon.

She wasn't in love.
She couldn't be.
But what if she was?

Chapter 17

Tucker took the last sip of his now-cold coffee and watched Max struggle to stay calm in the face of his grandfather's stubborn refusal to talk.

"Come on, Pops. Something's going on. Why are you being so mule-headed about this?"

"It's not mine to tell." Max Senior stared into his own cup, his bright blue eyes shuttered with frustration.

"So there is something to tell?"

"Don't put words in my mouth, young man. I'll knock 'em down your throat."

Tucker knew the words for the bluster they were—steeped in fear forged over fifty years—and kept his own counsel. Although Max wasn't doing the best job in the world of keeping his calm, Tucker sensed ganging up on the older man wasn't the path to getting what they wanted.

"You and Mrs. Beauregard are in danger, Pops. You need to let us help you."

"I've been taking care of myself for over eighty years. You think I don't know how?"

"It's not about taking care of yourself. It's about getting help when you need it."

Although Tucker had sworn he wasn't getting involved, visions of Cassidy's dead brother-in-law rose up in his mind's eye. Despite his vow to stay silent, the only way to help Max make his point was to take it out of the realm of personal safety.

"The people who've come after the women at Elegance and Lace are ruthless, Mr. Baldwin. If they think you know something, or if they think Mrs. Beauregard knows something, they're going to come after you, too."

"Jo?" The old man's hands trembled around his paper coffee cup, and Tucker hated causing him grief, but he hated the thought of leaving him in the dark even more.

"These people mean business."

"What people?"

Max caught Tucker's eye before he spoke. "You don't know?"

Max Senior was indignant. "I have no idea."

Tucker kept his voice low, unwilling to add to the alarm by allowing anyone nearby to overhear them. "There have been a series of break-ins at Elegance and Lace. People looking for something. And then two nights ago a body was left at the back door as a message."

"Who?" Mr. Baldwin's eyes grew wide as he processed the news of the murder before his gaze collided with his grandson's.

"Cassidy Tate's former brother-in-law."

Max covered his grandfather's hand with his own. "This is why we need your help. And why we need to know what we're dealing with. Whatever secret you're hiding. Or whatever you're keeping for Mrs. B. Someone knows. And they're not going to rest until they have the jewels."

Max Senior's jaw dropped, his face going ashen. "You know about the jewels?"

* * *

Cassidy had rehearsed in her head the speech she was going to give Mrs. Beauregard. Something sweet and kind, letting her know how much she cared and how well she thought of her and how much she appreciated the space they'd leased for Elegance and Lace.

It was at the transition into "How the hell could you hide priceless jewels in the floor of said shop?" that her polished speech sort of went sideways.

So it was a shock when she walked into Mrs. B.'s room and found Tucker and both Maxes surrounding the bed and realized she didn't have to ask any questions at all.

"Cassidy dear." Mrs. B. held out her arms, and Cassidy went straight into them. "I'm so sorry. So, so sorry."

Tight arms banded around her neck, and Cassidy was lost to the crushing hug. Over and over, murmured "I'm sorrys" continued to fall from Josephine's lips.

"Shh. It's fine."

Cassidy caught Violet's stare and slight shoulder lift so she held on and gave Mrs. B. one more tight squeeze before stepping away. Tucker pulled a chair up for her and she sat, taking Josephine's hand in hers.

When Max Senior took the chair on the other side of the bed—along with Mrs. B.'s hand—Cassidy knew something had happened since they were all together a few nights earlier.

His voice was gentle when he spoke, a lifetime of love in his eyes. "Jo. We have to tell them."

The same wild-eyed fear that had Mrs. B. hanging on her neck washed over her in another wave as she pleaded with Max Senior. "We can't tell them. We can't, Max. We can't do that to them."

"Jo. They're in this. They have to know." He lifted her hand to his lips for a quick kiss. "They need to know."

"No," she whispered. "Someone will hurt them if we do."

He pressed one more kiss to the back of her hand before lifting his gaze to his grandson. "Someone's already tried that and they gave him a run for his money. Now we need them to know what they're up against."

Where she thought the news of an attack would have caused even more grief and surprise, impeding Mrs. B.'s ability to deal with the situation, Cassidy was surprised to see resignation instead.

She knows.

And when Josephine nodded, her gaze still fearful but full of determination, Cassidy braced herself for what came next.

She felt Tucker come up behind her, his hand on her shoulder, and she took comfort in his touch. In the warmth and safety of his heavy palm where it lay against her body.

With a quick glance up at him, she covered his hand with her free one and settled in to listen. "You can tell us, Mrs. B. It's all right."

"My father was drafted into service to the British Crown by MI6 during World War II."

Cassidy had seen a few pictures of Mrs. B.'s father in her home over the years. Although she couldn't remember much of the details, as she recalled he was a slender man with white hair. Not the image that first came to mind of a superspy. "Did he smuggle secrets?"

Josephine's smile was distant, but Cassidy took solace in the fact that she was smiling. "Oh, no. Nothing that dangerous. He was a tradesman. A diamond cutter of the first grade."

"I thought much of the expertise in diamond cutting was in Antwerp? Especially at that time." Violet's question was spot-on, and Cassidy didn't even question how Violet knew something like that.

Her friend simply knew.

"A majority of it was, but not all. Besides, for what MI6 had in mind, they needed an Englishman. And there were none more loyal than my father."

Questions filled her mind, but Cassidy held on to them all. There'd be time enough for questions after she got through the story.

And what a story it was.

"As you may know, the Crown Jewels were placed in a secret location during the war, which has still never been revealed, even to this day."

Max shook his head, a low moan escaping his lips. "Please don't tell me I stole the Crown Jewels of England."

Violet smacked him on the shoulder—a very un-Violet-like move—before muttering, "Not unless you've hitched a ride to the Tower of London recently."

Although a spark lit in the depths of Mrs. B.'s gaze at the byplay between Violet and Max, she continued her story. "Not exactly. My father created fakes so there were admirable replicas of the jewels should they need to be used as decoys."

Cassidy didn't miss the relief that eased Max's jaw but Mrs. B.'s words jogged something loose. "What do you mean not exactly?"

"There were three stones that my father was also asked to keep safe."

"Real ones?" Tucker's deep voice punctuated the moment.

"Yes." Mrs. B. nodded. "They were presented to the King as a gift just before the war, and his wife had a premonition about them. She didn't want them."

"So your father took them?" Lilah asked.

"Disposed of them. With MI6's permission and in full accord of the King."

"Why didn't the Queen Mum like them?"

Again, Violet hit the nail with her history knowledge and Cassidy leaned forward, unable to hide her excitement. "We're really talking about King George the Sixth? And the Queen Mum. *The King's Speech* King George and all that?"

"Well, yes, of course."

"And you realize how amazing this all is?" The excitement bubbling in her gut took Cassidy off guard and she tried to keep herself focused on the matter at hand.

But the King and Queen?

The letter they'd found in Mrs. B.'s house had said it all, but still she'd resisted in the face of such a story. Had she, Violet and Lilah really been sitting on royal jewels that belonged to the British monarchy for the past three years?

Even the idea that the jewels were in Texas was just too impossible for words.

Tucker spoke and pulled them back on track. "How did the jewels end up here?"

"My parents never quite got over the ravages of war. London was bombed repeatedly and they both wanted a fresh start."

"So why not leave the jewels behind?" Tucker asked. "The real ones were safe then."

"My father was asked to protect them personally. It was an honor he took seriously. And when he announced he was moving his family to the States, to a vast open place called Texas, MI6 asked him to take the replicas with him. There was some fear that if they fell into the public domain someone could use them to do damage."

"Like use them to try to replace the real ones if they could find a way to get into the Tower of London," Max said.

At Jo's nod, Max continued, his voice dry as day-old toast.

"So why not destroy them? They're just a bunch of glass, right? There's no value there beyond the reason they were created. That reason was gone once the war was over so the fakes should have been destroyed."

"But that's where the real jewels come in." Josephine explained the purported history of the three rubies that were gifted to the King and Queen on a trip abroad. The difficulty they had in their travels home and the Queen's desire to have them removed without drawing undue attention to the matter."

"So Josephine's father secreted them with the fakes." Max Senior took over the story. "His history as a diamond cutter made it easy to blend the real jewels with fakes and he immigrated with them in his tool set. No one was the wiser."

Tucker struggled to take it all in, the story more unbelievable than he ever could have imagined.

Crown Jewels? *The* British Crown Jewels. Seriously?

Whatever he thought he knew or suspected about this situation had been blown to bits, the story of Mrs. Beauregard's father like something out of a movie.

A thriller that had no basis in reality. Especially not *his* reality.

"Is it possible your father told you this, maybe as a story or a way to connect with his homeland?"

Mrs. B.'s face was kind—understanding, even—but she held firm. "It's one-hundred-percent true. All of it."

"All of it," Max Senior added. "I helped Jo bury the jewels."

"And you never thought anyone would find them?" Tucker asked.

"We figured by the time anyone possibly discovered them, the provenance wouldn't matter any longer. We were deliberate in keeping all paperwork separate," Jo said, her gaze on Max Senior.

"And the appraiser we worked with helped us alter the fakes a bit to make them a little less identical to the originals."

Max moved forward from his position against the wall, his earlier concern for his grandfather back in spades at the man's mention of another witness. "You told someone about this? Someone besides the two of you."

"We've kept it a secret, but yes, I found someone I trusted to get the three rubies appraised."

"Is it possible they kept records, Pops?" Max moved even closer to his grandfather. "Do you still have the guy's name?"

"Gunner Davidson was a friend. He never would have done anything with the information. We were careful. And we were careful in choosing him."

While Tucker didn't doubt the man was a friend, stones of the kind Josephine's father had secreted out of England would be worth making a fuss over. And an experienced jeweler in Texas, in what he estimated was the mid-1950s, would have been hard-pressed not to discuss such a major professional evaluation.

Even though Max's line of questioning would need to be pursued further, Tucker figured it might be easier to turn the conversation to calmer matters. "Why did you bury them?"

"My father kept them locked up in the house throughout his life. But, well—" Mrs. B. broke off. "Max and I thought we should remove the evidence. My father left me his properties when he passed away and it seemed like the right place for them."

"You never wanted to wear them?" Lilah probed, her voice gentle.

"They weren't meant for me. It seemed wrong, somehow. And—"

When Mrs. B. didn't say anything else, Cassidy pressed, her voice gentle. "And what?"

"And I couldn't shake the superstitious part. My father never bought into it. He was an eminently practical man and had spent his life around jewels. He didn't ascribe properties to them beyond what he could measure through his loupe. But I never had an interest in them. In keeping them. They were a secret to me, nothing more."

"Some things aren't meant to be ours," Violet said.

Tucker didn't miss the way Josephine and Max Senior looked at each other after Violet's statement.

Nor did he miss the subtle shift in the room at the woman's reference to a curse.

Even though it sounded crazy to talk curses in this day and age, they had a dead body that suggested otherwise.

Robert dialed Cassidy's number once more and swore when it dropped over to voice mail. She was probably in one of her designing fugues again. He never could understand her when she went to that weird place in her head, focused on yet another wedding dress.

He'd gone along, of course. And to be honest, her focus on other things gave him time off from playing the perfect boyfriend. That crap got tiring after a while.

Cassidy seemed taken in by his "perfect boyfriend" persona, but he knew damn right well that her friends had their doubts. Lilah was a freaking ray of sunshine who kept those rays on bright all the time, but she noticed things and got in a good potshot every now and again.

Violet, on the other hand, hadn't made a big secret of not liking him. She kept up a polite veneer when they were all out together but it didn't take a genius to know that she wasn't his biggest fan.

Maybe he could use that...

The thought drifted in and as he considered it, exploring it from various angles, he realized it was his best bet. He could use that perpetual dislike to his advantage.

Cassidy had no reason to call him back. But if he called Violet, he could persuade her to help him with some party planning. She might not like him, but she was a businesswoman through and through. He'd appeal to that business sense and work it from there.

A quick internet search turned up a number for her and he dialed her up, listening as her phone rang before going to voice mail. He nearly hung up, but then thought better of it. He waited for the beep, then dived in.

"Violet. It's Robert Barrington. I know it's been a long time but I was hoping to get your help with a party I'm planning for my parents' fortieth wedding anniversary. Please give me a call when you can." He rattled off his number and settled in to wait.

"Have you lost your ever-loving mind?"

The words exploded from Max's mouth like gunshots, and Cassidy had to admit her thoughts weren't all that far from his.

They'd migrated to her house after their visit to the hospital and had settled in her living room with several plastic containers of sushi, a few bottles of wine and Bailey guarding the door, a boiled soup bone from Lilah between his paws. Although the guys had looked dubious at first, she was glad she'd ordered extra by the way each of them kept digging into the carryout trays for more rolls.

"I'm not stupid, Maxwell. I think it's the perfect opportunity to draw the bastard out." Violet kept her tone level—too level—and Cassidy knew that was trouble.

"Robert's at the center of this. There's no way you're taking a meeting with my wimpy ex." Cassidy thought through the remembered message and fought the shiver that gripped her shoulders.

First he'd left her a message. Then a second. And then he'd moved on to Violet, his voice as smooth and easy as the lies that had tripped from his tongue.

"Oh, come on, he's too stupid to be at the center of this." Lilah piped up. "Look at how badly he's bungled even an innocent get-together."

"Lilah's right." Tucker snatched another California roll, his coordination with chopsticks impressive. "He's not the lead on this. He's someone else's puppet."

"So we draw him out to the find the puppet master." Violet pressed her point. Cassidy knew the look of determination that had settled itself in Violet's green eyes. She'd seen that look often enough and knew it meant trouble.

Violet Richardson knew how to get her way. And if she didn't get it on her first try, she pushed and pulled and *maneuvered* until she did.

"Vi, you're talking about taking something into our own hands we have no business going anywhere near." Lilah's normally upbeat nature was nowhere in evidence. "We couldn't even manage to get a clean read off the video cameras of who dropped Charlie off behind the shop. How are we going to manage drawing out a criminal with an agenda and the skills to back it up?"

Cassidy knew the video feed had been a disappointment. The guys had taken a look at it and she, Lilah and Violet had reviewed the digital copies they could access 24/7 from their new security provider.

All they'd seen was a man, cloaked in a sweatshirt and jeans and with a ski mask covering his head.

She'd run the image repeatedly, hoping for some clue she'd recognize about the figure. Or that she could see a glimpse of Robert in a frame or two and know they'd caught their man.

But no matter how she'd scrutinized the feed, she got absolutely nothing off the image that was captured.

"Lilah's right. We need to turn this over to the police and wash our hands of it."

"It's too late. We're in danger now." Violet wouldn't be dissuaded and, if anything, her arguments had grown more fierce. "No one knew the full contents of that box. So no one's going to believe we didn't hold something back that came from what Max lifted."

"The police will know. And when nothing shows up fenced in the coming months, whoever's behind this will lose interest."

"Those stones have been hidden for more than half a century and that hasn't deterred anyone's interest." Violet poured another glass of wine, her frustration palpable. "And I, for one, am sick of playing the sitting duck."

"It's hard when things don't fall right in line, just like you planned." Max's pointed words hung over the group like a hangman's noose.

No one said a word, even as fury leaped, hot and strong, into Violet's vivid green eyes. For a moment, Cassidy got the distinct impression the argument was going to come to blows.

Or blows from Violet, at least.

Instead, something seemed to register at the last minute, because those flames of anger died, doused by a wave of reality. "Yes, it's damn hard. It's my job to make things happen and instead I'm sitting around like a damsel in distress. I've managed to acquire two bodyguards, I've put off about eighty percent of everything I had to get done this week, I haven't slept in my own bed and it's looking like I won't tonight, either—" She broke off and turned toward Lilah. "Sorry."

"Nothing to be sorry about. I know how much the princess loves her six-hundred-thread-count sheets."

The same look as before—the one that made Cassidy think her delicate friend was going to go all wrestler on someone—flickered again then quickly vanished as a husky laugh escaped Violet's throat. "Nothing but the best for me."

"'Course not." Lilah lifted her glass in a toast. "You're Violet freaking Richardson."

Just like earlier in the car, Cassidy took some comfort—even if it was minimal—from the fact that they could still laugh in the midst of such chaos.

But when she caught sight of the longing that stamped itself over Max's face, his gaze racing over Violet's laughing face, Cassidy reconsidered her assessment of the situation.

Max was worried about Violet.

Terrified, if she read his body language correctly. And her friend's tendency to throw herself into the middle of something was tying him up in knots.

Tucker stood to go get more wine from the kitchen, and Cassidy didn't miss the glint in his eyes that suggested she join him. She followed him into the kitchen, a comment about Violet and Max hovering on her lips when Tucker grabbed her and pulled her into his arms.

His mouth coursed over hers, his kisses full of a raw, base hunger.

She kissed him back, whatever she was about to say fading in the glory of being in his arms.

Until that moment she hadn't understood just how much she'd missed seeing him. Touching him. Being with him.

The corded muscles of his forearms lay under her fingertips, and she explored that sinewy surface as he pulled her even tighter against his body. With his teeth he tugged her lower lip into his mouth, and she felt an insistent pull deep in her core.

How did we find each other? she wondered as the moments spun out between them, the sensual kisses driving both of them slowly mad with desire.

And how was it possible she hadn't even known him a week ago?

The need for him was so strong—so *necessary*—she struggled to make sense of it all.

Was this what people meant when they blithely rattled off pithy little statements like "you know when you know" and "someday your prince will come"?

She'd thought she knew before. Twice before she'd started down the path of binding her life with another, only to run out on the first and now find out the second was likely a psychopath.

The part of her that hid from others wanted to hide from this, too.

And the bigger part of her—the woman who was tired of being alone and wondering if there would ever be anyone out there for her—knew she needed to hang on to what she'd found.

"Tucker." She whispered his name against his lips, torn between continuing to kiss him and getting back to the four other people having a meal in her living room. "We need to get back to dinner."

"A minute." He wrapped his arms around her, drawing her head against his chest. "Please give me a minute."

She took the comfort he offered and, sensing he needed

it as much as she did, returned it back to him. Her hands stayed low on his hips and she took solace in the warm, unyielding strength of his body.

Just one more moment.

For them.

Hard muscle flexed under her fingers as his body slowly swayed against hers, and she allowed her mind to drift with the gentle movement.

She'd thought it before, but after observing him for the past few days, she had a new appreciation for the term "warrior." She also understood how his agile mind played as important a role as his strong, solid body in this.

He'd worked, alone or as a team with Max, quickly assessing threats and dangers and strategizing against them. From initially handling things at Elegance and Lace, to planning how to get back in and get the gems, to how they were going to deal with Robert, he was in charge. In control.

Which was why his next comment was so jarring. "I let you talk me into drawing them out once and I can't do it again."

"Tucker." She laid a hand on his chest and tried to get a bit of space. "I know Violet. She's not talking about doing this alone."

"We shouldn't be doing it at all."

"We can involve the police. No, we *should* involve the police. Set it up like a sting. You know once he hears we have a lead Detective Graystone will be as anxious as we are to take Robert down."

Bailey trotted in, obviously sensing the tension, and he plopped into a seated position between the two of them on the floor. Tucker patted his head before taking a few steps back. "You heard Lilah. Robert's not the source. He's just a cog in the wheel."

"Then we take him down and remove one of the cogs."

"Why? So whoever's running the show can pull in a few more? These guys mean business."

"So do I."

"Why? So you can hang on to a gemstone that has a dark cloud over it?"

Cassidy puzzled through his comment, surprised at the depth of conviction she heard. "You believe there's something wrong with the stones?"

"I… No…" He shifted off the counter to pace her kitchen, his body caged by the small space. "Who the hell knows? All I do know is that almost seventy years ago someone in a position to keep an expensive set of gems discarded them like they were garbage."

"It's not like the royal family hurts for money."

"That's beside the point and you know it. So you stuff them in a drawer in a room of the palace. They disowned them."

Although she'd thought Mrs. Beauregard's story fanciful, Tucker made a sound point. Who discarded something so precious? Even with endless amounts of money, who would just give up something like that?

Donate it, maybe? Regift it if it wouldn't cause offense to the original gifter. Heck, make a fuss and put it in a museum.

And in that moment, the reality of what they were dealing with hit her. "They wanted it off British soil."

"Exactly."

Cassidy inhaled on a sharp breath. "And now it sits in my friend's safe."

Chapter 18

Tucker stood on the porch waiting for Bailey to return from his last romp of the evening and couldn't shake Cassidy's haunting words. Long after their friends had left, with Max promising to stay at Lilah's with Violet under full security, he was still thinking about Cassidy's conclusions.

They wanted the stones off British soil.

He wasn't a fanciful man. His earlier life and insistence on trying to live up to his father's impossible dreams had driven any sense of the whimsical straight out of him.

But he was a strong believer in his gut. And his was ringing bells something fierce.

He also couldn't shake the mystery of who the source of the information leak was. Josephine and Max had sworn up one side and down the other they hadn't shared the information and he believed them. Their sheer unwillingness to share details over the past few days—more than fifty years after burying the jewels—was a pretty good indicator neither of them had given up their secret.

So who was it?

The jeweler who'd evaluated the stones was the most likely source but there was no way he was the only one.

And even if he had talked, he'd have no idea the stones lay in the center of a concrete floor.

So who knew?

And who had they told?

"I can see the deep thoughts floating above your head like storm clouds."

Cassidy came up behind him and wrapped her arms around his waist as Bailey bounded up onto the front porch. He let the dog in, then firmly closed and locked the door before turning toward her, pulling her against him. "There's a lot to think about."

"I think I have a way to cut those deep thoughts off for a while."

He smiled at her, the moment more precious than he ever could have imagined.

He loved this woman. With everything he was, he loved her. Her warmth. Her loyalty. Her spirit of dedication to her work. Those and so many other facets he'd seen over the past week fascinated and enticed, drawing him ever closer into her orbit.

So why the indecision in telling her his feelings?

He cared. More than he'd ever imagined he could.

And although his thoughts as he looked at her had immediately filled with images of them making love, they morphed, grew more expansive. The physical was one part of what they shared, yet he saw so much more when he looked at her.

Felt so much more when he was with her.

He *knew* it wasn't a mirage.

Yet he couldn't struggle past the scars of his youth to actually put his feelings to words.

So he pushed everything he felt into the physical and hoped it was enough. Hoped she understood that everything he was or would ever be was for her.

As if in unspoken agreement, she fisted his shirt in her hands, dragging it up and over his head with swift fingers. A warm smile danced between her lips and her eyes were tempting and so full of promise.

He tried to keep up but she'd already danced out of his reach, dragging the sun dress she wore up her body and over her head as fast as she'd removed his shirt. The dress floated to the floor at his feet but he barely noticed, his attention fully focused on the naked woman standing before him. "You're… I mean…"

"Naked?"

One lone eyebrow quirked above the rich blue of her eyes before she lifted up on her tiptoes and nipped at his lip. "Cat got your tongue, Mr. Buchanan?"

He knew he was about three paces behind her—and reveled in the slightly befuddled haze that had drained nearly all thought from his mind—but he also wasn't a man to waste an opportunity.

Quick as a flash, he slipped out of his shoes, then dropped his jeans and briefs in one fell swoop.

"Ah. I see we're on the same page now."

He laughed at her words before he dragged her against his body. The wild, uncontrolled, unrelenting need for her nearly had his knees buckling before he caught himself. He boosted her up so her legs wrapped around his waist and captured one pert nipple between his teeth, just because he could.

She pressed herself into his mouth and his pleasure downshifted into primal satisfaction when she moaned low in her throat.

Any thought of taking things slow vanished at that delicious moan and he pushed them both on, flipping their positions so her back was against the door. She splayed her hands over his shoulders and positioned herself over him, then tightened her legs around his waist for leverage.

And then she began to move.

Pure ecstasy swept through him at the joining of their bodies. Their mouths met again and again, full of a desperate desire to ride the moment for all it was worth.

The play of their tongues—a sensual give-and-take—mimicked the hard, driving needs of their bodies. Tucker kept his hands tight at her waist, guiding their motion while supporting them both.

And quickly felt the moment spin out of his control.

Raw need.

Elemental hunger.

And a desperate yearning for all she could give him and more.

It was one of the most powerful moments of his life.

Enraptured, Tucker breathed her in, her name a rough whisper dragged from his throat. "Cassidy."

And when he heard her cries grow more urgent, signaling her release, there were no more words.

Only the glorious act of falling with her.

Tucker reached for Cassidy to pull her close and came up with nothing but a handful of bedsheet. Coming awake in an instant, he sat up and scanned the room. It was dark, but faint light drifted from her second bedroom along the hallway. Since he didn't see Bailey where he'd slept beside the bed on a soft pillow Cassidy had given him, Tucker figured where he found one of them he'd find the other.

He followed the sliver of light in the hall and pushed open the door to the room.

And found Bailey asleep at her feet while she sewed a long length of material.

He took the moment to watch her, pleased to stand and

look his fill. She'd pulled all her fiery hair up in some sort of messy twist that drew the eye. From there, he followed the long column of her neck, then over her slender shoulders, clad in a thin tank top.

Unbidden, a memory long buried rose up in the back of his mind. His grandmother kept a painting in her room of a young woman in her bath, glorying in the early-morning light. As a young boy he'd been fascinated by the picture, until the day his brother had found him and teased him, ruining the painting for him.

"Quit being a perv, Tuck. You can't even see her fully naked."

*He whirled, surprised at the voice and the sneer he heard under Scott's words. He didn't even know what that word meant—*perv?*—but he didn't like the way it sounded when Scott said it. "I am not."*

"Sure you are. What are you doing? Camping out in here to look at the naked woman? Come on. Dad wants us downstairs for the football matchup with Cousin Dell's kids."

Tucker hated football but he didn't dare say it out loud.

Scott played football therefore he had *to play football. And go sit in the bleachers on Friday nights and scream for Scott. And spend all Saturday morning after the game having breakfast in town so everyone could come up and congratulate Scott on how great he played while his old man glowed like a lightbulb.*

He'd rather be anywhere *else.*

"Tucker?"

His vision cleared only to be filled with Cassidy, concern filling her eyes, turning them a warm blue. "Are you okay?"

"Yeah. Sure. I'm fine."

"You looked so far away."

And he had been. He might have been standing with her but in his mind he was that eight-year-old boy, still angry and frustrated by everything he couldn't have.

And everything he wasn't allowed to be.

"Something jogged a thought."

"You want to talk about it?"

"No." He dropped into a small love seat opposite her. "It was just silly. I saw you sitting there and it made me think of some dumb memory at my grandmother's."

If she was upset he didn't share anything further, it wasn't apparent. Instead, her smile was warm and her question sweet. "Did she sew?"

"I don't know. I don't—"

Maybe it was the lack of pushing or the subtle acceptance that he didn't have to share every thought in his head, but before he could stop them, the words tumbled out.

The painting he'd loved. Scott's cruel taunts, from an older brother to a young, impressionable one. And another afternoon of endless torture playing a sport he hated.

She sat next to him and took his hand in hers. The warmth of her fingers touched something inside him, chasing away the cold that had settled in his stomach at the re-telling of a dopey old memory.

"Seems like we've churned up a few old ghosts over the past week."

What were the odds? Most people his age hadn't lost a sibling, yet both of them had, and they'd connected over that aspect of their lives. "It's strange. I lost my brother and you lost your sister. And neither of us have very good memories of them."

"Or anything to chase away the guilt over that fact."

Did he feel guilty?

Although he wouldn't have classified the emotion that

way, now that it was out there, he realized there was some truth to the thought.

Scott had lost his life and in the process—albeit a slow one—Tucker had gained his.

"I loved him. But I never had a bond with him."

"That was me and Leah. Of course I loved her. She was my sister. But we never had a bond. And then once I met Vi and Lilah, I felt bad about that because I *did* have that relationship with them. And then she died and all those feelings sort of jumbled up into one big mess."

"Max is my brother. I knew it from the first—he had my back and I had his. And then we went through enough situations where we *had* to have each other's back and it was as natural as breathing."

She rested her head against his shoulder and linked their fingers. "Maybe it's time we stopped feeling guilty about something we're immeasurably lucky to have."

"Maybe so."

Detective Graystone buried his head in his hands, a low moan of disgust punctuating the gesture. He had commandeered the front display area of Elegance and Lace, and his stiff pose was in stark contrast to the large, purple velvet chair he'd chosen. "Run this past me one more time?"

Max avoided a sigh—though Cassidy figured it was a close call—and launched into his story once more. "I took some of the jewels out of the case before I stowed it in the van."

Max had told the detective the same story about five times and no matter how many different ways Graystone challenged him, the order of the telling never changed.

"And despite getting video cameras installed, no one saw anything on the video feeds to corroborate your story?"

Although Cassidy knew it was his job, it amazed her that the detective missed no detail. Left absolutely nothing uncovered.

Before she could say anything, Violet interjected. "Lilah and I watched the feeds back at Dragon Designs. We saw Max open the back door of the van and open the box. You can see him rummage through the box, shove something in his back pocket and then put the lid back on. What we can't see, no matter how many times we run through the footage, is who came up to the van. We know he got in and out of the van but that's all we can see."

"Because he's wearing a ski mask and sweatshirt in Dallas in August? And presumably shoved the box under the sweatshirt."

"Yes." Lilah nodded. "And when you watch it you can see he'd clearly staked out our cameras because he had to have put the mask on out of frame."

The detective sighed, his mouth set in a grim line. "Whoever this guy is, he wasn't stupid about it. He must have worn different clothes until he found a parking spot near here."

"No cameras on any of the buildings nearby?" Violet asked.

"My officers are trying to track them but security is limited here. Nothing to reasonably follow someone traveling up or down the street. And you have a lot of buildings where the cameras are up for show, without actually capturing any footage."

Cassidy knew they'd been the same with their building so she could hardly fault her neighbors. She knew some of the higher-end design firms had top-notch security, but the rest of the businesses were small firms with little to steal beyond a few laptops. Heck, if it hadn't been for the break-in and Tucker's insistence on better security they still wouldn't have cameras at Elegance and Lace.

Of course, they hadn't felt at risk up until now.

"Your landlord said her home was broken into by a masked man." Graystone flipped through his notes, nodding when he found the one that corroborated the thought.

Cassidy appreciated the thorough attention to detail but her unease about Robert hadn't diminished and she decided to go for broke. "There is one more lead you may want to look into."

She recounted her experience with her former fiancé and his sudden interest in contacting her, then Violet. The detective scribbled several pages of notes before glancing back up, his gray gaze sharp. "I don't suppose either of you have any intention of calling him back."

"He is looking for our services," Violet pointed out.

Violet might have nerves of steel but she was well matched by Detective Graystone. "Miss Richardson. While I appreciate you've lost several days of productivity at your business to this matter, do you honestly think Mr. Barrington's call was a casual outreach?"

"It could be."

"And you'd need to lose about a trillion brain cells to even remotely pull off that dumb look you're aiming for."

Violet's wide-eyed stare narrowed, then considered him before she nodded, and Cassidy didn't miss the grudging respect stamped there. "Fine. Robert Barrington could be the answer to drawing out whoever is behind this."

Lilah reached for one of the cupcakes she'd laid out earlier on the oversize coffee table that sat in the middle of all of them. "I think the detective wants to take back what he said."

"What's that?" Violet asked.

"You really are that dumb."

* * *

Cassidy stood at the security pad and hit Enter after punching in the code. She waved at Tucker and gave him a thumbs-up. As soon as he and Max were on their way back to their office—Tucker's SUV getting smaller as it wove down Dragon—Cassidy whirled on her friends.

"What the hell is wrong with you two?"

"I had a good idea."

"And we all discussed it and discarded it last night, Vi. We're not drawing Robert out. Or whatever slimeballs he's working with. We're in over our heads and this isn't some mystery novel or movie of the week. Someone's after us and has tried to hurt us."

"Which is why we need the detective's help."

Cassidy shook her head, refusing to believe Violet could be so stubborn about this. "It's why we need to turn in the jewels and be done with this."

"Don't you get it?" Violet shot the words right back, her normally serene expression nowhere in evidence. "It's too late. No one is going to believe us if we hand over the three jewels. There are always going to be rumors. Questions about whether we kept something. Those jewels are the only bargaining chip we have to draw out the person behind this."

"And then do what? Kill him? Or them?" Cassidy never lifted her voice, but the words settled with the power of nuclear bombs. "Because that's the currency these people deal in."

No matter how she thought about it, that was the lone thing she came back to, over and over.

Her brother-in-law had made his choices and had been killed for them. They hadn't fully figured out what he'd done, but he'd obviously had some information and had attempted to sell it to the same person Robert had.

"So what are we supposed to do? Leave ourselves open to further attack?" Violet reached for her cup of coffee, her eyes bleak. "I'm not suggesting drawing these people out because I have some death wish. Nor am I interested in keeping those jewels. But we have to protect ourselves and use whatever leverage we can. And as far as I'm concerned, the Dallas PD isn't up to the task."

"Reed's been on our side. And he could have had a few kittens over the fact Max took those jewels at all," Lilah pointed out.

Cassidy didn't miss Lilah's use of the detective's first name, but her observation was quickly overridden by Violet's dark tone. "Which I'm still mad at him for. Really mad."

"So don't let your hormones make your decision for you."

Cassidy's eyes widened in shock at Lilah's bold statement, in lockstep with Violet's.

"I'm… I mean…"

"Exactly." Lilah nodded. "So what are we going to do? I agree with Cassidy that these people mean business and we're foolish if we think we can best that. And I also agree with Vi. This can't be over until it's been dealt with. Greedy, nasty people assume everyone else operates from the same playing field."

"Meaning what?" Violet's cheeks were still flush from the hormone comment, but her words were all business.

"We can say there are only three rubies but that doesn't mean whoever's after them will believe us," Lilah said. "While someone obviously knows about the jewels buried in the floor, we don't know if they know the full extent of what's included."

Cassidy reached out and took Lilah's hand while Violet took the other. Their friend had lived with nasty and greedy and come out the other side.

So when she spoke once more, Cassidy and Violet listened.

"Here's what we're going to do."

Robert's stomach clenched hard over the sick, roiling waves that already danced there as the phone number appeared on the dashboard of his Mercedes. On a deep breath, he hit the controls on his steering wheel. "This is Barrington."

"Robert."

Cassidy's voice drifted out of the speakers, enveloping him like the sweetest music. "It's Cassidy Tate."

The need to control—to dominate—leaped up and strangled every other emotion. "Took long enough."

"I know." She tsked lightly under her breath. "Violet and I were just talking about how much business we've been keeping up with. It does make for some busy days. How have you been?"

He suffered through the pleasantries—knew they were a requirement to make this come off as authentic—clawing his way through each and every word.

"So this is an exciting time for your family. Big Rob and Marjorie are celebrating their anniversary. What were you thinking of for the event?"

"Something small. Intimate." Like he'd actually throw something for his parents. Two people who were as content to sit out in their garden at their postage stamp–size house as they were to go out to dinner.

"Then I know just the place. There's a new event center—very boutique—down here in the Design District. We've begun recommending it for select events and have had some very pleased clients. What does your schedule look like early next week?"

"Today would actually be much better."

"Oh…" He heard her fumble, yet that sweet tone remained intact, the Cassidy Tate veneer firmly in place.

She never ruffled. Never said what she felt. Never argued.

And now she wasn't going to see what was actually coming straight at her.

"I think I could do four. I know the owner's out this afternoon but she's usually happy to give me the keys. Why don't you meet me in front of Elegance and Lace and then we could head from here. Would that work?"

"Perfectly."

She rattled off directions he didn't actually need and hung up.

And as he disconnected, Robert took his first easy breath in days.

"That was even easier than I thought it'd be." Cassidy laid her phone on Lilah's kitchen table and stared at the three enormous rubies laid out side by side.

"He bought it?" Lilah set a few mugs on the table, the rich scent of coffee adding to the warmth of her bright yellow kitchen. "All of it?"

"All of it. He even hemmed and hawed like we thought he would when I suggested early next week for the meeting."

Bright, midday light streamed in through the kitchen windows, highlighting the facets of each ruby. Cassidy reached out and touched one of the stones, almost surprised by the cool surface. It looked like it should be warm, radiating heat the same way it reflected the light in dramatic arcs over the table.

Instead, the stone was very, very cool. And that absence of warmth was almost more off-putting than the stones' history.

"They are beautiful." Violet picked up one of the other stones. "Gorgeous edges and lines. Perfect facets, really. And that rich color."

Cassidy set her stone back down, the color suddenly reminding her of blood.

The same blood that had covered her former brother-in-law.

She'd lost no sleep over Charlie but she'd never have wished an ending like that on him. Violent and miserable, then left out like a piece of trash.

"Cass?" Lilah blew on the top of her mug, her eyes wide over the rim. "You okay?"

"I'm trying to be but I can't stop thinking about Charlie. And Robert, too, for whatever he's in the middle of. It hits me at the strangest times, a vivid image that just fills my mind and takes over."

Violet laid the ruby back on the table, then covered all three with the same cotton cloth Max had used to carry the stones in his pocket. "No matter how horrible and misguided, he was still your family. Or had been at one time. It's okay to be sad about that."

"And Robert? What about him? I was on the verge of binding my life to his. And now? I find out the man I might have called my husband is a murderer." She broke off, a sudden rush of tears tightening her throat. "Or might be."

The tears and a raging well of anger had her off the chair and pacing into the living room. She'd thought she was okay with this. Had deluded herself into thinking it.

But sitting in that bright kitchen the truth had broken through, a dark oil slick sluicing over the light, suffocating the surface.

"You didn't marry him."

"But what if I had?" She whirled on Lilah, the pain so raw and fierce she thought her knees might buckle. "If it hadn't been for Leah's death and his checking out of the relationship, I might have."

Leah?

The thought hit her so swiftly and powerfully she dropped to her knees.

Oh, no. Leah.

"Cass?" Her friends raced toward her, flanking her as they got her to her feet.

Violet crooned in her ear as she led her to the couch. Limbs numb with the reality of the situation fell into the cushions with all the finesse of a rag doll.

"What is it? Tell us, honey."

"Leah." She whispered her sister's name. Saw the confusion that stamped itself like a matched set on her friends' faces.

"What about her?"

"Charlie. Robert. Murder and theft and the supposed puppet master Lilah mentioned, controlling it all from a distance." Cassidy took a sharp breath, the need for oxygen desperate even as her lungs burned with the effort. "What if my sister didn't commit suicide?"

Chapter 19

Tucker pressed Lilah's doorbell again, a sick sort of intuition coating his stomach with acid. When he finally saw her bright blond head through the frosted glass on the side of her door he took a deep breath.

They were there.

They were fine.

But his calm was short-lived when Lilah opened the door and gestured them in. "You'd better get in here."

He shoved through the door, the sound of tears crystal clear as he barreled toward the living room.

And found Cassidy heaped in a ball against Violet's side, her shoulders shaking in uncontrollable sobs.

Reaching for her, he pulled her close, pressing his lips to her head. "Shh. Cassidy? Shh." Over and over he crooned nonsense words, all while fear gathered in his gut with the oncoming strength of a hurricane.

"What is it?"

The sobs slowly faded, and she lifted her eyes to his. It was like looking into a tossed sea of blue. "I love you. Whatever's wrong, it doesn't matter. I'm here for you. I love you."

Her eyes widened, a mix of shock and the already clear-ing pain of whatever had brought the tears, as she digested his words.

"What?"

"I love you."

She straightened, and he saw the strength that lived inside her pokering up her spine. "I'm a mess and you're telling me this now?"

"You have a better idea?"

"I'm a mess, Tucker Buchanan!" She leaped off the couch and began to pace. Tucker noticed her friends had disappeared somewhere to give them privacy and he was grateful for it.

"So?"

"So how can you tell me you love me now? There's no moonlight. Or soft kisses in said moonlight. And I have snot running down my nose!"

His lips twitched in the face of her anger. "Sorry to ruin your fantasy."

"It's not a fantasy. It's how it was supposed to be."

"Well, get used to reality."

She dashed at her eyes and took a hard sniff. "I'm a mess."

"You're beautiful. And I couldn't wait to tell you any longer."

"Well." She exhaled on a huff, a small hiccup from her crying jag escaping with the sigh. "Well."

"Well, what?"

"I love you, too."

Satisfaction exploded through him like the sweetest vic-tory and until that moment, Tucker hadn't even realized he'd been waiting for her answer.

But now that he had it, he dragged her close and crushed

his mouth to hers. When he finally lifted his head, he uttered a single word. "Good."

With a lone finger, he snagged a lingering tear at the corner of her eye. "Now, what's wrong?"

Whatever he'd been expecting, the suggestion her ex-fiancé and her former brother-in-law had somehow had a hand in her sister's death was far from it. "How did you get to this? From what you said, your sister committed suicide."

"A fact that never sat well with me. We weren't close but there was no indication she'd ever had that urge. Or such a hopeless outlook on her life that she'd end it."

"She was in a bad marriage. And if what's come to light about Charlie is any indication, he was likely scamming during their marriage, as well. That could devastate someone. Could impair their judgment." Tucker tried to counter her words.

"I've felt my judgment has been impaired and I don't want to kill myself."

Thank God, he thought, but pressed on. "You also didn't get married. Didn't end up in a marriage with a criminal. It could take its toll."

"I suppose."

Now that the storm had passed, he settled on the couch and pulled her next to him. "What was it you and the girls wanted to discuss?"

"We need your help getting prepared."

"For what?"

"We're meeting Robert at four o'clock today."

She'd expected the anger. And the repeated mutterings that suggested they were insane. And even the grudging trip to the bank to secure a safe-deposit box.

What she hadn't expected were the guns.

Four semiautomatic handguns and one high-powered rifle lay in a row, their gleaming dark frames drawing the eye.

Tucker and Max seemed oblivious to the firepower as they stood over a large drafting table in the back of their studio, walking through how they were going to handle the op.

Op.

That's what they'd called it ever since she, Violet and Lilah had walked them through how they were going to handle Robert Barrington.

"Cassidy brings him in here." Max pointed toward a set of blueprints. "We're waiting here and here. Lilah and Violet keep eyes trained from the loft space up here."

It was Violet who'd had the idea to use one of Max Senior's empty buildings off Slocum. She'd recalled from their last district meeting that the tenants had vacated and he hadn't yet re-leased the space.

Large and open, the warehouse had minimal places Robert could run to once he understood he'd been cornered. The space also boasted a loft where Violet and Lilah could hide out of sight, yet have a ready view of what was happening so they knew the exact moment to call the police.

Although it was a fact she avoided thinking about, her two best friends were also crack shots. Violet had learned from a young age, and Lilah had become quite proficient over the past few years.

They were prepared.

"You know what you're going to tell him?" Tucker lifted the large envelope and held it up.

"Yes."

"Want to run it by me?"

Cassidy shook her head, anxious to get started instead

of talking about the details endlessly. "I don't want to rehearse it too much. I know what I'm going to say."

He pressed a hard kiss to her lips. "Then let's go do this."

The late-afternoon quiet closed in around her, and Cassidy realized—with no small measure of surprise—how she no longer liked the silence of the shop.

It was funny, she thought. Not even a week before, she'd been headed in for her usual early-morning work session when she'd found the shop broken into.

She'd always loved the quiet. The alone time with her designs, the soft smells of silk and coffee floating around her as she worked.

And now it just felt empty. Devoid of life.

The door jingled, and she jumped, the jarring sound buzzing through her like an electric shock. Robert was here.

She inhaled a deep breath, unwilling to let him see the fear coursing beneath her skin. She could do this. Say hello. Make small talk. Get him to the warehouse.

That's all they needed.

"Robert!" She pasted a bright smile on her face and walked toward him. His arms were already extended, his smile as fake as hers.

"Cassidy. It's good to see you, love."

Disgust crawled over her skin like maggots but she held her own. "How are you?"

"Fine. Fine. I appreciate you taking the time."

Robert moved closer, and she fought another shudder. He'd always been a dominating sort of personality, using his large form to get into people's space. She'd observed it often enough when they were together.

How could she have not seen it for what it really was?

Intimidation.

"So. You ready to go see the space?"

"In a minute."

Sirens went off in her mind—loud and clanging—as he took another step closer. "Why wait?"

"I think you know."

She took a step back, then another, but waited too long to run. He tackled her with his large body, wrapping her arms tight against her body before he dragged her toward the back of the store.

"How the hell long is this supposed to take?" Tucker paced the cavernous warehouse, his voice echoing across the yards of concrete.

"Calm down, Tucker!" Lilah hollered down from the loft. "Violet's got eyes on the security system. He just drove up."

Something violent fisted in his chest, and Tucker cursed himself.

He shouldn't have let her do this. He should be there with her. They shouldn't be doing this at all.

Max's hand settled over his shoulder, his friend's presence reassuring. "It's almost over. Come on. She knows what she needs to do and knows how to get him here."

"I know."

"It'll be over soon."

"I know, damn it." He fingered the safety on his gun. "So where are they?"

The seconds dragged on, every moment agony.

Where were they?

"Oh." The word was faint, uttered above them from the loft but it was enough to draw Tucker's gaze.

Before he could ask what was going on, a second word followed. "No!"

* * *

Cassidy struggled against Robert's grip but his hands were tight around her. She'd tried several times to get an elbow into his gut—anything to give her a bit of leeway—but his hold was relentless.

She didn't remember him to be this buff when they'd dated.

"Sit down!"

He tossed her toward a stool in Lilah's kitchen, the motion hard enough to slam her against a row of cabinets. She scrambled to her feet, prepared to run, when she heard a loud click. She stilled, the sight of a gun in his hand stopping her cold.

"Robert?"

The image she'd held on to since that morning—trapping him in their clutches at the empty warehouse—altered with startling speed.

He'd gotten the upper hand.

And all she could do was think of Tucker there, waiting for her. Of Violet and Lilah, stowed up in the loft, wondering where she was.

"Let's not play stupid. We both know why I'm here. Where are the gems?"

The thought to lie flitted briefly in her mind but she knew it was futile. "I don't have them."

His hand shook but not enough to give her any sense his aim would be off. "Where. Are. They?"

"Do you honestly think we kept them?"

"Then you're going to take me to them. I need them or I'm a dead man. And if you've got any sense, you'll get rid of them or you'll be dead, too."

"What did you get yourself into?"

Her question hung between them and for the first time,

she saw a glimpse of something familiar in his eyes before it vanished. "Where are they?"

"Did you kill my sister?"

She knew he meant business and knew his only concern was the rubies, but she couldn't keep her earlier thoughts quiet. She had to know.

"Hell, no."

"No?"

An incredulous look came across his face. "I barely knew your sister. Why would I kill her?"

"Did she know something about this?"

"You'd have to ask Charlie about that." A crooked grin lit up his face, and she recoiled at the dead look in his eyes. "Oh. Right. Charlie's gone, too. I dumped him on your loading dock."

A hard breath escaped her at the raw truth of his words. "You killed him?"

"No," Robert snapped. "What do you take me for? I disposed of him. Big difference."

What did she take him for? She'd nearly taken him for her husband.

The thought sloshed through her stomach like a set of vicious blades, mediated only by the most fortunate fact that she hadn't gone through with it.

What would life have been like?

"Did Charlie kill my sister?"

"What do you think?"

"I think he did. Knowing what I know now, I definitely think he did."

"He probably did. He'd been drugging her for a while. That little meltdown they had over the holidays was another sign of it."

"Oh, no." She shook her head. Leah. *Oh, Leah.*

Robert moved into her space, his looming form taking

up her entire vision. A frustrated red painted his skin, and she watched the mottled color creep up his neck.

"Where are the jewels?" His scream echoed off the stainless-steel kitchen.

Whatever bargaining power she'd thought she had evaporated. "In my bag at the front door. There's an envelope. Details are in there."

The gun wavered along with the indecision stamped across his face, but he nodded. "Show me."

He perp walked her toward the front of Elegance and Lace, the gun poking into her back as they moved.

Robert was going to kill her. She knew it with sudden clarity.

When he realized the envelope had no jewels in it— and that she didn't have them—he'd kill her as sure as she stood here.

For the first time, she was grateful everyone was at the other warehouse. They were protected. Tucker was safe. Lilah and Violet would remain unharmed.

The envelope stuck up out of her bag, and Robert pointed toward it. "Pick it up."

She bent over and air exploded around her the moment her head felt below her waist. Glass shattered and Robert screamed as he fell in a heap next to her, writhing in pain.

Tucker burst through the door, Max on his heels as a wail of sirens pierced the air.

They'd come.

Robert screamed again as Tucker lifted him off the ground, slamming a fist into his face. Blood dripped onto the floor from an open wound in Robert's shoulder as Tucker picked him up once more, slamming him into the floor.

Max shoved his gun into his back pocket and moved

in to break them up, his body straining as he pulled the two men apart.

The sound of sirens grew even louder, drowning out the grunts of all the men. Police streamed into the shop, guns drawn, just as Max pulled Tucker free of Robert's struggling form.

The police screamed out orders and everyone put their hands up as the officers got caught up on the situation. Despite Robert's screaming protest of his innocence and the continued threat of Tucker's dark stares at the man, Violet and Max managed to calm the situation, Violet's arrival with video footage putting the matter fully to rest.

Heart in her throat, Cassidy hugged Violet and Lilah, nodding under their repeated need for assurance that she was unharmed. From their arms, she watched Tucker struggle to stand still as he waited for the police to let him move.

His gaze locked on hers the moment the officers gave him leave to go to her.

"I thought I wouldn't get to you." Hard, tortured breaths ripped from his throat as he dragged her against him. "I thought we'd be too late."

"I'm fine. It's okay."

"I knew better. And I don't know why I went along with this asinine plan to—"

"Tucker. Shh." She hugged him tighter and knew he had a point. "When Detective Graystone gets here we'll tell him everything. We'll put this behind us."

They stood like that for a few moments, heads bent, emotionally miles away from the swirling chaos that surrounded them.

Robert continued screaming, his belligerent tone directed at anyone who would listen. Although she tried to muster up any sort of sympathy for his horrible choices, she couldn't find a drop.

She only cared about her immense good fortune that Tucker Buchanan had found her.

On a smile, she lifted her head. "What are we going to do with each other now that our lives are going to go back to normal?"

"I'm going to love you. Every single day of my life, Cassidy Tate."

"When can we get started?"

His lips came down on hers, full of the only chaos she was interested in. The crazy, messy madness of love.

And she was going to spend every single day for the rest of her life enjoying every single minute of it.

Epilogue

The Duke kicked the dead man lying in the grass, his serene backyard now marred once again by blood. Robert Barrington's sightless eyes stared up at him and he kicked the body out of sheer anger.

While he'd had low expectations for the society boy, he'd had equally low expectations of the women.

They baked cakes and sewed dresses and planned weddings. And they'd bested him.

With one more swift kick to the body out of sheer frustration, he stalked off across his yard, anxious to get some distance.

He'd tally the man's bail money against his investment in this operation and move on.

He always moved on.

The manila envelope that had been among Robert's possessions when the police combed through the crime scene lay in his hands. His contact at the courthouse had been more than obliging with the file, his overwhelming gratitude that his daughter had been released from a local prostitute ring ensuring his discretion.

The fact the ring of whores was his own was the Duke's business.

He opened the envelope to reveal several eight-by-ten photographs. Something akin to arousal coursed through his blood as anger and triumph mixed together. Three enormous rubies reflected back at him from the photos.

One photo showed a row of three, numbers beside each gem. Three individual photos followed, close-ups of each ruby. Their corresponding numbers lay next to each, with a strawberry beside for perspective. The rubies were as large as the fruit.

The women had no idea what they'd given him. They might assume the jewels were safe, but he didn't need to go after the gems.

He only needed to go after the women.

As long as he got his hands on one, he'd have the rest. And then he'd have it all.

*****

The
DANGEROUS IN DALLAS
series continues soon with
TEMPTING TARGET

If you loved this novel, don't miss these other suspenseful stories from Addison Fox:

THE MANHATTAN ENCOUNTER
THE ROME AFFAIR
THE LONDON DECEPTION
THE PARIS ASSIGNMENT

Available now from Harlequin Romantic Suspense!

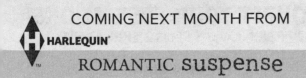
Available March 3, 2015

#1839 A REAL COWBOY

Cowboys of Holiday Ranch • by Carla Cassidy

When a masked intruder appears in her son's window, Nicolette Kendall knows she needs help. Cowboy Lucas Taylor is the perfect man for the job—hard, ruthless and emotionally distant. But even as his guarded heart begins to crack, they must unravel a mystery to save her child.

#1840 THE MARINE'S TEMPTATION

The Adair Affairs • by Jennifer Morey

Georgia Mason wanted adventure—and now she's tumbled into a deadly game of cat and mouse between marine Carson Adair and a murderer who has destroyed his family. Carson has to protect the spirited librarian as he uncovers secrets someone is killing to keep.

#1841 THE RANCHER'S RETURN

by Karen Whiddon

Ex-con turned rancher Reed Westbook didn't kill his brother, and the only woman who could prove it just showed up on his doorstep. Kaitlyn Nuhn knows who the real killer is, but to stop a powerful enemy, Reed must trust her.

#1842 THE BOUNTY HUNTER'S FORBIDDEN DESIRE • by Jean Thomas

When Chase McKinley's brother vanishes, all leads turn up murdered or missing except for Haley Adams. Armed with the last thing his brother sent her, Chase and Haley race against time to solve an international conspiracy.

REQUEST YOUR FREE BOOKS!
2 FREE NOVELS PLUS 2 FREE GIFTS!

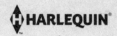

ROMANTIC suspense

Sparked by danger, fueled by passion

YES! Please send me 2 FREE Harlequin® Romantic Suspense novels and my 2 FREE gifts (gifts are worth about $10). After receiving them, if I don't wish to receive any more books, I can return the shipping statement marked "cancel." If I don't cancel, I will receive 4 brand-new novels every month and be billed just $4.74 per book in the U.S. or $5.24 per book in Canada. That's a savings of at least 14% off the cover price! It's quite a bargain! Shipping and handling is just 50¢ per book in the U.S. and 75¢ per book in Canada.* I understand that accepting the 2 free books and gifts places me under no obligation to buy anything. I can always return a shipment and cancel at any time. Even if I never buy another book, the two free books and gifts are mine to keep forever.

240/340 HDN F45N

Name	(PLEASE PRINT)	
Address		Apt. #
City	State/Prov.	Zip/Postal Code

Signature (if under 18, a parent or guardian must sign)

Mail to the **Harlequin® Reader Service:**

IN U.S.A.: P.O. Box 1867, Buffalo, NY 14240-1867
IN CANADA: P.O. Box 609, Fort Erie, Ontario L2A 5X3

Want to try two free books from another line?
Call 1-800-873-8635 or visit www.ReaderService.com.

* Terms and prices subject to change without notice. Prices do not include applicable taxes. Sales tax applicable in N.Y. Canadian residents will be charged applicable taxes. Offer not valid in Quebec. This offer is limited to one order per household. Not valid for current subscribers to Harlequin Romantic Suspense books. All orders subject to credit approval. Credit or debit balances in a customer's account(s) may be offset by any other outstanding balance owed by or to the customer. Please allow 4 to 6 weeks for delivery. Offer available while quantities last.

Your Privacy—The Harlequin® Reader Service is committed to protecting your privacy. Our Privacy Policy is available online at www.ReaderService.com or upon request from the Harlequin Reader Service.

We make a portion of our mailing list available to reputable third parties that offer products we believe may interest you. If you prefer that we not exchange your name with third parties, or if you wish to clarify or modify your communication preferences, please visit us at www.ReaderService.com/consumerschoice or write to us at Harlequin Reader Service Preference Service, P.O. Box 9062, Buffalo, NY 14269. Include your complete name and address.

HRS13R

SPECIAL EXCERPT FROM

H HARLEQUIN®

ROMANTIC suspense

*When a masked intruder appears in her son's window,
Nicolette Kendall needs help from reserved cowboy
Lucas Taylor. But even as his guarded heart begins to
crack, they must unravel secrets to save her child…*

*Read on for a sneak peek of
A REAL COWBOY, the first book in the
COWBOYS OF HOLIDAY RANCH series
by* New York Times *bestselling author*
Carla Cassidy.

He stepped outside and looked around. "What are you
doing out here all by yourself in the dark?"

"You told my son that cowboys only bathe once a
week, and now Sammy won't get into the bathtub."

By the light of the room spilling out where they stood,
she saw his amusement curve his lips upward. "Is that
a fact?" he replied. "Sounds like a personal problem to
me."

"It's all your fault," she said, at the same time trying
not to notice the wonder of his broad shoulders, the slim
hips that wore his jeans so well.

He raised a dark eyebrow. "The way I see it, you started
it."

This time the heat that filled her cheeks was a new
wave of pure embarrassment. "Look, I'm sorry. When I
told my son those things, I'd never really met a cowboy
before. The only cowboy I've ever even seen in my entire

life is the naked singing cowboy in Times Square. I now have a little boy who refuses to take a bath. Can you please come back to the house with me and tell him differently?"

Amusement once again danced in his eyes as he gave her a smile that made her feel just a little bit breathless. "Basically you've come to say you're sorry about your preconceived notions about cowboys, because I think it would be nice if you apologized before asking for my help about anything."

"You're right. I am sorry," she replied, wondering if he wanted her to get down on her knees before him and grovel, as well.

"Okay, then, let's go." He pulled the door of his unit closed behind him and fell into step next to her.

"A naked singing cowboy…and you New Yorkers think we're strange." He laughed, a low, deep rumble that she found far too pleasant.

She realized at that moment that she wasn't afraid of cows or horses, that she wasn't worried about falling into the mud or getting her hands dirty.

The real danger came from the attraction she felt for the man who walked next to her, a man whose laughter warmed her and who smelled like spring wind and leather.

Don't miss A REAL COWBOY by Carla Cassidy,
available March 2015
wherever Harlequin® Romantic Suspense
books and ebooks are sold.

www.Harlequin.com

JUST CAN'T GET ENOUGH
ROMANCE
Looking for more?

3605

Harlequin has everything from contemporary, passionate and heartwarming to suspenseful and inspirational stories.

Whatever your mood, we have a romance just for you!

Connect with us to find your next great read, special offers and more.

Facebook.com/HarlequinBooks
Twitter.com/HarlequinBooks
HarlequinBlog.com
Harlequin.com/Newsletters

♦ HARLEQUIN®

A *Romance* FOR EVERY MOOD™

www.Harlequin.com